MAMLUK

J. K. Swift

Mamluk
Hospitaller Saga Book 2

Published by UE Publishing Co.
Vancouver, BC, Canada
Copyright© 2018 by J. K. Swift
All rights reserved.
Print Edition

Cover design by Chris Ryan, collecula
www.collecula.com

This is a work of fiction. Names, characters, places, and incidents are either products of the author's imagination or used fictitiously. Any resemblance to actual events, locales, or persons, living or dead, is entirely coincidental. No part of this publication may be reproduced or transmitted in any form or by any means, electronic or mechanical, without permission from the author.

www.jkswift.com
New Releases Mailing List
http://eepurl.com/hTAFA

BOOK DESCRIPTION

Only the port city of Acre remains in the hands of the Crusaders. The boys in Brother Foulques de Villaret's Army of Children are approaching manhood, but their training is far from complete. Foulques needs more time. The Hospitallers, Templars, and Teutonics all need more time. Before preparations can be made, the Mamluks are at the gates of Acre. And in their midst, is a man Foulques knows only too well: a terrifying Mamluk warrior named Badru Hashim, *the Northman*.

Mamluk is the second book in J. K. Swift's **Hospitaller Saga**. It tells the story of the siege of Acre, a long, bloody struggle for the last Christian-controlled city during the waning days of the Kingdom of Jerusalem.

THE KHANJAR

Question: What weapon should a soldier carry with him at all times?

Answer: The *khanjar* should never be left behind, neither in war nor in peace. It has many advantages and can be used with all other weapons. It is useful with lances and with arrows, with swords and maces, and with javelins, and with all these together. So learn all there is to know about it.

—From the Mamluk military treatise: *Complete Instructions in the Practices of the Military Art (Nihayat al-Su'l wa'l Umniyaya fi Ta'lim A'mal al-Furusiyya)*
Translation by David Nicolle

CHAPTER ONE

SULTAN QALAWUN SAT on the raised dais inside his temporary command pavilion, a blood-red tent erected on the high ground of the surrounding desert. His ranking emir were assembled around him, their armor dull, caked with the dust and blood of war. Only their faces and hands were clean, for they had all used the cauldron of water outside the tent to wash away the filth of battle before presenting themselves to their sultan. Even the lamellar cuirass of his eighteen-year-old son bore the glorious smears of war. Qalawun wondered how many Mongols the young man had killed. The wild look in his eyes spoke of at least one, but Qalawun doubted it was many more than that. It was all right, though. The boy had not yet caught time's eye. He would have ample opportunities to prove himself.

Ah, youth, Qalawun thought.

He flexed the aged muscles in his sword arm and glanced down at the golden mail covering it. Matching greaves protected his thighs and a conical helmet sat on a nearby table. Nothing was solid gold of course, for that would have been far too heavy to wear and beyond useless as armor.

Although this delicate, gold-plated mail was probably not much better. It had been some time since he had worn a true set of armor.

He looked around at the tent full of hardened warriors. The few that met his gaze did so with only respect and adoration in their eyes. And why not? He had defeated the Mongol hordes not once, but twice now. Twenty years ago, on the plains of Ain Jalut he had fought under the command of Sultan Baybairs himself. While the rest of the world cowered at the relentless onslaught of the barbarians from the steppes, the Mamluks had stood their ground and sent the Mongol wave crashing back upon itself. Being the barbarians that they were, they proved themselves incapable of learning from that first encounter and Qalawun used the same strategy, the same formations, to break them once again.

Qalawun nodded to his most trusted emir and vice-sultan, Turuntay, who was a thick, heavily bearded man. Like Qalawun himself, Turuntay had been a Kipchak Turk before the sultan's men took him from his village when he was still young enough to forget who he was.

"Bring him in," Turuntay said.

Two warriors dragged a man into the tent on his knees with his hands tied behind his back. He fell onto his side when they deposited him roughly on the carpeted ground.

"Kneel," Turuntay shouted. "You are in the presence of Sultan al-Malik al-Mansur Saif ad-Din Qalawun al-Alfis-Salihi, defender of the words of Allah, His holy territories, and all His people."

The Mongol's eyes flicked open but he made no attempt to sit up.

"Get him up," Turuntay said to the men on either side of the captive. They yanked him upright to his knees and steadied him there with their fists wrapped in his ragged shirt. The Mongol straightened as best he could and stared directly at Qalawun with his almond-shaped eyes. His clean-shaven face was swollen around the mouth and cut in several places, but other than that he seemed unharmed.

Qalawun leaned forward. "You are the Mongol general," he said.

It was not a question. Qalawun's vizier stepped forward and began to interpret the sultan's words to the barbarian in his own tongue, but the man spit at him.

"I do not need an old man to tell me the words of a dog," he said in strongly accented, yet perfectly intelligible, Turkic. One of the warriors holding him had his scimitar half pulled from its scabbard before Qalawun stopped him with a shake of his head.

"You speak our words," Qalawun said.

The Mongol's lips curled back. "You think they are so special, your words? So difficult to learn? They are nothing. You think you won something today, but the will of heaven cannot be stopped. The bloodline of Jhingis Khan cannot be stopped. His grandson will return, and you will never speak your words again unless the Great Khan wills it so."

Qalawun leaned forward in his high-backed chair. "Your talk bores me, Mongol, for I have heard it all before. Twenty years ago at Ain Jalut. Then, as now, your barbarian kin fell to Mamluk swords and arrows by the thousands. It took longer for us to clean your blood off our weapons than it did to slaughter your horde."

Qalawun turned to the emir on his left. "Kitbugha. Let him feel the hand of a Mamluk."

Kitbugha stepped forward and backhanded the Mongol across his face, snapping the general's head to the side and eliciting a groan of pain.

"Kitbugha was in your Khan's army at Ain Jalut. I took him prisoner at that battle. I do not know why I did not kill him, for I killed so many that day, one more would have made no difference. But Allah stilled my blade and put pity in my heart. I allowed Kitbugha to serve me. I saw to his education, and in time, I made him into a man. A Mamluk."

Qalawun nodded to Kitbugha and he stepped back into place beside the sultan. Then Qalawun stood and leisurely took the Mongol general's face in one hand. He dug his thumb under one cheekbone and his fingers under the other and applied pressure on the nerves there to turn the man's head to look at him. The palm of his hand covered the Mongol's mouth, in case he tried to spit at him.

"If Jhingis Khan himself were still alive, and he led his horde against us, it is his head I would hold in my hand right now."

The Mongol squirmed against the perceived blasphemy until Qalawun squeezed his fingers and the man's eyes watered.

"The Mongols will always be inferior to my Mamluk warriors. That is truly heaven's will. And do you know why?

Your soldiers are herdsmen and bandits who, for a few short years, play at war. They ride their ponies at their enemy, loose their arrows, and run away before they can be caught. That is the way of the steppe warrior. And it has worked until now because you have never come up against other skilled horse archers. You see, the Mamluks have their roots in the steppes as well."

Qalawun released his grip and eased himself back into his chair. The Mongol's mouth opened and closed to ease the pain in his jaw.

"Do you know what 'Mamluk' means?" Qalawun asked.

"Dog," the Mongol said. "Dogs with only one god."

"In a way you are right. Most of us did not accept the teachings of Allah until we were men, like Kitbugha, here. Mamluk means 'owned.' Most of us were bought at a young age. We were selected for our physical attributes and then trained in the warrior arts since we were children. My own name means 'one thousand dinars' for that is what my master paid for me. We are slaves. Warrior slaves whose entire lives are devoted to war. We know nothing else. If it helps, you may blame your losses of today, and twenty years ago, on the poor quality of your armor and swords, the inferior bows with which you launch your poorly crafted arrows, or even the superior strength and speed of our larger Arabian stallions over your steppe ponies. But these are excuses."

Qalawun stood once again. He reached out his hand and slowly wound his fingers in the Mongol's long hair. He made a fist, pulling the man's head back. The barbarian's nostrils flared and his chest heaved, but his dark eyes stared into Qalawun's own with a seething hatred.

"We Mamluks are not Egyptians. We are not Arabs, nor are we all Turks, though we often choose to speak that language. We come from all manner of countries and backgrounds, but many of us are horsemen from the steppes. We are cultured, educated, disciplined versions of yourselves. Everything you aspire to be. Today, barbarians of the steppes have been defeated by men of the steppes. As it happened those many years ago at Ain Jalut. As it will happen again."

A small, jeweled dagger appeared in Qalawun's hand. He drew it across the Mongol's throat and the man's eyes went wide.

"How could it ever be otherwise?"

The Mongol opened his mouth to say something, but blood had already filled his throat and was beginning to flow out of the fine slit in his neck and spread downward. In a few short moments, the rags on his chest turned redder than the finest silk. The Mongol was dragged from the room before he was truly dead, lest he spoil the sultan's carpets any more than he already had.

Qalawun scanned the room. His emir, on the whole, seemed pleased with his handling of the enemy general. His son, Khalil, however, wore more of a scowl than usual. Qalawun turned his back to the boy and made his way to his chair.

"Next I would have the knights of the cross brought before me," Qalawun said to no one in particular. The warrior nearest the door threw aside the ornate silk curtains and disappeared outside. Seconds later he returned with an escort of guards and seven prisoners. Joined at the neck with a line of chain, their hands tied behind their backs, these men were obviously not Mongols. Their pale skin marked them as Franks, but the way their hair was cut short on top and the unkempt style of their beards suggested they were much more than simple soldiers. Five had been stripped of their armor and wore only light breeches and sweat-stained undershirts of gray cotton. But for whatever reason, two of the men still wore their red battle tunics over mail hauberks. Splayed across each man's chest was a white cross. They were Hospitallers and Qalawun knew full well how they liked to claim this white cross was meant to symbolize peace, or a moment of stillness upon the blood-red battlefield of war. It was Qalawun's turn to scowl. He had fought the Holy Christian Orders all his life. These were not men of peace.

With a curt nod of his head, the Hospitallers were knocked to their knees with the pommels of swords.

"Who amongst you has the authority to speak with me?" Qalawun said in fluent French.

All the Hospitallers lowered their eyes, save one of the men still wearing his red tunic.

"I am Brother Dumont, a captain of the Knights of Saint John of Jerusalem, currently stationed at Margat," the man said.

"You command these men?" Qalawun asked.

"Our commander fell in the battle," Dumont said. "But yes, I believe I am the highest ranking one of my brethren who yet lives."

"You realize that by siding with the Mongols you have violated the peace treaty we have had with your grand master these past years?"

We were ordered here by our prior. That is all I know."

"Is that so? All of you come from the fortress of Margat then?"

Dumont nodded.

"And I suppose the grand master of your order in Acre knows nothing of this treachery?"

"I am not privy to the knowledge of my order's leaders."

"No, of course not," Qalawun said. "Your God's Holy Orders are as secretive as its priests, no?" He leaned back into his chair and let the silence in the tent build.

"What will you do with us?" Dumont asked.

"A fair question, Captain. The truth is I cannot decide. Perhaps my son will have some ideas. Khalil?"

Qalawun's son stepped forward. "Yes, Father?" He did not speak French, so he had no idea what the Hospitaller and Qalawun had been discussing.

"What would you do with the Hospitaller prisoners if you were in my position?"

"Father?"

"I ask for your opinion, my son. What do you think we should do with the prisoners?"

Khalil's eyes narrowed. "They are sworn enemies of Islam. They must be executed of course."

Captain Dumont shifted on his knees and Qalawun suspected he might understand enough Turkic to grasp the plight of his situation.

"Yes, of course," Qalawun said. "And how would you execute them?"

The boy did not hesitate. "They must be tied to posts in Cairo's square and lashed every day until they die, so the people understand what we protect them from."

Qalawun fought to keep his eyebrows from arching at the response. He nodded and said, "I see." He turned to the vizier. "Clear my pavilion. I should like to confer with my son."

Less than a minute later Qalawun and Khalil were alone.

"Do you know why I asked for your advice just now Khalil?"

"To see me shamed in front of your emir," Khalil said.

Qalawun closed his eyes and shook his head slowly. "No, Khalil. Despite what you may think, that was not my intention."

Khalil threw up his hands. "And what else am I to think? I know you had no intention of ever following my advice."

Qalawun felt his blood rise and the heat radiate up into his face. "Have you ever seen a man whipped to death?"

Khalil shrugged. "I am not sure. Perhaps when I was a young boy."

Qalawun shook his head. "A skilled master of the leather can keep a man alive for weeks. In fact, it is more likely the man would starve to death than die from the whip."

"All the better. The longer the Christians lived the better the spectacle for our people," Khalil said.

Qalawun stood and took a step toward his son. "Spectacle? A man suffering the leather cries out for only one or two days. Any more and the pain closes down his body. He loses consciousness. What good would it do for our citizens to see us whip a silent, bloody piece of meat day in and day out, while the carrion eaters circle overhead?"

Khalil stared straight ahead, his gold-flecked brown eyes seething with emotion, but whether he felt anger toward himself, or at his father, Qalawun could not tell.

"I sought to give you an opportunity today to impress the emir," Qalawun said.

Khalil turned to look at his father. The boy's eyes softened, somewhat. "Why would I need to impress any one of them? My sultan is not amongst them."

Qalawun forced one of his rare smiles. "Without the emir, there can be no sultan." He stepped forward and put his hand on Khalil's shoulder. "They are all Mamluk. You are not."

"So you have always told me," Khalil said.

"I tell you so you are prepared. When I am gone, the only way you will take my place as sultan will be if the emir allow you to do so. For that to happen you must earn their respect."

Under his hand, Qalawun felt the tension in Khalil's body shift.

"What do we do with the Hospitallers?" Khalil asked.

Qalawun removed his hand from the boy's shoulder and nodded. "You are right. They must be punished. And not only the knights of Margat who sided with our enemies. Their entire order must suffer."

Khalil's face lit up. "Yes, Father."

"But not today. Our army is tired, our resources depleted."

"Then when?" Khalil asked.

"Not as soon as you would like, Khalil. But by Allah's might, they will suffer. I make this promise to you, not as your father, but as your sultan."

"And the prisoners?"

"Ah, yes. Go now and have them assembled. Execute all but one of the Hospitallers in front of the emir. Do it yourself, but give them a swift death. They are warriors, after all, and they fought bravely. Cut off their heads one by one and let the captain live so he can tell his superiors what happens when the Mamluks are betrayed."

This seemed to appease Khalil, for he stood up straight. "Yes, My Sultan."

Qalawun watched his son stride from the pavilion. As the curtains fluttered in the early evening breeze, his gaze settled on a puddle of red on the carpet between him and the doorway. He bent over, his back and knees protesting, and swiped three fingers through the remains of the Mongol's lifeblood. Qalawun stood upright, and with his eyes fixated on the doorway, wiped his hand down the front of his chest, leaving a rusty smear across the golden mail.

He closed his eyes to focus his senses. Outside, he heard the commotion of men being forced to their knees. Seconds later Khalil grunted and his blade sang as it separated head from body. The stroke had been swift and true, and it brought a satisfied smile to the old man's face. He felt the wrinkles on his face tighten as they resisted the unfamiliar sensation, and he became keenly aware that, unlike his son, Time had found him. But he had much to do before he surrendered to its ravages.

Qalawun, on this day, arguably the most powerful man in the world, suddenly felt very old.

CHAPTER TWO

FOULQUES DE VILLARET plowed through the early evening throng of people scrambling along the streets of Acre hustling to finish the last tasks of the day. Or, as he crossed from the Venetian quarter into the Genoese slums, begin the revelries of the night. Lost in thought, with his simple black cloak wrapped around him and his hood pulled over his head, he strode through the alleys ignoring the catcalls of women and the unwelcome stares of men.

Admiral. Foulques had never heard anything so ridiculous in all his life. What had gotten into the grand master's head? Or rather, who? Foulques sensed the hand of his uncle in this move. Even from England, he seemed to have more control over Foulques's life than Foulques himself. He could have arranged it with the grand master, for Guillaume de Villaret had the influence. But he could have had the good grace to ask Foulques before having him exiled to the island of Cyprus. He could understand that his uncle was trying to look after him, as he always had. Everyone knew it was only a matter of time before Qalawun and his Mamluks attacked. Guillaume was no doubt just trying to save his nephew by getting him out of Acre before it fell under siege.

Out of Acre. The thought chilled him more than he cared to admit. Acre was the only place he had ever called home. Could he ever know another? He was told the city's beauty was unequaled in all of the Levant. In Foulques's mind, even Jerusalem itself could not compare, though he would never say the thought aloud. Acre's main bazaar was a place of wonder, intoxicating with the colors and scents of spices gathered from the four corners of the world. Its deep harbor of azure blue water was so clear that you could see fifty feet into its depths and count the sea creatures glistening under the sun. Some felt threatened by the myriad of people, the sheer number of languages spoken on the city's streets, but that was one of the things Foulques treasured about his city. As a child he had spent countless hours wandering through the market listening to the strange words of traders and travelers from afar. When he could not understand what was spoken, he would make up stories about them. As the years passed, he found he no longer had to rely on his imagination so much, for there were few conversations he could not follow. But for all its glory, the city had its share of darkness as well.

With these thoughts rambling back and forth through his mind, Foulques did not see the guard seated at a small table outside the gambling hall's main entrance until the man stood. He placed himself between Foulques and the closed door.

"Far enough. The Greek does not allow priests or monks in any of his establishments," the guard said in Arabic, holding a hand out in front of Foulques's bowed head.

Foulques stopped more than a full arm's length away. He lowered his hood and let the split down the front of his robe fall open to reveal the sword beneath. He wore no mail, but the way the guard's eyes widened, Foulques was sure the man no longer thought he was a priest. Still, he did not move from in front of the door.

"Forgive me. I did not know you to be a man of the Hospital," the guard said, this time in broken French.

"I have business inside," Foulques said, in Arabic.

"Perhaps I could take a message? Who is it you wish to speak with?" The words flowed out of the guard's mouth quickly, like he was both grateful to be speaking his native tongue and eager to be rid of the Hospitaller.

"A Genoan. Vignolo dei Vignoli. I was told he is inside."

"Give me a moment and I will see if the man you seek—"

"No need. He is here," Foulques said.

He stepped forward, giving the guard the choice of either initiating a physical confrontation with a soldier of the Order, or making an undignified leap aside. It was not a difficult choice.

Foulques pushed open the door and paused to let his eyes adjust to the dimness of the room. A few years past, Stephanos the Greek had moved from a rented hut, half of which was carved into the ground below street level, into a much larger building that boasted a solid paver stone floor and a ceiling high enough to keep some of the smoke out of its patrons' eyes. Other than that, it was not much of an improvement. It was still in a seedy area on the edge of the

Venetian Quarter, and its clientele consisted of an odd mix of every type imaginable, from Genoese dock laborers and mercenaries to the occasional young man of noble blood.

As Foulques's vision grew used to the lack of light, and his lungs to the thickness of the smoke-filled air, he saw that all eyes were upon him. A half-dozen men stood around an oval table, drinks in hand, a scattering of coins placed before them. Stephanos, a thick man with an even thicker head of curly gray hair, sat on a keg of ale behind the table. His hooded eyes took in every movement of the place with a seemingly detached interest. Another similar table stood off to the side, but it was empty as it was not yet midday.

A tall figure detached himself from their midst and took a few hesitant steps toward the knight. "Foulques? Brother Foulques! My good friend," Vignolo dei Vignoli said in a loud voice that carried to all corners and all ears. The rest of the hazard players gathered around the table immediately lost interest in the Hospitaller and returned to their game.

Once he closed the distance, Vignolo lowered his voice. "I would say it is a pleasure to see you, Foulques, but that has rarely been the case in the past. I suspect it should prove no different on this occasion."

"Have you had your fill of honest work, then?" Foulques said. "The Hospital has been more than generous to you these past few years."

"And I suspect even more generous shortly?"

Vignolo flashed one of his self-sure grins, revealing white teeth and a handsome face that seemed at odds with the dismal room in which they stood. It had been over seven years since Foulques, with five hundred young peasant children from the Alps in tow, had first met Vignolo on the docks of Genoa. At the time, Foulques had had serious doubts about the man's character and purity of soul. But Vignolo had come through for the Hospital, and later, for Foulques himself. Foulques owed the Genoan his life, and that knowledge weighed more heavily on the knight than he cared to admit.

"Let us have it, then," Vignolo said. "Tell me the size of ship your grand master needs and where we will be going. And I will be blameless later if you leave anything out, though I know you will."

"We should sit," Foulques said. A rhythmic thumping sound began in a room directly above them and a sprinkle of dust drifted loose from the ceiling. He fought back a sneeze and glanced around the room. "Somewhere other than here, however."

"Nonsense," Vignolo said, pulling out a stool from under a nearby table. "There is a perfectly good seat right here."

Foulques did not miss the casual glance Vignolo cast back toward the hazard table, nor was it possible to ignore the feel of Stephanos the Greek's eyes following Vignolo's every move. No doubt Vignolo had gambled away more than he had come with. That would explain his relatively welcoming demeanor toward Foulques.

After the two men had sat down, and a tired but strong-looking woman dropped off a couple of mugs of mead, Foulques wasted no time in getting to the point.

"The Hospital has need of your talents, Vignoli, but it is

not of the usual variety. It will require you being away from Acre for an extended period of time."

Vignolo shrugged and leaned back on his stool with both hands wrapped around the clay mug in front of him. "You would have me leave all this behind? I can only hope my compensation will reflect the hardships I should endure."

"I have been authorized to pay you far more than you are worth. You can be sure of that."

Vignolo's eyes narrowed and he slowly leaned forward. "What is wrong, Foulques? You have the smell of a desperate man about you. Exactly how long will we be gone?"

"I cannot say," Foulques said. He forced himself to meet Vignolo's eyes with his own.

"Our destination? Surely that you can enlighten me on."

"The island of Cyprus."

"Cyprus?" Vignolo laughed and took a long pull off his drink. "You let me think we were headed for the dark heart of Cairo, not the home of the King of Jerusalem. I have not had any direct dealings with the young King Henry himself, but his brother is no stranger to me. And I must say, he and I have more in common than you know."

"Prince Amalric's appetites for both women and drink are no secret," Foulques said.

"You left out gambling. He is a young noble with no titles to weigh him down, yet all the family riches of Cyprus are at his fingertips. How else is he to fill his time?"

Foulques shook his head. "I did not come to debate how royals should live their lives. We have other concerns."

"*You* have other concerns. You always do. Me, I have

debts. When do we leave?"

"Just like that? What happened to the income from your estate on Rhodes?"

Vignolo rolled his eyes. "My steward has petitioned the Byzantine Emperor. He claims his workers have not been paid for three years, and until this misunderstanding gets sorted, the Emperor has confiscated all my holdings on Rhodes."

"A misunderstanding, is it?"

"It is my steward. He is stealing from me, I know it."

"How would you know it? Have you even been to Rhodes?"

"Do not lecture me, Foulques. What would a monk know about business matters?"

Foulques reached inside his robe and pulled out a purse. It was not large, but it was stuffed with as much coin as it could possibly hold.

"As I have told you before. I am no monk." He dropped the purse on the table between them. It hit hard, with a loud, satisfying clink of metal.

Vignoli immediately covered it with his hands and pulled it close. In a hushed tone, he said, "You are a mad monk, is what you are. This is not the place to be throwing full purses around." He cast a nervous glance toward the hazard table. Foulques followed his eyes. Everyone seemed to be absorbed in the game. "Now tell me what you want done so we can get out of here."

Foulques leaned back on his stool. "I need you to make a seaman out of me."

A twitch started at the corner of Vignolo's mouth. It quickly spread into a full-blown smile, accompanied by a series of head shakes when he realized Foulques was serious.

"You? A seaman? Anything else, Brother Foulques? The moon, perhaps?"

"Yes. I want you to turn a hundred of the Schwyzers into seamen as well."

Vignolo broke into open laughter at that. The moment he was able to contain himself, he stood up and wiped his eyes.

"Well, you mad monk. We had best be on our way. My life's work is before me." He held up the coin purse. "I trust more of these will follow?"

Foulques nodded. "As many as it takes."

Vignolo turned and shouted at the hazard table. "Stephanos!" He tossed the entire purse in the Greek's general direction. Several pairs of hungry eyes followed its flight, but it was the stocky man on the stool with the crazy gray hair whose hand shot up and snatched it out of the air.

"Watch that for me until I get back, will you?"

CHAPTER THREE

THE SUN OF the Levant was unforgiving at midday, especially when seated upon a sweating destrier. Thomas found himself longing for a set of mail the likes of which the leader of his eight-man patrol, Brother Alain, wore over his padded hauberk. The small, finely crafted metal links of the knight's armor hugged every crevice of his body as he swayed in his saddle, emulating the movements of muscle and bone. While Thomas's scale mail fell over his own frame with all the comfort and grace of an ale barrel. A knight had let Thomas try on his mail a year ago, when Pirmin had organized an impromptu celebration of Thomas's thirteenth birthday. Thomas doubted it actually was his birthday, but Pirmin was quite adamant. And when he got it in his head to organize a celebration of any kind, there was no stopping him. Thomas had been shocked at how the steel pulled the heat from his body, even as it clung to his torso like a second skin.

A rivulet of sweat leaked from under his helmet and stung his eye. He felt his scar tighten and tug all along the length of his face, right down to his jaw, as he tried to blink the stinging sensation away. His mount veered out of formation a step or two as he turned his head back to see why his rider was squirming in the saddle. Thomas hastily set him back on the path with a firm nudge of his knees.

Brother Alain was the only knight in the eight-man patrol, but all the others were experienced brother-sergeants. They rode two men abreast, and Thomas, since he was the most inexperienced, was in the second to last set. Only Brother Alain and Roderic, the sergeant at his side, carried lances. They were weapons reserved for the knightly class, or the most deserving and well-trained of the men-at-arms.

As though Brother Alain could feel Thomas's coveting eyes on his back, he turned in his own saddle and scanned his men until his gaze settled on the youngest member in his troop.

"Brother Thomas. Join me here in the front, if you will." A new bead of sweat fell into Thomas's other eye.

Brother Alain spoke a few words to the man at his side. Roderic turned his horse away from the column and trotted toward the rear. He gave Thomas a nod as they passed each other and then Roderic took up a position at the very back as the sergeants jostled to fill in the gap Thomas left.

They continued on in silence for a few minutes, but Thomas could feel Brother Alain watching him from the corner of his eye. "It is good to be nervous," Alain said.

"I am not nervous," Thomas said, a little too quickly.

Alain nodded. "All the same, it is nervous men who tend to outlive the complacent ones."

Thomas was about to protest, but as he searched for the

right words, he suddenly realized Brother Alain had stopped his horse. Thomas brought his own mount to a halt and twisted back to look at the knight. His hand was raised and the column behind him had pulled up into a tight formation.

"Do you hear that?" Alain asked of no one in particular.

The sergeant behind him nodded. "Steel," he said.

Thomas wanted to take off his helmet so he could hear better, but that would be a mistake. Instead, he strained his ears beneath his arming cap and thought he could just make out the sounds of voices coming from up ahead on the road.

"Fighting," Alain said. "Sergeants! With me." He nudged his horse into a trot, pulling Thomas along with a nod of his head. "Stay close to me, Brother Thomas."

Thomas concentrated on doing as Alain said. He kept his destrier close enough to smell the oiled leather of the knight's saddle. He could have reached out and put a hand on Brother Alain's shoulder. His horse was so well trained that the moment Alain nudged his own destrier into a gallop, Thomas's horse matched the new pace instantly without any instruction. The wind blew under his helmet, bringing with it a welcome coolness, and at the same time an excited beat to his heart.

Up ahead they could see a circle of men and women standing protectively around three or four carts. Whirling around them on white steeds, a dozen desert dwellers thrust at them with spears, or loosed arrows from short bows. More than one figure lay unmoving on the road with one of the deadly shafts embedded in his back or chest.

The Hospitallers picked up speed. Thomas blew out a

breath to calm his insides. This is what he had trained for. He had spent years imagining this moment. He was one of God's warriors racing to the aid of those in need. And what is more, he led the charge. He risked a sideways glance at Brother Alain. The knight's image blurred as the wind stung Thomas's eyes and he felt tears leak from their corners. A grin stretched his lips and spread across his face, straining the long, pale scar to its limit.

There must have been a dozen Bedouins darting in and out of the small group of wagons and their defenders. Most were on horseback, but a few stood on the ground off the side of the road, launching black-shafted arrows from bows as curved as Satan's horns. Alain targeted one of these footmen with his lance and Thomas found his own horse being forced to veer away from the wagons, where the main fighting was sure to occur. Carried along with Alain's charge, Thomas recognized this was an attempt by the veteran knight to protect the young sergeant at his side. Disappointment flared in Thomas.

The Bedouin in Alain's sights panicked when he saw the destrier bearing down on him. He threw his bow aside and launched himself toward a nearby tree. Alain's lance skewered him in mid-air. The momentum of the charge tore the weapon from the knight's hand and forced him to steer his mount sharply to the left to avoid careening into the foliage at the side of the road. Thomas reined his destrier in and wheeled the stallion out of the way to give Alain room as he shot past in front. As Thomas turned his mount back toward the wagons, movement on the other side of the road caught his eye. A man, clad head-to-foot in the black robe of a desert dweller, raised his wickedly curved bow and loosed an arrow at Brother Alain's back.

Thomas opened his mouth to shout a warning but his voice refused to obey. Sitting there in his saddle, his sword in hand and mouth hanging open, every muscle in Thomas's body suddenly froze. The Battle Furies had taken him.

He had been warned of this in his training, time and time again. The stress of battle affected men differently. Some lost their minds, flying into an uncontrolled blood frenzy, sometimes attacking both friend and foe alike in blind rage. The spirits of the battlefield, the Furies, loved men such as these, for they fed off the misery and chaos they caused. The spirits would hover about the battle, stealing men's thoughts and coaxing them into greater and greater acts of violence and mayhem until the warrior was utterly spent, or himself destroyed.

But there was also another type of Fury that preyed on mortals. These were the ancient ones, the Terror Furies, and they were much more dangerous. For they no longer received sustenance from the simple suffering of humans. A mortal's death was the only thing that could curb their hunger. For a time. To this end, they would find a man in danger and steal his ability to move. Then, at the exact moment of death, the Fury would feed.

All this, and more, coursed through Thomas's mind as he watched the Bedouin draw his bow. The arrow sprang forward, its gray feather fletchings sending it spiraling toward the unaware knight's back. The archer misjudged the distance, for instead of taking Alain in the middle of his back, it floated upward to the high point of its trajectory and slammed into the top of the knight's helmet. There was a loud metallic clang and Alain's head slammed forward, but the curved surface of his helmet turned the projectile aside, and it glanced off into the woods.

The sound of the arrow hitting Alain's helmet broke the Fury's hold on Thomas. Breath rushed into his lungs and he flexed the muscles both in the hand holding his sword and the one holding his horse's reins. He jammed his heels into his destrier's side and a scream burst from his throat. He could move. And he knew, so long as he kept moving, the Terror Fury could not harm him. The lesser Furies could, perhaps, but that would not be a useless death.

The archer turned toward Thomas and nocked a new arrow. Thomas felt his mount spring into a gallop as the bowman raised his weapon and sighted down the shaft. Thomas hunched low in his saddle, his sword held before him pointed at his foe as had been drilled into him time and time again. He saw the bow limbs snap forward but he lost sight of the arrow. The next thing he knew he was going forward over his horse's neck. He tried to grab a handful of mane as he flew by, but the stallion's neck was bent so far forward and Thomas's forward momentum so great, that the coarse hair was ripped from his grasp. He caught a glimpse of something black protruding from the horse's chest, and as both he, and his mount, tumbled into the road, he saw the gray feathers splattered with blood. His horse screamed and Thomas knew he had to throw himself from his saddle or risk being crushed to death by the stallion, but there simply was not time. He saw the hard road, felt it tear at the skin under his leggings, saw his horse's legs above him blocking out the sky, then the road again. He felt a crushing weight over one leg, a suffocating presence on his chest, the sky presented itself once again, then he was on one knee with nothing but blackness in front of him.

His sword arm was straight out in front, and it dawned on him then that his gloved hand still clutched his blade. The blackness took shape. Thomas looked up, his vision unhindered by the loss of his helmet, and a set of brown eyes wide with agony, stared back. The Bedouin fell first to his knees, then to his side, dragging Thomas's blade out of his hand.

Remembering his earlier battle with the Terror Fury, Thomas told himself he must keep moving. He pivoted on his knee and looked in the direction of voices coming from behind him. Alain and Roderick were running toward him on foot. Behind them, near the wagons, the other sergeants were sitting calmly atop their destriers while a few fleeing riders made their escape through the woods. Thomas knew he should join the men at the wagons, but realized his sword was still in the form on the ground beside him. He turned back and reached down to retrieve it, but as soon as he placed his hand on the pommel, the Bedouin's body bucked and a high-pitched moan escaped his lips. Thomas flinched and withdrew his hand. He looked at the man's face. His covering had fallen away and Thomas stared into the clean-shaven face of a boy younger than himself. Surely no older than thirteen.

A boy. Mary, Mother of God.

Thomas looked again to his sword embedded up to the hilt in the boy's stomach.

I must remove it. The boy will die…

As soon as he touched the handle, the boy cried out and squirmed in pain. He grabbed onto Thomas's hand with a strength that belied both his size and age. He said something Thomas did not understand and shook his head. His eyes were wide and they would not let Thomas look away.

Thomas was dimly aware of voices behind him, and although he could hear the words, he could not comprehend their meaning, nor tear his eyes from the boy's own.

"Lung shot from the air in the blood," Roderick said.

"Afraid so. This one will not be seeing the stables again," Alain said.

"You want me to put him out?"

Thomas did not know if Alain slit his stallion's throat himself or if he had Roderick do it. But the horse let out one last cry before its suffering was over.

The boy, however, took much longer to die. Thomas sat, the boy's hand clutching his own, until the end. He would not allow the Furies to feed on this one.

CHAPTER FOUR

Badru Hashim pulled his marble white mare to a halt alongside Yusuf and his own mount and let the reins hang loosely in his left hand. He eased his feet out of the stirrups and let his long legs dangle freely only a foot off the ground. After a graceful shake of her long, shapely head, Badru's horse accepted her master's permission to graze the scant foliage at the side of the forest road.

"He said he would be here by midday?" Yusuf asked.

"I expect him shortly. For a merchant he is exceptionally punctual and has never once failed to do what he promised."

"People keep their promises better to some men than others," Yusuf said.

Badru could not tell if Yusuf was being complimentary or impertinent. "People choose who they disappoint in life. I have had my share of disappointments, and I have learned that it is possible to limit a great deal of them with a small measure of forethought."

Yusuf slid down from his saddle. As he allowed his animal to graze, he placed his hand idly on Badru's knee and looked up at him from beneath his shadow.

"Why do I feel you speak of the present more than of the past?"

Badru could not help but look away from Yusuf's handsome face. His fine features harbored not the slightest sign of guile or concealment. His questions always came at Badru like an arrow shot from the most powerful of horn bows, straight and unflinching.

Yusuf's voice dropped in volume. "Am I one of those disappointments you speak of?"

Badru felt anger sweep through him. "Of course not! Why would you say such a thing?"

Yusuf shrugged. His hand dropped from Badru's knee and the huge Mamluk was instantly conscious of the small spot of warmth that fled with it.

"Something is bothering you, Badru. You have claimed in the past it is only the responsibility you feel for keeping your men fed and fulfilled, but I have suspected for some time that it is more than that. Please. Do not deny it. That does neither of us any good."

Another wave of anger flowed through him, and for a moment Badru considered reprimanding Yusuf for his audaciousness. But then the anger turned on itself and he was left with a knot of helplessness in his breast as he looked upon Yusuf's guileless features. His face was bright with a hopeful patience. He was the one man in the world who dared speak to him in such a manner. He no doubt sensed the emotion coursing through Badru. Yet he did not press him and that fact gave Badru the courage to speak.

"You are right. As always, you are right. If I only knew

myself as well as you seem to know my thoughts…"

"Then what is it, Badru? Do we not have everything we always dreamed of? How many times did we lie on your pallet in that Frankish whore's estate and fantasize about being anywhere but there? We would steal moments of our lives from her to be together. Moments of our own lives. And now that Allah has chosen to give us our lives back, what do we have to long for?"

Badru knew what Yusuf was trying to say. He had been a house slave, a servant of the privileged. Freedom had been his dream, not Badru's. A Mamluk without a master was nothing more than a self-serving mercenary.

"I tire of these meaningless contracts," Badru said. "We sell our ship and the lives of the men for silver. The silver of greedy men with no higher purpose in this life than to possess what others have. We take gold for killing rich men's enemies, for bringing them young girls and boys to satiate their lust or to serve in their kitchens. Sometimes both. I do not think this was Allah's plan for us."

Yusuf was quiet for a moment. He let out a breath, considering Badru's words. He would weigh them carefully, for it was rare that Badru offered up much of his inner thoughts.

"For the past eight years you have given your men a purpose. Over thirty men owe you their lives and well being. Is that worth so little to you?"

"Perhaps I only hold them back from the path Allah would have them walk."

"You have given them their freedom, Badru. They are free to follow you or not, and every one of them has chosen."

"A true Mamluk can never be free," Badru said. He felt a familiar pain begin to build at the base of his skull. Instinctively, he closed his eyes and surrendered himself to the white rain until Yusuf's voice pulled him back out.

"What is it you see when you do that, Badru? You go somewhere."

Badru looked at Yusuf. His eyes were bright, shining with life, and his face held the half-smile that never failed to ease Badru's mood, whatever the cause. That smile was a sign that all was right in Yusuf's world. He could have asked Badru for all the terrifying creatures in the Mid-Earth Sea and Badru would have sought each and every one out without hesitation. For him.

"It is a silly thing," Badru said. "You will laugh."

"Tell me. Now I must know," Yusuf said.

"It is one of my earliest memories. I do not know how old I was. Less than five though, for I had not yet begun my training in earnest at the tabaqa. Why do you laugh? I have told you nothing yet."

"I can see you as a child. Need I say more?" Yusuf said, his eyes crinkled at the edges and Badru could tell he was doing his best to contain another outburst.

"All right. Enough of this. It is a foolish story." Badru tried to nudge his horse forward but Yusuf wrapped both of his slender hands around his ankle.

"No, no. I am sorry! Please, continue. Or I swear, I will pester you until we are both older than the sands of the Sahara."

Since Badru knew Yusuf was not exaggerating, he took a

moment to collect his thoughts and continued.

"I was housed together with hundreds of other children. I was quiet, and big for my age, so I had trouble fitting in with the others. Perhaps I did not understand many of them, for they had come from many different lands. I remember often being alone."

Yusuf was no longer laughing. The half-smile was gone and Badru regretted being coaxed into telling him this story. He began to speak faster, eager to be done with it.

"But there was a servant woman, a Georgian I think, who showed me much kindness in those times. She would come sit with me and tell me stories."

"What was her name?" Yusuf asked.

Name? Badru shrugged and shook his head. "I have long since forgotten. But I remember her stories, or at least parts of them. She was the one who told me I had Norse blood, and in the land of the Norsemen, when it rained, the rain was white. The drops so white and thick that, when the wind blew, two people could hold hands, yet not see one another's face."

"Snow…" Yusuf said. "She spoke of snow. Have you ever seen it?"

Badru shook his head. "No. But some days she would come and sit with me. We would close our eyes and imagine we were surrounded by nothing but the cold, the wind, and the white rain. All the world would disappear. Everything but the warmth of her hands."

"What happened to her?"

"All I remember is that once I entered the tabaqa proper,

I never saw her again."

"Why not?"

"I think she was a nursemaid, and since the beginning of our training marked the end of childhood, she would have no longer been allowed to see us. For we were men, then, and had no need of a nursemaid."

Yusuf crossed his arms in front of his chest and his eyebrows arched. "Surely she could have sought you out, at least to visit."

Badru shrugged, and looked off to the trees at the side of the road.

"How old were you the last time you saw her?" Yusuf asked.

"Seven. Perhaps eight."

A silence fell between the two men and Badru avoided looking at Yusuf until he spoke again.

"Thank you," Yusuf said.

"For what?"

"For sharing her story. And a part of yours."

Badru was grateful when a sound not belonging to the forest drew their attention to the bend up ahead in the road. It grew steadily until they could clearly discern the sound of wood rattling against metal, and the squeal of an axle in dire need of a good greasing.

A small wagon drawn by two stocky ponies appeared. Its driver, a short man with a stature matching that of his beasts of burden, was the sole occupant. He raised a hand in greeting and continued his slow, clamorous approach.

Mehmet was a careful man. That was why Badru liked

him. It was not easy to purchase supplies unnoticed for nearly thirty Mamluk warriors and the handful of followers they had picked up over the last few years. But Mehmet and Badru had agreed upon a system that worked for them both. Six years ago, Badru began taking on land-based contracts in addition to his usual sea jobs. This meant he needed to maintain a herd of horses for his men.

He frequently employed mercenaries for some of these jobs. For these rough men, virtually any mount would suffice, but for his Mamluks, their training and status demanded the finest war steeds. He could never hope to afford to buy so many horses on a regular basis, so at Yusuf's suggestion, he purchased breeding stock and oversaw the rearing and training of his own small herd. He took to the new venture with a passion he did not know he possessed. He found himself spending weeks on end with his horses and was miserable when he had to set sail on the Wyvern.

This did not surprise him in any way, for he had always considered himself a child of the desert. If he had not been sold to a slave trader in Marseilles who happened to own one of the fastest galleys on the Mid-Earth Sea, he would have been content living his life without ever learning to sail. But duty demanded otherwise.

"He looks troubled," Yusuf said.

"He always looks that way," Badru said. "He is a miserable man at the best of times."

As the wagon approached, Badru nudged his horse forward a few steps and Yusuf followed, leading his own on foot.

"Peace be with you," Mehmet said. Beneath a light blue turban, the bottom half of his round face broke into a sudden smile, splitting his thick beard with yellowing teeth.

"You are late, Mehmet," Badru said.

"And you brought company," the merchant said, nodding down from his seat at Yusuf. "That is unlike you. Expecting trouble?" He pulled the brake handle on the wagon for the second time.

"You were a sack of flour short last time," Yusuf said. "I am here to confirm the order before we release payment. Please untie the canvas so I may inspect the contents."

Yusuf moved toward the cart and placed a hand on the nearest tie-down, but Mehmet leaned over and intercepted him by grabbing his wrist. Yusuf pulled his wrist away and eyed the man warily.

"It will unknot easier if you know where to start, is all," Mehmet said. "Give me a moment and I will have it off for you."

His sudden movement was a reflex, an uncontrolled response to something he did not want to happen. Badru silently chided himself for not seeing the signs before today. He had become accustomed to Mehmet, perhaps even trusted him to a certain degree. For three years the man had brought foodstuffs in exchange for well-trained horses. It was not always easy for Badru to come up with enough coin to keep his men fed, but horses were another matter. Often the horses were worth far more than the goods Badru received in exchange, but he hoped by making the transaction worthwhile to Mehmet, it would stop him from asking too many questions. It was an arrangement that had benefited them both greatly, but unfortunately, the sheen of perspiration glistening across Mehmet's forehead told Badru this mutually beneficial relationship had come to an end.

Mehmet climbed slowly down off the cart, his eyes looking everywhere except at the two men before him. "You know, it was not easy getting this shipment out of the gates. The guilds demand clear records of everything leaving the city. They want goods coming in, not going out…"

Badru shifted his weight in his saddle and his horse responded. She took three steps toward the wagon. Yusuf saw Badru approach and he backed away. Mehmet had his back to Badru and he continued to spout incessant chatter while his fingers fumbled with the knots holding the canvas covering in place.

"Merchant," Badru said, looking down at the man's back. He would no longer honor the man by using his name. "Merchant. Still your hands. We both know there is nothing under those tarps."

Mehmet's shoulders slumped and his fingers clawed at the knots on the rope one last time before he slowly turned around. He squinted up at Badru. Gone were all traces of the unnatural smile he had worn minutes ago. In its place was the miserable, distrusting face of a man who had forged a life in a world where many could not.

"I am sorry, Badru. I had no choice. They threatened my family."

"Tell me how many and where they are," Badru said.

"Four, maybe five. Frankish dogs, all of them. They are

close. That is all I know."

Franks. They were always Franks.

He had killed his mistress, Veronique Boulet, eight years ago. After all this time, one would have thought the coin on his head would have dried up. Was it her husband who continued to fund these bounty hunters? Badru doubted it. Like Badru, he was also a free man now. No, more than likely the money was from a consortium of French slavers who could not allow their reputations to be diminished by the actions of a former slave.

"Let me go before they arrive. I can still be of use to you, Badru. Let me prove it."

Badru glanced to both sides of the road before looking back at Mehmet. "It is an impossible task to go through life without disappointing someone." He leaned forward over the merchant and held his eyes captive with his own. "My friend and I were talking about this very thing just before you arrived. I feel that the best a man can do is to choose who he disappoints. In this case, you chose well."

Mehmet's eyes widened and the miserable look on his face shed at least a few years.

"You will not regret—" His words choked off. He put his hand to his throat to investigate and it came away wet and slick. Badru wiped the short, curved blade of his khanjar on the side of the merchant's turban. Mehmet followed the movement even as his hand pressed against the gash at his neck, attempting to hold in the blood flowing freely under his beard, giving it a freshly oiled hue.

"You chose wisely," Badru repeated. "Know that I will do

no harm to your family, for you have paid for your treachery."

It took a few seconds before Mehmet's legs gave out and he slid down the wheel of the wagon with blank eyes staring up at Badru. He came to rest propped up against the wheel, with his hand still on his neck, and a stripe of blood marring the side of his pale blue turban.

A man stepped from the trees onto the side of the road a hundred yards away. Another emerged on his left, and together they began walking toward the wagon. Badru sensed motion behind them and saw Yusuf staring intently the way they had come.

"How many?" Badru asked.

"Three. Two with crossbows."

"When the fighting starts, you get under the wagon, between the wheels."

"No. I can help you, Badru."

"That is the best way for you to help."

"You think I cannot fight? You have so little confidence in my abilities that you would have me hide like a coward? I will not!"

The two men ahead were closing the distance. Badru could now see that one had a crossbow while the other had a sword still sheathed at his side. Five men. That in itself was not worrying, but the fact that three had crossbows posed an unpredictable threat. It was a coward's weapon. One that required almost no skill to use, but so deadly even the best armor was no match at close range. Even the Pope had outlawed its use… against Christians only, of course.

"Yusuf, I cannot focus on my adversaries if you are at risk. Please, do as I say." Badru was aware of the quaver in his voice. He hated the sound of it.

One of the two men from up ahead pointed at Mehmet and called out in French, "Fantastic! One man less to pay. I was hoping you would do away with that shifty bastard."

Badru was out of time. He sat up straight in his saddle, well aware that because of his height, his chest was positioned well above his horse's head and presented the crossbowman with an impressive target. They stopped walking thirty paces away. Badru did not have to glance over his shoulder to know the men behind were still approaching.

"You *are* a big one," the leader said, letting out an appreciative whistle. He raised his voice and spoke in broken French. "You come nice. I make big money. You come dead, I make little money. Both good. Nice better. Understand?"

The crossbowman aiming at Badru chuckled and his aim wavered for a second. But he drew in a breath and his weapon was steady once again.

"The Furusiyya demands I allow you to leave if you so wish it," Badru said in French.

The leader let out another low whistle. "By all that is sacred! The bear can talk. No wonder they want you alive."

Badru drew his sword. He noted with satisfaction how his young mare's ears stood at attention, and her muscles tensed, at the soft music of steel gliding against leather and wood.

"However," Badru continued, "a decent man has already died here today because of your actions. Therefore, you will not be permitted to leave."

Two quick taps of Badru's heels into his horse's side and she leapt forward, hitting a canter after only a single stride. With his scimitar clutched in his right hand, Badru threw his arms wide and allowed the mare's momentum to bend his body back at the waist, until his shoulder blades came to rest on her rump. The rear edge of the saddle dug into the small of his back, but he exhaled and willed his muscles to relax, molding himself to his horse's back. There was a buzz overhead, the sound of wind rushing past wooden vanes at great speed. He stretched his right arm back, allowing his horse to support the weight of his sword and shoulder, and then he began his rise.

Halfway up, he felt his blade stick as it made contact with the crossbowman's chest. There was no need to swing it, for the curved blade drew itself into the cut. Badru wedged his elbow against his horse's side and let her thousand pounds of momentum take over. Once his sword began its work, there was no more pressure on Badru's arm. The blade ripped into the man diagonally across his chest, opening him like a ripe peach.

The other man passed by Badru on his left, his sword not yet cleared from its scabbard. As Badru wheeled his horse around, he heard a Mamluk war cry. Two riders thundered up the road behind the three other bounty hunters. One of them managed to loose a frantic bolt in their general direction but the other's head was separated from his shoulders before he had acquired a target.

Badru was confused for a brief moment. Why were his

Mamluks here? He had not ordered them to come. He left the thought alone as he charged the Frankish leader. The man had managed to draw his sword, and by his relaxed grip, Badru could tell he had training. But Badru's mare also had training, although no real experience. Badru seized upon the opportunity to give her some.

He could have run the Frank down but opted instead to pull back hard on the reins and put his horse into a rear. She rose on her hind legs and kicked out with her fronts, hitting the man in the chest with one of her hooves. He spun like he was caught in a whirlwind and fell to the ground hard. Badru stroked his mare's neck and praised her in one of the tongues of the desert dwellers as she pranced around her fallen opponent. Mehmet would have been pleased with this one.

Badru walked her to the wagon and dismounted. He handed her reins to Yusuf and said, "Why are Safir and Kemal here? I told them to stay with the ship."

"I asked them to come," Yusuf said.

"And the other times I have been alone?"

Yusuf looked away and shook his head. "You have never been alone."

"You overstep your position," Badru said.

"And you take too many risks. If we lose you, we lose everything!"

Badru blinked at the intensity in Yusuf's voice. He did not need to be reminded of his responsibilities.

The two Mamluk warriors walked their horses toward them, leaving one headless body and another bloodied corpse in their wake. A third man dragged behind Safir's horse with a rope around his neck, his fingers clawing ineffectually at the hemp.

"Only one lives, Emir," Safir said. He unwrapped the rope from his saddle and tossed it to the ground.

Safir and Kemal dismounted. The Frankish leader had pushed himself up to a sitting position. His sword was within reach but he wisely left it where it lay.

"Pick it up," Badru said. "If you defeat me, you and your man will go free."

The Frank spat on the ground. "I do not believe that for a minute, heathen."

Badru shrugged. "I may be many things, but I do not lie. It is my intention to stake you to the ground and open up your back in front of your man. Then I will cut the ribs from your spine with this." He patted the khanjar at his belt. "And when your screams have quieted down, I will pull the lungs from your body and heap them quivering on the ground for all to see."

Badru looked at the man with the rope around his neck. His face was red, his eyes darted everywhere at once, and a vein throbbed at his temple. "You will live to tell what happened here today. But you will never be the same."

His next words were addressed to the leader. "As Allah as my witness, so shall it be. Now, take up your sword."

CHAPTER FIVE

Three knocks sounded on the door. They were tentative, careful even, yet precise. Foulques set his quill down and leaned back in his chair.

"Enter," he said.

Thomas Schwyzer opened the door, stepped through quickly, and then eased the door closed. The only sound it made was when the latch caught.

"I was told to report to you, Commander," he said.

The young man standing at attention before Foulques looked to be about fourteen. Certainly no older than fifteen. Foulques motioned for him to approach his desk. He was tall and lanky, yet he moved well enough thanks to the years of physical discipline he had endured. Even so, he almost tripped as his foot snagged the edge of a lush Persian carpet spread over the floorboards.

Thomas's eyes could not help but stray about the room, taking in the eastern carpets, the tapestries on the walls, and the sheer fabric curtains covering windows of glass so fine you could almost see through them.

Seated behind his uncle's ornately carved desk, even

Foulques himself must look like he had just stepped out of the bazaar. His usual black Hospitaller tunic was replaced by the loose-fitting silks and linens that the Arabs preferred, but his head was uncovered, leaving his mass of black hair to float unfettered around his head.

"The East has much to offer," Foulques said, sweeping his arm around the room. "Why else would so many Franks come to these lands?"

Thomas shifted his feet, and looked like he was preparing an answer, but he said nothing. After an uncomfortable silence, Foulques stood, walked to the window, and looked out. Even though he could see nothing, he liked to stand there and bask in the sun's light. "Your studies go well?"

"Yes, Commander," Thomas said, finding his voice.

"Weapons Master Glynn speaks highly of your abilities," Foulques said, turning back to face Thomas. "Especially with the dagger. Not the noblest of weapons though, I must say." It was a curious choice of weapon, Foulques thought. While most young men were seduced by the nobility of the sword, Thomas had recently all but given it up and specialized in mace and dagger.

"I have been told you requested extra hours working in the hospital. Do you seek to replace your martial training with something you see as less strenuous?"

"No, Commander. I would use the hours I have free in the evening after Vespers."

Foulques nodded. "It is good you have an interest in medicine, for that is the founding vocation of our order. However, God has willed you should become a soldier, not a physician. Do you understand this?"

Thomas looked down at the ground. "Yes."

"How many patrols have you ridden out on?"

"One a week for the past year."

"Have you taken the lives of any of the enemy?"

Thomas looked up and one of his dark eyes twitched.

"I have killed a boy," he said, finally. "Though I thought him a man at the time."

Foulques had already known the answer to his question. But he wanted to hear how the event was weighing on the young man's soul.

"Boys grow into men. Men who would undermine the one true faith. You carried out God's will and that is the end of it. Think no more on it, for there will be more. Many more."

Foulques turned back to the window and gazed out. "If I grant you permission to work extra hours in the hospital, then you must do something for me."

The boy's head snapped up and he straightened. "Of course, Commander!"

"You will learn to read and write. First in Latin, then Arabic."

A confused look flooded Thomas's face. "Arabic, Commander?"

"Of course. Latin may be the word of God, but Arabic is the language of medicine. Although Frankish doctors are loath to admit it, the Arabian hakim are vastly superior. The works of the great Greek and Roman physicians have been lost to the West for centuries, but not to the East."

"But the writings of Galen and Hippocrates have already been translated to Latin," Thomas said. "One of the monks showed us copies."

"Copies, yes. Copies of Arabic texts. The originals are long lost, so the Latin versions are translations of Arabic works. I feel the Latin copies possess a sometimes diluting layer of interpretation that the Arabic texts never intended."

"You have read them?"

"Yes, and so should you, provided it does not interfere with your military training. But not only the works of Galen and Hippocrates. Arabic medicine is the medicine of the Islamic world, not just the Arabs. That means that the Persians and Nestorians in the east and even the Spanish and Jews in the west have all contributed to Arabic medicine. You will become familiar with these works as well."

"The Jews? But they are the enemy of Christ," Thomas said.

"So we are told. But as His soldiers, then is it not our duty to learn from the enemy? The truth is, as Hospitallers we owe the Jews and Muslims a great deal for keeping the knowledge of the ancients alive. Knowledge long ago lost in the west, due in no small part to the Church's fear of the common man exploring the divine mysteries of the human body. The Church is content to have us refuse medical treatment and pray while sickness ravages our body, leaving our lives in the hands of God alone."

Foulques felt his face begin to flush, but he could not help himself. To the horror of many priests and monks, he saw nothing wrong with using the corpses from battlefields to further medical knowledge. Surely some good could come from the violent deaths of both Mohammedans and Christians alike. So long as they were buried or cremated properly after an examination, where was the harm in furthering their knowledge if it could save lives?

"But surely the Church's position has changed," Thomas said. "We are, after all, an exempt Order subject only to the Pope himself. If the Church was truly against the study of medicine, why would they have allowed the Hospitallers to form in the first place?"

Foulques's eyes narrowed at the boy's question and he wondered if he, himself, had ever been so naive. "Although both the Templars and the Hospitallers are sworn to poverty, we control vast fortunes that rival that of many monarchs. In fact, a good deal of that fortune has been earned by lending money to Kings. But often wealth is merely the illusion of power. For the moment only the Pope himself has the power to command us, but that will not always be so. Change is the only constant in life." Foulques spoke the words, but in them he heard his Uncle Guillaume's conviction, a certain righteousness that he was not certain he possessed.

Foulques fixed his gaze once more on the window. He thought of his uncle, somewhere in England, and the games he must be playing to keep the supply ships coming with grain, weapons, and men. Supply ships that could just as easily be sent under a Templar flag, or even the black cross of the Teutonics. Word had it that support for the Germans grew greater in England with every passing year. "We tread softly here," Foulques said, continuing to stare out the cloudy glass. "Much softer than you can possibly imagine. Especially now. The Mohammedans are not the only wolf baying at our door."

Foulques took a deep breath, then wheeled around. "But I did not summon you here to lecture. In return for me allowing you to study in the hospital, I have a task that you are to complete for me. But it is for me alone. No one is to know of our conversation today. Is that clear?"

"Yes." Thomas's eyes darted around the room once before answering. Foulques could tell all this talk was making him nervous. He reached down to his desk and lifted a rolled up scroll with the names of three hundred of the original Schwyzers. With the help of Glynn and Brother Alain, Foulques had created the list, but the marshal would only allow him to take one hundred. He needed someone closer to them, an insider, to make the final cut.

"First you must learn to read the three hundred names on this list. Then you will learn to write well enough to prepare your own list of the one hundred young men you think are the most suitable. They must be strong of arm and skilled in combat. But above all, loyal. Select only those you would trust with your life, and make no mistake on it, for that is precisely what you will be doing. You have sixty days to complete your task before we depart."

Thomas's eyes widened. "Depart? Where are we going?"

"Our hospice on the island of Cyprus," Foulques said. "Ready all your possessions to take with you, Thomas, for once we leave, Acre will no longer be your home."

Or my home.

Foulques turned back to the window so the boy would not see his own eyes cloud over.

CHAPTER SIX

A L-ASHRAF KHALIL STOOD at attention beside his seated father. He held his helmet under one arm and watched the three Hospitallers approach slowly through a gap in the Mamluk army. In the distance, behind the Christians, were the towers of Margat squatting against the blue waters of the Mid-Earth Sea.

The sun glinted off the armor of the knights as they approached and the front man held aloft a flag pole bearing the white cross of the Order on a field of red. From afar, they made a brilliant display, but as they neared the small hill where Qalawun had set his pavilion, Khalil could see the grime on the men's armor. Their stilted gait hinted at a weariness set deep in their bones and the dullness in their eyes told the story of a siege that had gone on long enough. They had come to surrender the fortress and seek terms with the sultan.

Khalil found himself smiling. It had been over three years since he had executed those Knights of Saint John who had sided with the Mongols. His father had promised him then that the knights would be punished for breaking their truce, but three years was an eternity for a young man, and Khalil had almost lost hope that this day would come. But come it had. The sultan had, in secret, begun to raise an army in Damascus. No small feat in a land filled with spies and court officers forever trying to clamber into better positions with little regard for those they must throw to the lions. The sultan had raised an elite force of over fifty thousand men before he mentioned it casually over a roast lamb dinner one evening to his son. Three days later Khalil was marching beside his father at the head of a good portion of that army.

The knights of Margat had mounted a strong defense, until, one by one, the towers of the fortress began to drop to the sappers of the sultan's army. In a few more days their walls would be on the ground and they would be defenseless. The Christians had no choice but to surrender.

At the bottom of the hill, Turuntay and his men relieved the knights of their weapons, but when they tried to take the flag bearer's pole he pushed the Mamluks away and clutched the flag to his chest. Turuntay looked to his sultan for guidance and Qalawun gave him a nod to let him keep it. For now.

Turuntay guided the men up the hill and presented them to the sultan. The shortest and eldest of the three stepped forward and introduced himself as the Prior of Margat. He spat his words and curled his lips in disdain at the sultan himself.

Though Khalil had been studying French for the last few years his efforts were half-hearted at best and he struggled to understand the uncouth knight. In his mind, it was these invaders who should be learning Turkic, or at least Arabic. Why should he have to twist his tongue with the Franks' barbaric language?

Khalil looked back over his shoulder and picked out Ibn al-Salus from the group of soldiers standing nearby. He was the son of a merchant from Damascus and held the position of apprentice clerk in the sultan's court. The young man wore no armor, which was just as well, for judging from the strength of his build he would not be able to bear anything heavier than leather. But Ibn al-Salus had been a playmate of Khalil's when he was growing up and was the closest thing Khalil had to a friend. Khalil always found ways to keep him nearby even though the difference in their societal classes often made it awkward. He summoned Ibn al-Salus with a nod of his head and the young man came to stand behind Khalil.

"What are they saying?" Khalil whispered as his father began to speak directly to the Frank.

"The sultan offers terms. If the Hospitallers surrender their walls and weapons, they will all be allowed to leave with as much as they can carry," Ibn al-Salus said.

Khalil bit his tongue. Allowed to leave? With whatever they could carry? These were the same traitors who had sided with the Mongols and now his father would simply allow them to walk away bearing treasures?

The Frank muttered more unintelligible words. Khalil cast an impatient glance toward Ibn al-Salus.

"I think he said that would be acceptable. His men-at-arms would relinquish their weapons but the knights must be allowed to retain their swords."

The sultan coughed a few times into his hand and then sat up straighter in his seat as he fixed the Hospitaller in place with his dark eyes. After a long moment of silence he nodded once and said a few words in French.

"You father says he is only interested in taking the fortress of Margat, not the dignity of the brave men who defended it."

Khalil had heard enough. He shrugged away from Ibn al-Salus's hand on his shoulder and backed away from the throng of Mamluks around the sultan's dais. Ignoring the harsh looks from them all, he turned and strode swiftly away, his fists clenching uncontrollably.

He could not comprehend his father's thoughts. For three years he had labored to punish these men and now he let them walk away like they had never done anything wrong. Where was the justice in that? He found a flat rock overlooking the castle in the distance. The fortress was bleak and gray, in the middle of nowhere. Hardly a strategic position worth all this fuss.

Minutes later he heard footsteps crunching on the rocky path behind him. He turned, expecting to see his boyhood friend Ibn al-Salus, but was surprised to see the helmeted head of Turuntay, his father's highest ranking emir striding toward him.

"Khalil, there you are. I have been looking for you," Turuntay said.

"And you seem to have found me," Khalil said.

Turuntay walked up to the boulder Khalil sat on and took a step closer than Khalil felt comfortable with, no doubt trying to intimidate the younger man. Khalil stood straight up, his face almost grazing the chain hauberk of the stocky warrior general.

"Well?" Khalil said, his face inches from Turuntay's own.

"The sultan summons you," Turuntay said, his eyes and tone of voice did not show the slightest hint of respect.

"And I will attend him once the stink of the Christians has faded from his presence."

Turuntay's lips spread into a line. "You will attend him now. For he sent me to bring you to him, and unlike some, I bend to the will of my sultan. Now, you can follow me or I can drag you kicking and screaming like a petulant child. Think carefully on your next words."

The general's speech hit Khalil like a slap in the face. Never before had he been so direct and insulting.

"And why should he so suddenly desire my counsel? He showed little need of it just now."

"You are correct. He has no desire for counsel. We are to break camp and begin a forced march at dawn tomorrow."

"March? The army is not to be disbanded?"

"Disbanded?" Turuntay laughed. "You think we have spent these past months raising an army this size for the sole purpose of taking one remote Hospitaller castle manned by a handful of knights? But I need not tell you any of this, if you had stayed at your sultan's side instead of running away to sulk."

"Tell me what? Where is our destination?"

"We march to gather our forces and swell our ranks until our numbers are greater than any force ever assembled in the lands of Mohammed. With this force we will drive the Christians back into the foaming sea, and with time, the stain they have made upon this land will be washed away and forgotten."

Khalil's heart began to hammer. Drive them into the sea? But that could mean only one target, one destination…

Turuntay seemed to read Khalil's mind, for he smiled and nodded eagerly, his eyes moistening with emotion.

"Yes, Khalil. The time has come. We march first to Tripoli, then on to the last great city of Christendom. Acre herself. Once we have control of the Christian stronghold, there will be nowhere from which they can launch any further counterattacks. The only direction they will be able to run is back into the sea."

CHAPTER SEVEN

Pirmin called it the shining star of the Pisan Quarter. A place fit for princes and princesses, the hidden jewel of Acre that welcomed only the most deserving of patrons. And yet, the first thing Thomas thought when he stooped to enter the door of The Three-Legged Goat Taverna and Inn was *what was that smell?*

Physik Rafi had said on more than one occasion that Thomas had a good nose about him. A skill that came in handy in the Order's apothecary when identifying unguents and herbal concoctions. But this was one of those moments when it would have been desirable to be less gifted. As he stepped into the low-ceilinged, dimly lit room, an odor hit his face with the force of a slap. It was a sour combination of smoke mixed with equal parts sweat, urine, and honey. Overwhelmed by that and the noise, Thomas stood rooted in place just inside the entrance.

"Come on, get in there," Pirmin said pushing Thomas in the back. He skittered a few steps forward until his thighs smacked up against a table with three men sitting at it with clay mugs of ale in front of them. One of the mugs performed a rocking motion back and forth, back and forth, and for its finale tipped over and covered the table in a deluge of sticky ale.

"Hey, boy!" shouted a squat man with black hair and a thick, spiky beard crisscrossed with white lines where scars on his face would not allow any hair to grow. "By a witch's cold hole, you—"

"Watch that foul mouth of yours, Manny," Pirmin said as he wormed through the doorway. He came to stand beside Thomas and rose up to his full height, his golden hair brushing the lowest of the ceiling beams that supported the floor above like he was built in place when the building itself was erected. They both wore non-descript tunics of brown linen without any crosses or other insignia that might mark them as men of the Hospital. At fourteen, Thomas was taller than many men, but still had the willowy build of a youth. Pirmin, being three or four years older, had an impressive physique and seemed to be adding another five pounds of mass every week.

"Ah, Pirmin. Did not know the boy was with you. He surprised me is all. I just spent my last copper on that mug."

Pirmin produced a small purse Thomas had never seen before from beneath his belt. He slapped two coins down on the wet table. "Well, I will not have a man spend his last copper on a drink. Unless it is for me, of course."

Manny covered the coins with a wet slap of one broad hand before either of the other two men at his table could blink. "Thanks, Pirmin. I will get you back next time."

"You seen Jean around?" Pirmin asked.

"Yeah, he was in the back last I saw. You wrestling tonight?"

"Did not plan on it, but you never know. Me and Thomi are here to celebrate."

He slapped Thomas on the back and motioned for him to follow. They pushed their way further into the long, narrow room and sat at a small table two men had just vacated, leaving behind two mugs. Pirmin inspected the mugs and gave a satisfactory nod.

"Drinks are cheaper if we use a dirty mug. Shaping up to be a good night already, Thomi."

Pirmin waved to catch the attention of a girl with a tray warping under the weight of three full serving pitchers, but he need not have. Thomas had noticed her glancing in the big youth's direction several times already. She set the tray in the middle of a long table full of men. She told them to fill up their own mugs, and after slapping away a couple of hands reaching for her breasts, she took up one of the pitchers and carried it over to Pirmin and Thomas.

She and Pirmin locked eyes as he held out his mug. She poured using both of her slender hands. Thomas was struck by how tiny and graceful they were in contrast to the thick, callused hands of his friend. And yet, she showed remarkable strength in the casual way she controlled the heavy pitcher. Thomas was still staring at her hands when Pirmin spoke.

"You are a sight for thirsty eyes, Corrine."

Thomas had the feeling that the same comment from any other man in the room would have elicited a slap from those porcelain hands, but instead, she blushed and the hard lines around her eyes softened as she looked at Pirmin. Then she seemed to notice Thomas for the first time.

"Who might your friend be?"

"This is Thomas. And he is more brother to me than any man ever had."

She reached out one of her hands, and just like that, cupped it under his wrist. Her touch was warm and softer than the finest calf hair glove.

"If you want that mug filled, you will have to hold it steadier than that." It was Thomas's turn to redden, now. He lifted his mug a little higher and her hand left his own to help with steadying the pitcher, but the warmth on his wrist stayed with him as she boldly looked him over. Her gaze lingered on the old scar stretching the skin from the corner of his eye to his jawline, as most people's did. Thomas looked down at his full drink.

"You should bring him around more often," Corrine said.

Pirmin pulled two coins from his purse. "One for the drinks, the other for you."

"Pirmin, are you trying to buy my favors?"

"The sweetest things in life are never bought," Pirmin said, subjecting her to one of his best white-toothed grins.

She shook her head. "And what would Emma say if she heard you talking like that?" She turned and took a step in the direction of her abandoned tray and pitchers, but looked back over her shoulder. "Good thing she is not working tonight." The fingers of her left hand performed a graceful dance along her hip as she walked away.

Thomas was still watching her thread through the crowd when Pirmin said, "What a beautiful night, eh Thomi?"

Thomas smiled and remembered he held a full tankard in his hand. He took a sip and it made his eyes water. A thought occurred to him. "Where did you get the purse?"

"The purse or the coin within?"

"Both."

"The purse was a present from Emma. She sewed it herself, but it came with nothing but a sprig of lavender inside."

Pirmin was being evasive. He wanted Thomas to ask about this Emma, but Thomas would not be deterred. "And the coin?"

"I would rather not say," Pirmin said.

Thomas was quiet for a moment. He took another drink. "Did you steal it?"

"No! Of course not. I earned it, fair and simple by doing a few things for Max. Do not look at me like that."

Max was well known as the "procurer" for many of the boys in the Hospitaller compound, and a good number of the monks, as well. He always had some trinket he was trying to sell or trade. No one knew how he came across these items, but it was starting to all make sense to Thomas now. In fact, both Pirmin's knife and the loaner at Thomas's belt had come from Max. Neither of them had their own weapons. All swords and armor were returned to the armory at the end of training each day.

It was not easy to get leave of the Hospitaller fortress and enter the city proper. But Pirmin had been sneaking out of the compound since he was a young boy. Of course, he had also been caught more times than Thomas could count. Pirmin may have had the good looks of a Greek statue but he had the striped back of a slave. Father Dusseault liked to say that Pirmin was more half-wild dog than man, and no amount of punishment could curb his desire to wander.

"Relax, Thomi. I smuggle things through the gates to Max. Sometimes I pay merchants, or go with Max when he does. All honest work. Go ahead and drink up. Nothing I have done to earn this coin will make Saint Peter's list, I swear."

Thomas knew Pirmin had already flirted with more than his share of sin in his short life, but lying to friends was not one of those. Thomas gave in and took another long pull off his ale. It was warm, thin, and had a bitter bite. It was undoubtedly inferior to the brews the nuns made in the Hospitaller compound, but at that moment, Thomas was convinced it was the best thing he had ever tasted.

Pirmin nodded and gave Thomas a knowing grin. "Did I not tell you? Look around at this place. Have you ever seen more life anywhere in the Kingdom of Jerusalem?"

Thomas laughed. Pirmin was a lord of exaggeration. Neither one of them had ever been anywhere but Acre, not that the current Kingdom of Jerusalem extended far past her borders these days.

"I can think of a half dozen taverns that come close," Thomas said. "But you are right. This place has no rival in all the Levant. Here is to the Goat." He held out his mug. Pirmin held aloft his tankard and they clanked them together. They each drained off a good third of their mugs before coming up for air.

"Speaking of lists and my good friend Max," Pirmin said, "did he make yours?"

Thomas was not prepared for the question. "Pirmin, you know I am not supposed to talk about that with anyone."

"Come on. I am not anyone."

"Is that why you brought me with you tonight? Did Max pay you to bring me here?"

"Thomi… it is not like that."

Thomas leaned back against the wall. The fact Pirmin did not get angry at the accusation meant Thomas was closer to the truth than he liked. He should have known.

"I never should have told you about the list," Thomas said.

"You had to. It was driving you crazy spending all those extra hours with the monks and their letters. Max just thinks it would be a good business opportunity for him to go to Cyprus for a while. He wanted me to put in a word for him in case he was not already on the list."

"And what did you say?"

Pirmin shrugged. "I said he was probably already on the list. But I would bring it up next time we spoke."

"And he filled that fancy purse for you," Thomas said.

Pirmin grinned. "What are friends for if not to buy one another the odd tankard?" He leaned forward and put both elbows on the small table. Thomas had to pull his drink away to keep it from being spilled. "So? Is he on it?"

"He is not," Thomas said, holding Pirmin's stare. "I am

only permitted one hundred names and Maximillion is not one of those."

"Yah, but he could be, right? Do you know how to write it? I think Max does. I could get him to show you how if need be."

Thomas let out a breath. Pirmin would dog him forever on this. When he set his stubborn mind to something…

"Thomi. He is a friend. And he wants to go see a bigger piece of this world. I said I would do what I could."

Thomas had never had much cause to interact with Max. Like Pirmin, he was three or four years older and was a little gruff at times. It would be a simple matter to put his name on the list, as he had not yet submitted it to Master Foulques.

"All right, I will do it," Thomas said. "But I will have to take someone's name off, first."

Pirmin clapped him on the shoulder. "Excellent. It should be a simple thing to pick someone that does not know about it."

"No one knows about it," Thomas said. He was about to question Pirmin about the sheepish look on his face when Pirmin's eyes caught on someone standing in a doorway at the end of the room. The man was waving him over.

"Drink up, Thomi, and I will show you yet another way to fill a purse. He got up and Thomas followed Pirmin through the doorway. They entered a good-sized open space created with tables pushed up against the walls. A group of men stood around one table with a stack of coins on it. A man detached himself from the group as Pirmin and Thomas approached.

"Evening, Jean," Pirmin said.

"I have a new one for you, Pirmin. He has been here every night this week and has not yielded once. He brought friends too, so the purse is well worth our while. If you think you can beat him, that is."

Jean nodded toward a group of a half dozen men milling along the far wall. It took only a second for Thomas to surmise who would be Pirmin's opponent. A scowling, black-haired, bull of a man stood with his arms crossed, sizing up Pirmin. He wrinkled his nose and said something to the men around him that elicited a round of laughter.

"Looks strong enough," Pirmin said. "Smelling, that is. I will need soap after this one."

"Do not take him lightly, lad," Jean said. "He has dropped all comers. He has a fast start and aims to put a man on his knees first thing."

Thomas knew what Jean was talking about. There was not a boy living in the Levant, and most girls for that matter, who had not tried his hand at the game of Fingers at one time or another.

The rules were simple: two opponents faced each other and interlocked their fingers. Each one then attempted to make the other yield by bending and twisting his opponent's fingers in the most painful positions possible. No head-butting allowed. That was it. If there were any other rules, Thomas was not aware of them. The game was popular amongst drinking men, so broken fingers were the norm rather than a rare occurrence.

Thomas pulled Pirmin aside. "You sure you want to do

this tonight? He looks like he has some strength in those hands." The thick-set man had laced his fingers together and was working them against one another while he stared at Pirmin. He was shorter than Pirmin, but was broader across the chest. His arms were short, his forearms massive, and Thomas thought that would give him a leverage advantage in this contest.

"He is a hairy little troll, I give you that," Pirmin said.

"Do not be afraid to yield," Thomas said. "I will not be feeding you your soup if you cannot hold a spoon for the next month."

"Thank you for the words of encouragement," Pirmin said. He winked at Thomas and stepped into the open area to begin the contest. Pirmin was a head taller than the stockier man, but as they jammed their fingers together, Thomas saw Pirmin's eyes flicker with surprise at the man's strength.

A third man stepped forward to play the part of master of fights, but aside from telling the men to begin and warning them not to head-butt, there was little else for him to do.

The cheering started as a few shouts of encouragement, but as the men's movements became wilder and more strained, the shouting began in earnest. Back and forth they struggled, taking turns grunting with exertion or pain as fingers and knuckles creaked and cracked. More than once the onlookers let out a collective groan as one man bent the other's fingers over in a painful lock, but no one yielded.

Pirmin's face had reddened and he had not smiled in a

long time. He was no longer having fun.

His opponent pushed both hands forward toward Pirmin's chest, and then quicker than a snake, whipped only his right hand around and down to the outside, forcing Pirmin up on his toes. The shorter man wedged his elbow in tight against his body and looked like an immovable rock, while Pirmin danced on his toes trying to stop his left wrist from giving away to the point where he could no longer resist the pressure on his fingers.

Thomas recognized the danger. Yield, he thought. This game is not worth broken fingers. No sooner had the thought entered his mind than Pirmin hopped slightly to his right and twisted his right hand by bringing his elbow up level with his hand. The movement turned his opponent's wrist sideways with his little finger pointed upwards. Thomas recognized the position as a sword or knife disarming technique they often used in practice. It was an excruciatingly painful joint lock, one which could very easily result in a broken wrist.

The stocky man yelped once, then his face twisted in fury when he realized his left wrist was being attacked. He let out a yell and flexed his wrist and forearm with all he had, pushing Pirmin back. But that was what Pirmin was waiting for.

While his opponent was channeling all his power into his left arm, he gave up control with his right. Pirmin suddenly stepped to his left while circling his left arm up to chest height. Using his newfound leverage, he twisted over his opponent's wrist once again into the same position as the other arm and bore down on the fragile joint. The man screamed as the connective tissues holding his wrist onto his forearm were stretched to their tearing point. In a desperate bid to escape the pain, his legs gave out and his knees crashed onto the floor.

"Yield!" Pirmin shouted.

The man resisted and attempted to rise, but Pirmin put more pressure on his wrist and the man's knees hit the floor once again. This time he could not get the words out fast enough.

"Yield! I yield, God damn you."

He was still kneeling on the ground, cradling his arm, when Pirmin picked up his winnings and steered Thomas to a new table near the entrance of the tavern. Corrine brought them two new mugs of ale and Thomas noticed Pirmin's swollen fingers had a slight tremor to them as he wrapped them around his tankard.

"You know you cheated," Thomas said. "It is called 'Fingers' for a reason."

"Yah, well the bugger almost broke mine," Pirmin said. "Even if I had yielded he would have gone ahead and done it, I am sure." He gave the fingers on his left hand a quick rub. "I admit the troll was stronger than he looked."

"He looked plenty strong to me," Thomas said.

Pirmin gave his hands one last shake and then held up his mug. "To the troll! This round is on him."

It was almost midnight when they left. Pirmin was still talking about Corrine when three men stepped out of the shadows before them. Another four closed off the path to their rear. Thomas felt the pleasant glow of the evening's drinks flee from his system, and he was left with a cool tremor running along his spine as he recognized the squat form of the man Pirmin had bested in the tavern earlier. All the men he could see were armed with swords. Two of them were drawn. Thomas was about to draw his own knife when Pirmin whispered, "Easy Thomi. There are too many. Let me talk this out."

A tall man standing next to the stocky form of the troll spoke up. "My friend here says you owe him something."

"The big monkey almost broke my wrists," the troll said, his words slurred with drink.

"Almost is the key word here," Pirmin said. "You may have trouble holding a spoon for a few days," he shot Thomas a sidelong glance and one corner of his mouth turned up in a grin. "But I would wager my entire purse nothing is broken."

The tall man said, "The time for wagers is over. How about we just take that purse off you and call it a night."

Pirmin looked slowly around at the seven men surrounding them. "Normally, I might argue your point, but it is getting late." He pulled the purse from his belt and tossed it to the tall man. It flopped through the air and hardly made a sound when he plucked it out of the air.

"Feels a little light," he said. "Maybe you are trying to cheat us. But then, that would not be the first time, would it?" He drew his sword and the man next to him followed suit.

Thomas and Pirmin drew their knives, both woefully

aware of how outnumbered they were. Thomas could sense the blood pumping in Pirmin, saw his chest heave with breath and his muscles tense, and then he launched himself forward at the three men. For a split second Thomas envied the ability of his friend to burst into action. He lost no time to any agonizing decision-making process. He saw something that needed doing, so he did it. But this was sheer lunacy.

Pirmin had already crashed into the three men in front by the time Thomas had cleared his own knife from its scabbard. He considered turning on the men coming up from behind, but quickly discarded that idea. He stepped forward to help Pirmin.

Pirmin was embroiled with the three men in a tangled mass of arms and legs. One of the men was on the ground wrapping himself around Pirmin's thigh, another was on his back. The troll had one hand on Pirmin's throat, while the other was locked around Pirmin's knife wrist.

Thomas considered knifing the man riding Pirmin's back, but he hesitated, for no blood had yet been drawn from what he could tell. Instead, he wrapped his arm around the man's neck and attempted to pull him off his friend. He choked him with the crook of his elbow until he came away, then he felt a heavy blow to the back of his head.

His vision clouded and he remembered thinking he was grateful it was not a naked blade. Then he felt more blows on his face and body, and when his vision cleared, he was on the ground with boots flying at him from all directions. A big shape next to him was receiving a similar treatment. Dull, thudding pain shook his entire body and every breath became a struggle. Thomas could do nothing but curl into an even tighter ball. Then, mercifully, the barrage ceased.

He heard the tall man's voice, a little out of breath. "Let Malcolm finish the big one, if he can hold a blade. Make the young one watch so he learns something from all this."

Laughter erupted in a full circle around Thomas and Pirmin, as rough hands jerked Thomas to his feet. He coughed and had to spit out a mouthful of blood before he could catch his breath. His sides hurt with every inhalation, but he could tell his ribs were not broken. Someone grabbed him by the hair and turned his head. He saw the troll with a short sword in hand, standing over Pirmin.

"I am going to start with your fingers, you bastard. This will not be quick."

Panic dulled all the pain in Thomas's body and his chest heaved. Pirmin groaned and stirred on the ground. In a moment of clarity, Thomas knew he would rather die than live and watch his friend be killed in front of him. A voice inside accused him of being selfish.

The troll stomped down on one of Pirmin's wrists and he raised his sword over the youth's hand. He stayed there for what seemed an eternity. A glint of light flashed in the left side of the troll's chest and then faded away with a soft, sucking noise. The troll tottered from one foot to the other and then pitched forward head first onto the ground. He lay there unmoving, crossed neatly over the inert form of Pirmin.

As Thomas raised his head, he saw another cross. This

one brilliant white and unmoving, piercing the blackness of the night like a harvest moon. Above the cross was the gray beard of what Thomas thought must surely be an apparition brought on by the heat of the moment. Only when the figure spoke did Thomas begin to think he was not imagining the spectral figure.

"Unhand the lad," Marshal Clermont said.

"Shit! He killed Malcolm," one of the men holding Thomas said.

"Get out of here, old man. This is not your business," said the man who had taken Pirmin's purse.

Marshal Clermont lunged and anyone with an untrained eye would have sworn he did not move at all, for he had returned to his starting position, sword by his side. The tall man clutched feebly at his throat. Blood, black because of the lack of any light source, poured around his hand and dripped off his elbow. Then it turned red as nearby lanterns beat back the darkness.

"Make way for the watch! Clear a path. What is going on here?" Several new figures materialized out of the gloom. The men holding Thomas swore and took their hands away as an officer of the city guard approached. Thomas dropped to one knee as a fresh wave of pain lodged itself somewhere deep in his ribs.

The city soldiers fanned around in a semi-circle with their spears leveled. The officer drew his sword even as he said, "Any man with a naked blade in his hand will be cut down by my men."

After very little hesitation everyone sheathed their

swords. Everyone, that is, except for Marshal Clermont. He flipped the point back and brazenly rested it on his shoulder once everyone else had stored their weapons.

"What happened here?" the city guard commander asked.

"He killed two of our friends," one of the men who had been holding Thomas said. He pointed at the bodies of the troll and the corpse of the tall man with the gaping neck wound lying nearby. Pirmin was still on the ground, but at least he was moving.

"I did not ask you," the officer snapped. He turned to the marshal and waited.

Marshal Clermont nodded. "I killed these two men and was about to kill the rest when you intervened."

"You see? We did nothing!"

"Shut up," the commander said, without looking in the man's direction. The muscles in his jaw moved back and forth as he looked at the Hospitaller. "What would you have me do with these men?" he finally asked.

Marshal Clermont looked at each of the men in question. Thomas had seen this appraisal of his before, when he looked over men in the training yard. Thomas suspected he was not impressed with what he saw.

"Let them go. The city will have need of all types of men in the near future. But escort these two lads back to the Hospital. I fear they have become lost."

The marshal did not wait for the officer to respond. Instead, he turned to Thomas. "I know his name is Pirmin. What is yours, boy?"

Thomas licked his lips and took a moment to get his tongue moving. "Thomas, Marshal. Thomas Schwyzer."

Marshal Clermont narrowed his eyes and nodded. He turned and strode away into the night. Thomas did not know it at the time, but those would be the first, and the last, words he would ever speak to Master Mathieu de Clermont, "the Mongoose" of the Order of Saint John.

CHAPTER EIGHT

Foulques and Brother Alain stood at the docks of Acre looking out at the Hospitaller 'fleet.' Dozens of Schwyzers carried barrels and bundles wrapped in canvas from a mountain of supplies on the dock to two small merchantmen moored to the nearest wharf. A third ship, a galley with banks of oars on either side, was anchored out in open water. Impressive in both size and years, it was the only warship they had. When Vignolo had first seen the ship, he asked Foulques how old it was. Foulques had no idea, nor did anyone he asked. So Vignolo announced he would row out to her and see exactly what dark arts were keeping her afloat. He left Foulques and Alain co-ordinating the loading of the merchantmen. That had been two hours ago, but finally, Foulques could see the small skiff returning.

By the time Vignolo joined Foulques and Alain on the dock, the mountain of goods had become a small hill.

"What are your thoughts?" Foulques asked Vignolo.

The Genoan let out a deep breath and sat down heavily on a canvas-wrapped crate full of foodstuffs. "I hope you can all swim." Brother Alain shot Foulques a panicked glance. "It is worse than I thought," Vignolo continued. "She is a brute, all right. Been repaired so many times over the years, there is enough wood on that ship to build three. Her prow has seen the worst of it, though. Seems sturdy enough now, but whoever owned her before the Hospitallers thought she was a battering ram. There are more layers on her prow than you would find on a Venetian virgin."

"But it will get us to Cyprus, correct?" Foulques asked.

Vignolo nodded. "She has not fallen apart yet, so there are forces conspiring to hold her together that are beyond my understanding. But I know some Rhodes men who would enjoy looking at her."

Vignolo was about to say something else, but he seemed to lose his train of thought as his eyes caught on something behind Foulques.

"What is it?"

Vignolo scanned the entire dock, left and right, before he spoke. "Do you know who that Arab is over there? The one standing in the shade of the harbor master's hut?"

Foulques looked over his shoulder. He immediately picked out the man Vignolo had noticed. A thin man stood under the eaves of a small shack nestled between a warehouse and a tavern. At first glance, he appeared to be seeking shelter from the morning sun, but he did not lean against the building in a relaxed manner. He stood erect under the eaves of the building, staring in their direction intently, as though calling them toward him with the force of his stare. And that was exactly what he was doing. It was Monsieur Malouf.

"Stay here," Foulques said. "I will be right back." He

turned toward Malouf, but Vignolo reached out and grabbed him by the arm.

"Do you know that man?" Vignolo asked again, but with more force this time.

"I do," Foulques said.

"Then you would be best served by pretending you never saw him."

Foulques grabbed Vignolo's wrist and slowly removed his hand from his arm. "Since you seem to know who he is, then you also know that we have seen him because he has wished it so."

As Alain looked on in confusion, Foulques turned his back on the two men and walked toward Monsieur Malouf.

As Foulques approached, Malouf leaned against the building and used a tiny knife to trim his fingernails. He looked up. "Peace be upon you, Admiral Foulques."

"And Peace be with you, Monsieur Malouf." Foulques joined him in the shade and he too leaned against the wall. The two men looked out over the harbor and Foulques waited for Malouf to speak.

"You know, I have always liked the way you call me 'Monsieur.' It must sound strange to anyone else. You, a Frank, addressing an Arab man with a French title."

Foulques shrugged. "That is how my uncle introduced you to me when I was a child. It does not feel strange to me."

"Yes, Guillaume always did have a penchant for tradition. That is one of the things I like about him. Any word from your uncle?"

"Not directly, no. But I am told he will be sending reinforcements to us soon."

Malouf crossed his arms and nodded. "That is good. The Mamluks are coming. And they will not be merciful. You have heard, no doubt, what they did at Tripoli?"

"Yes," Foulques said. "Marshal Clermont was there with a Hospitaller force. It was a slaughter. They were fortunate to escape, but Tripoli is not Acre."

"You have much faith in your city's walls. I hope it is well placed," Malouf said.

"Why did you come here Monsieur Malouf? You risk much by being seen with me in public."

Malouf held his hands out, palms up. "A father will do anything for his daughter."

"There was no need for you to seek me out. I am a man of my word. I have not forgotten our bargain."

"Ah, but I am sure you understand my concern. In Cyprus, you will be a long way from your responsibilities."

Foulques turned to look at Malouf. "I have not forgotten Najya. She is in no danger. Even if the Mamluks should attack, Acre will not fall."

"And if you are wrong? Forgive me Foulques, for I do not doubt your convictions. But you must understand, in my life I have learned it best to look at problems from all possible sides."

"And what do you suggest?"

"Go to her, Foulques. Convince her to leave the city. She will go if the request comes from you."

Foulques said he would do his best to convince her, but he knew in his heart she would not like the idea. When he returned to where Vignolo and Alain were standing, he realized Vignolo was staring at him.

"What?" Foulques asked.

"What did he want?" Vignolo was scanning everything that moved around him.

Foulques looked back to where Malouf had been standing, but the old man was gone. "He wants me to pay his daughter a visit."

When Foulques looked back at Vignolo, the Genoan was staring at him open-mouthed.

"That is not what I expected to hear," Vignolo said.

CHAPTER NINE

When Foulques arrived at Najya's home, he spotted her outside tending to one of the two beehives flanking either side of the door. Her home was her workshop, and her workshop her home, for bees had been a large part of her life for as long as Foulques could remember. By the time she was twelve people already knew she was the one to contact if they came across a swarm on their property that they needed removed.

Foulques accompanied her on several of these 'queen rescues,' as she liked to call them. Not because he was particularly enamored of bees, or honey. Quite the opposite; he was secretly terrified of the stinging insects.

He had heard stories of a man his uncle knew who disturbed a hive under an old wagon. He was stung multiple times and his face swelled up beyond recognition. He quit breathing at one point and he had to be treated by one of the brothers of Saint John. Ever since then, the image of the man's grotesquely swollen face had left its mark on Foulques's memory.

However, as much as he distrusted the tiny insects, he

found Najya's enthusiasm infectious whenever she went on one of her rescue missions. When they spotted the blanket of bees hanging off a tree branch, the soldier bees swarming around their young queen as she searched for a home to start a colony, Najya's voice would become hushed and brim with excitement. At the same time, she would take on an air of concern for the homeless insects and her movements would become so careful, so deliberate.

That was the difference between her and Foulques when it came to the bees. He would move carefully around the insects out of fear. Najya would do it out of concern for their well being. And the bees seemed to know it, for she could walk up to the branch, cooing and talking quietly the whole time, pick it up carefully with her slender, bare hands, and drop it into a sack to take home. There she would put the queen and her court, as she liked to call them, into one of the empty wooden hives she had built herself and which stood waiting for just such an occasion. To Najya, finding a new home for the queen was worthy of any royal coronation Foulques had ever witnessed.

He stood there, across the street from her home, and watched her work. He was near enough that if he had spoken in a normal voice she would have heard him, but so engrossed was she in her work, he could have been standing right next to her and she would not have noticed.

She wore a long, simple tunic of white linen, hemmed in golden thread. Over this was a sheer wrap of blue silk. It was as gossamer as the wings of the creatures she so loved, and Foulques could not help but look on in fearful fascination as she reached her arm down the open top of the larger of the two hives, which was almost as tall as she was. Bees spouted up all around her, but she talked quietly to them while swinging a tiny brass brazier, which emitted a constant stream of fine smoke. Foulques waited until the smoke pluming from the brazier had placated the bees enough for him to approach.

She finally noticed him and she stood there smiling, the sun sparkling off her large, light brown eyes and emphasizing just how sheer her wrap really was. With smoke still swirling around her, she looked like she had just come to life from the margins of a monk's illustrated fairy tale.

She held up a hand. "Wait there, Foulques, while I close up their home." She set the brazier down, which was still spitting forth spirited tendrils of smoke. Then she carefully placed the large, irregularly shaped lid back over the hive, talking quietly as she worked.

"People are going mad in this city. Last night someone broke into one of my hives and stole honey! I have had my workshop here for ten years, and not once has anyone ever stolen anything from me."

She brushed off her hands, stepped lightly over to Foulques, and kissed him on first one cheek and then the other. Foulques looked nervously around, but Najya laughed. She looked like an Arab, often dressed as one, but her customs and actions were all her own. She was unpredictable, but always genuine, and that was why everyone, including Foulques, loved her.

"Have you come to say goodbye, then?"

Foulques looked down at his hands. "In part. But really, I am here to try and convince you to leave the city before the Mamluks arrive."

"If they come," she said.

"They are coming."

"Well, you are too late," Najya said.

Foulques knew this was going to be difficult.

"Look, Najya—"

"My brother was already here. Several times, in fact. If he cannot convince me to leave, what chance do you think you have?" She cocked her head and looked at Foulques out of the corner of one eye. "Did he send you?"

"No, of course not." Foulques was relieved he did not have to lie.

She crossed her arms and gave Foulques one of her all-knowing half smiles. "Tell me Master Knight. If your Order was not sending you to Cyprus, would *you* be leaving the city? Now come inside and have tea with me. People will be staring at us soon and you do not want that, do you Brother Foulques?"

And that was that. His conscience was clear. He followed Najya inside for tea.

CHAPTER TEN

Khalil focused on the irregular up-down movements of his father's chest. Resisting with every fiber of his being the urge to look at the horn scroll tube resting on a large pillow at the foot of what would surely be Sultan Qalawun's deathbed.

Khalil knew they were watching him. Someone was always watching him. But that was quite possibly the only reason he was still alive. His servants were watched, his friends were followed wherever they went, and anyone they talked to was noted. So how could he have been responsible for poisoning the sultan?

Vice-Sultan Turuntay and his Royal Guards were beyond thorough in their investigation. They had a long list of suspects, men and women of power and ambition, like Khalil, but in the end, the culprit turned out to be quite unremarkable. One of the sultan's bath attendants, a Christian slave taken at Tripoli, confessed to pricking him with a venomous needle. Turuntay accepted that, for no trace of poison was ever found in any of the sultan's food, so it had to have been administered by other means. The sultan's team of hakim had been astute in recognizing he had been poisoned in the first place. They had conflicting theories on what type of poison had been used, but the slave died by ingesting some other deadly substance before she could be questioned further. Whatever was killing Qalawun was much slower acting. It was shutting down his organs one by one and there was nothing anyone could do.

There was a sudden commotion outside the tent entrance. There were only four servants, Vizier Baydara, and two of Turuntay's trusted men inside the tent with Khalil. The vice-sultan, himself, was not present.

Khalil heard a soft, yet commanding, voice giving instructions to the guards outside.

"You will hold my emir's weapons in safekeeping, for he is a Royal Mamluk of the Cairo Tabaqa, come to pay his respects."

A handsome, clean-shaven Arab stepped gracefully through the doorway. His hazel eyes were lined with a trace of black and they shone forth from his delicate face like the last rays of sun setting behind an oasis. Those eyes took in the room and everyone in it with a single glance, and when he opened his mouth his words rang with conviction.

"My Master, the venerable Emir Badru Hashim, would have words with his sultan."

A second form, stooped and massive, then filled the door so fully that the braziers set just inside the tent dimmed as they were robbed of oxygen. The man moved into the room and they roared back to life casting the newcomer in shadow for a moment. He continued moving forward slowly, as though an unseen force pushed him along like the waters of a raging river carrying a colossal boulder.

Unlike the handsome man who had announced his master, the Mamluk's peculiarly gray eyes stared straight ahead at the sultan's bed as he moved unerringly toward it. He acknowledged the presence of no one else. One of the sultan's own guards took a backward step out of his path. Even the lanky form of Vizier Baydara was forced to scramble aside as the man named Badru Hashim dropped to his knees beside Qalawun.

"My Sultan."

Khalil's head vibrated when he spoke, like someone had beat a large drum with a heavy hand. Once.

"I have returned to you. As Allah is my witness, and by all codes of the Furusiyya, no man or woman has dominion over me. My service, my life, is once again yours to command."

Khalil was close enough to see his father's face twitch, and then his eyes fluttered open to slits, as though the Mamluk had the power to call back men from the dead.

Who was this man?

Qalawun's eyes continued to open, growing wider and wider. When they were fully open, the sultan turned his head and looked at the Mamluk. Then they grew wider still, though Khalil would have thought it impossible. Qalawun took in air through his mouth, his chest began to move, and his face gained color. Then it reddened, veins snaked up along his neck and into his cheeks, his chest arched up, and in the old man's eyes Khalil saw something he did not think his father was capable of experiencing. Terror. Not rage, not surprise. Pure terror. He had awoken into a nightmare.

The sultan's chest heaved, he opened his mouth and a single, strangled word came forth.

"No..."

The giant man faltered. He blinked. This was, apparently, not the outcome he had expected.

The tent flaps flew aside and Vice-Sultan Turuntay stormed into the space. Five Royal Guards followed.

"Get that man out of here!"

The man in question was slowly rising to his feet. When the first guard took his arm, he dislodged his hands with a violent shake. He withered the second guard with a stare and walked past him toward the entrance under his own power. He did not once glance at Turuntay as he exited the tent.

As Turuntay and the guards went to the sultan's side, Khalil found himself being pulled along in the stranger's wake by irresistible forces. Standing outside he saw the Mamluk walking swiftly away, his servant half running to keep up.

Khalil saw his friend, Ibn al-Salus, on his way somewhere with a rolled up carpet under one arm. He shouted his name and ran to meet him. Ibn al-Salus gave him a questioning look.

"You see those two men?"

"Yes...?"

"Go to them. Do whatever you must to make them stay until I have had a chance to speak with them. But keep them out of sight. Somewhere that Turuntay will not see them."

"All right, but I—"

"Do it! Whatever it takes. Understand?"

He ran back to the tent without waiting for his friend's response.

The sultan's hakim were gathered at his bedside when Khalil entered the tent. Turuntay and Vizier Baydara were in one corner speaking in hushed tones. They stopped talking when Khalil approached.

"Who was that man?" He directed the question toward them both. Baydara looked at Turuntay, but the vice-sultan avoided both Khalil's and the vizier's eyes. He knew something.

"I ask again. Who—"

"He is a disgraced Mamluk released from your father's service years ago," Turuntay said.

"Disgraced? How?"

"His blood is mixed, his tendencies barbaric, and he has eyes the color of the dead. What else do you need to know while your father lies dying in front of us?" Turuntay said, gesturing toward the prone form of Qalawun.

Baydara nodded his thin face. "We should pray to Allah. The hakim say it could be over at any moment."

Sultan Qalawun died within the hour. Khalil stood at foot of the sultan's bed for the whole duration, never once letting the horn scroll tube out of his sight. In that time, the sultan's highest ranking emir, one after another, silently shuffled into the tent to stand watch over their master. Soon after the sultan let out his last breath, Vizier Baydara, with all the pomp and grace required by custom, walked to the pillow on which the scroll rested. He drew his khanjar, sliced the golden cords tying the horn to the cushion, and picked it up. He broke the wax sealing its end. He removed the parchment from within and began to read.

"I, al-Malik al-Mansur Saif ad-Din Qalawun al-Alfis-Salihi, the sultan of Egypt, name my son Khalil as my successor. Let all those emir loyal to me also support him in this, my final wish."

There was a pause on Baydara's part, Khalil noted, before he went down on one knee and held the scroll out to Khalil with both hands. Khalil snatched it from his hands and waited for the vizier to say the words. When he finally did, they were completely bereft of emotion.

"What is your command, My Sultan?"

Khalil had given this moment so much thought over the last few days he had trouble believing it was actually here. But here it was. Time was no longer his enemy.

"We attack," he said.

The tent was silent, save for the inhalations of twenty men.

"We cannot attack," Vice-Sultan Turuntay said. "We must return the sultan to Cairo and honor him."

Khalil heard no respect in his words. No deference, whatsoever. A Mamluk should know better.

"I *am* the sultan," Khalil said. "My father has given his life in preparing the greatest army ever seen. And you would dishonor him by disbanding it?"

"Not I," Turuntay said. "Custom demands we respect the grieving period."

Khalil glared at Turuntay. "Custom demands? It sounds like it is you who demands." Khalil caught himself before he said more. This was not the time to confront the vice-sultan. "Customs change. Once Acre has fallen, we will grieve for my father. There will be time, then. Time enough for the whole world to grieve."

But you, Turuntay. You I will permit to grieve much sooner.

CHAPTER ELEVEN

THE SHORT JOURNEY from Acre to Cyprus had gone without incident. The late winter sun was not yet too hot, but it was still brilliant enough to make the gentle waves of the Mid-Earth Sea sparkle like gem stones. The galley was not the fleetest of ships, that much was true, but it was stable. And that suited Foulques's mood, and stomach, just fine.

As Vignolo directed his young crew on the docking procedures, Foulques saw Brother Thomas standing alone at the railing. The tall youth stared out over the small bay, his eyes seeing none of its beauty. Foulques knew how he felt, for he had the same misgivings about their new home. He went and stood by his side.

"Admiral," Thomas said, bowing his head in greeting.

"Congratulations. That was officially the first successful voyage of the Hospitaller Navy," Foulques said. "I wanted to tell you that you did a fine job choosing the one hundred members. They are all good men."

"Ninety-nine," Thomas said.

Ah, the true source of the melancholy, Foulques thought.

He should have known.

"I am sorry Pirmin could not be with us, Thomas. Unfortunately, the marshal felt he needed him at Acre. I do not always agree with Marshal Clermont, but this was his call to make. There was nothing I could do."

Thomas nodded. "I understand," he said.

Foulques was fairly certain he did not. How could he? The marshal knew Foulques wanted Pirmin for his own use. The lad was going to be an amazing warrior. He did not know how to tell Thomas that his friendship with Pirmin had come to an end purely due to Foulques's own enmity with the marshal.

Foulques pushed away from the railing. "Carry on, Brother Thomas. Carry on. It is all any of us can do."

※

FOULQUES ENTERED THE meeting chamber expecting to find a room full of advisers and servants to King Henry, the King of Cyprus, and currently the leader of the Kingdom of Jerusalem. But it was empty, save for one small man sitting behind a rather non-descript table of rough-sawn wooden slabs set atop two trestles. The doors closed behind the Hospitaller and the first thing that went through Foulques's mind was, *Who is this young man?* He could not have been more than twenty years old.

The man motioned for Foulques to approach, and it was that small gesture that gave him away. Only royalty could exude that much confidence, disdain, and suspiciousness all in the wave of one hand.

"Welcome to Cyprus, Brother Foulques," King Henry said. "Or should I address you as Admiral?"

"However you prefer, Your Grace."

"You are younger than I had envisioned," King Henry said.

Foulques gave the King what he hoped was a courtly bow, but truth be told, he had never mastered the art of politicking, and one of the King's eyebrows arched at his attempt.

Without preamble, Henry said, "I do not want more Hospitallers here."

"And I did not wish to come," Foulques heard himself say before he could curb the thought. He cleared his throat. "What I mean to say, is, I would rather be in Acre defending her walls with the rest of my brethren."

A silence filled the room. Then Henry said, "Good. We understand each other. My brother has allowed too many Templars here already. It is too late for me to throw them out, but I have restricted their land and will not approve any expansions to their temple. I tell you this because I want you to know what a compromise it is for me to allow your Order to bring a hundred soldiers onto my island. Your hospice on Cyprus has served my people well. I will not begrudge you that. But to ask me to supply land and buildings to house soldiers is not something I wish, nor welcome with open arms."

"Then why, may I ask, did you, Your Grace?"

The two men stared at each other. This open hostility was unexpected, for Grand Master Villiers had assured

Foulques all the arrangements had been made for Cyprus to become the home of the future Hospitaller Navy.

"I have the falling sickness. Did you know this?"

Everyone knew it. "I have heard as much, Your Grace."

"Of course you have. Amalric has made sure of that. My brother is embarrassed by my affliction. His wife even more so. But I cannot blame her. Did you hear how I succumbed to a rather severe set of convulsions at their wedding? That I shit myself there on the travertine floor of the church in front of three hundred guests?"

Foulques paused before answering. "Yes, Your Grace. I had heard that."

King Henry squinted and cocked his head at the Hospitaller. "You are a direct man, Admiral. That was not the response I expected."

Foulques shrugged. "If I may say so, nothing of this meeting is as I expected."

"What do you know of the falling sickness?" Henry asked.

"Very little. Only what I have read."

"Which is?"

"The Greeks called it the Sacred Disease. They considered the convulsions attacks on the individual from various gods. Different types of convulsions were attributed to different gods. Hippocrates, however, thought this was nonsense. He believed the convulsions were caused in the brain and were treatable."

"What do you believe?"

"I, of course, do not believe in the existence of pagan

gods. And even if such beings did exist, why would they waste their time tormenting humans?"

"My brother and his priest say I am possessed by demons. They have me pray thirty times per day and then question my faith when the convulsions come. Are they right? Is God my answer?"

"Yes. In all things, yes. But I think your brother is wrong in this. Prayer alone will not give you the relief you seek."

"We have come full circle," Henry said. "If I allow you to stay here, will you put your Order's physicians at my disposal?"

"To be blunt, Your Grace, I do not know much about this topic, nor do I know how far the Hospital's knowledge extends on it."

Henry waved away Foulques's comment. "It does not matter. All I ask is that you bring someone with a keen mind to your hospice in Cyprus. Someone who will give me honest answers to my questions."

Henry reached up one thin hand and pinched the bridge of his nose while he closed his eyes. He was pale and the motion exposed an inner exhaustion that Foulques had failed to notice before.

"I believe Julius Caesar also suffered from the falling sickness," Foulques said.

Henry looked up between his fingers. "Did he? I did not know that. I suppose I should feel relieved, Brother Foulques? For if he could forge the greatest empire ever seen, surely I should be able to rise to the occasion and stop the remnants of a tiny one from disappearing altogether?"

Foulques stayed quiet. Truthfully, he did not know what he had hoped to achieve by mentioning that obscure fact, but Henry was right. Any way one looked at it, the comment came out as piteous.

"There is a hakim at the Palais des Malades in Acre," Foulques said, finally. "If there is any worthwhile treatment available, he will know where to look."

Henry sat up. "Can you bring him here?"

"I will speak to my superiors, but I believe it can be arranged. Whether the hakim will come, or not, is another matter, but I suspect he will rise to the challenge."

Henry leaned forward and laced his fingers together on the simple table in front of him. "Do it then. Once he arrives you can begin building barracks for your men. Until then, they will have to sleep in tents. But I hear they were all born in caves in Germania, so they should be used to living in the elements, no?"

"Alps," Foulques said, quietly.

"What?"

"I said they have come a long way to fight for God's Kingdom."

"Have not we all?" the King said, letting out a deep breath. "At any rate, it looks like no one will be fighting any time soon." He cocked his head when he saw the blank expression on Foulques's face. "Have you not heard? The sultan is dead. The Mamluk army is in disarray. My advisers tell me they must now return to Cairo and choose a new sultan. The Kingdom of Jerusalem lives on. For a time."

Foulques could not believe what he had just heard.

"Your Grace. Are you sure? Is Sultan Qalawun truly dead?"

"Of course I am sure. Now the waiting begins. In time, I will be forced to send emissaries to sue for a new peace treaty. But not until I know who I will be dealing with."

Foulques's heart was pounding. The air he breathed suddenly tasted a little sweeter. Who knew what the new sultan would decide regarding Acre. Perhaps he would even be able to return there some day.

Henry steepled his fingers in front of his chest. He looked like a man who was trying to pray, but could not quite bring himself to clasp his hands together. "I would like to know your opinion, as a military man. If the Mamluks come at us again, which I feel is inevitable, what are the odds of Acre falling?"

Foulques was surprised at the question. "Acre will never fall, Your Grace. Her walls are too high and too strong. A hundred men could keep a thousand at bay. Her only weakness is her port, but the Mamluks have no navy."

"Neither do the Hospitallers," Henry said. "Yet."

In those words, the wisdom of his superiors came into focus. Acre was not going to be his battle to fight. He and those 'cave-dwelling' children of his were the future of the Order. They were in a race for control of the seas, and in such a race, there was no better place to prepare than an island.

He remembered his long voyage to the Alps to recruit the Schwyzer children. It seemed a world away now, in both time and distance. They were so young. Did they even remember the snow-covered mountains and lush, green valleys they came from? And what would they think of this new home of theirs? Well, he supposed, it looked like they would find out together.

Cyprus. A place neither Foulques, nor the Schwyzers, had ever asked to come.

CHAPTER TWELVE

On the high ground, overlooking the Mamluk encampment, stood a solitary red tent, the *Dihliz* of the sultan. Although it was in the middle of the camp, it was set up with a good deal of open space between it and all the other neighboring shelters. The Dihliz was ringed with torches and guards, with a single walkway leading to its entrance. Anyone who set foot within the ring of fire, and not on the walkway, would be killed by the guards, no questions asked.

This was a new law set out by a new sultan. The sultan no doubt thought it would make him appear strong, unapproachable by the unworthy. But Badru Hashim, as he strode along the walkway with a guard at each side, thought the new law made the sultan look cautious, perhaps even afraid.

Two more guards stood at the entrance. "Emir Badru Hashim," one of Badru's escorts said. "He has been summoned."

The older guard at the entrance said nothing, but abruptly turned and disappeared inside.

Badru and the three remaining guards stood outside, waiting. They waited for twenty minutes and no one said a single word. Badru liked that. These were disciplined Mamluks who knew their place in the world. Badru and Yusuf had already been detained in the camp for two days. What was another hour to him?

But it was not an hour. The first guard reappeared moments later and motioned for Badru to enter. He kept his head down after he entered, for he was aware of someone sitting in the sultan's chair. Badru strode to the center of the carpeted floor and went down on one knee. He bowed his head and waited for the new sultan to speak.

"Rise, Emir Hashim," Sultan Khalil said.

Badru started at the mention of his name. It was a strange sound to hear the sultan use the name of one so far beneath his station. But Badru had been away a long time. Perhaps things had changed in the sultanate since he had been gone.

"I am sorry for keeping you waiting for so long. With the death of my father, these last few days have been rather... trying," Khalil said.

Badru turned his eyes up from the thick carpet at his feet to the young sultan's face. The sultan met his gaze and held it.

"I believe I owe you another apology on my father's behalf," the sultan said.

Was he playing with him? Badru wondered. Of course he was. The sultan looked at Badru, perhaps waiting for a response of some kind. But there was nothing Badru could say. One could not simply accept an apology from the sultan.

"My father treated you poorly the other day. But he was an old man on his deathbed. Who is to say what thoughts capture a man's mind at such a time. I hope you will not hold it against him."

"Of course not," Badru said, finding his voice. "He is—was the sultan. It is not for a man such as myself to understand or question his actions."

The young sultan nodded in agreement. He stared at Badru for a long moment before he said, "Is it true, Emir? That you are of the Cairo Tabaqa? And if so, why is it that I do not know you?"

"You would have been a small boy when your father released me," Badru said.

"And why did he do that?"

The brusqueness of the question caught Badru off guard, but it should not have. How many nights did he lie awake on his pallet wondering just that?

"Only he can answer that question," Badru said.

Sultan Khalil smiled and slid back on his chair. He slouched in it in a way no trained Mamluk ever would. But then, Badru reminded himself, Khalil was not Mamluk like his father had been.

Some time during the years Badru had served Veronique Boulet, he had come up with an acceptable answer to Sultan Khalil's question. Great lords were always buying and selling Mamluks for their stables, striving to get the perfect mix of men for their house's goals. No doubt the sultan had simply been offered a price he could not refuse.

"Well, we are both a long ways from Cairo now," Sultan Khalil said. "Though I hope to be back there soon. And you, Emir. Where is it that you would like to be?"

"I—I have not given the matter much thought, My Sultan."

"Guards. Clear my tent."

The guard who had escorted Badru inside said, "My Sultan, is that wise?"

The sultan's eyes narrowed at the guard and Badru could tell the guard regretted the poor phrasing of his question immediately.

"Of course it is not wise," Khalil said. "Wisdom is for old men and sorcerers! Do I look like an old man to you? Or a sorcerer?" He waved his hands over his head like he was casting a great spell.

"Of course not, My Sultan," the guard said.

"This sultanate has been ruled by old men for far too long. If we are to rid ourselves of the Christian pestilence that has been eating at our culture for generations, our actions must be bold, daring. Saladin was wise, my father was wise. And yet the Christians are still here!" He looked at Badru. "Emir Hashim. If my guards leave us alone, do you promise not to kill me?"

"I do, My Sultan," Badru said, without considering whether, or not it was a rhetorical question.

"There. You see? And I believe him. Now get out. All of you."

When they were alone, Sultan Khalil stood up and stretched. "I did not think being sultan would require so much sitting."

Badru said nothing. He was having a hard time making sense of the young sultan.

"Why did you come to see my father?"

"To offer my service. He was about to embark on the greatest undertaking of our age and I wanted to be a part of it."

"Do you think he refused you because he knew you killed the French whore he sold you to?"

The words caught Badru by complete surprise. Games. He had forgotten just how much his kind liked to play games with people.

"You know of that," Badru said. At least the sultan had not mentioned it earlier when the tent was full of Mamluk warriors.

"I do. And I know I could turn you over to my guards and have you executed. You have committed the gravest of crimes for a Mamluk." The sultan began pacing idly around the room.

"I do not deny it. I will accept my punishment."

"I said I *could* have you executed. I could also ask you why you did it, since you clearly do not deny that you did. But I have to tell you something, Emir Hashim." He stopped in front of a brazier and blew on the glowing coals until wisps of smoke rose up into his face. He stepped back. "I do not care why you killed your French master."

He paused, letting his words sink in. "When I look at you, I see a man who can help me."

"Help you? How can I possibly do that?"

Khalil let out a long sigh and sat back down in his chair. "I am a new sultan in a court surrounded by my father's men. I need one of my own. One I can trust with my secrets. In return, as the undisputed messenger of the prophet Mohammed, I can absolve you of the heinous crime you committed against your master."

Badru looked up and met Khalil's eyes. He thought the young sultan was going to offer him riches, all the gold he could possibly stuff in his saddlebags. Instead, he offered more. Much more. He was young, but he knew the rules of the game and, it appeared, he played to win.

"What must I do?" Badru asked.

✹

BADRU SAT ON the dirt floor of the large provision tent with the scabbarded, curved blade of his khanjar on the ground in front of him. He wore no armor, no shoes, and no shirt. The only article of clothing he had on were his loose, sand-colored breeches, which were corded tightly around his ankles and at his waist. His bare, massive chest rose and fell to the rhythmic commands of his breath. His gray eyes, though open, could have belonged to a dead man for how little they moved, or even blinked.

The tent was four or five strides across, and until recently, had been filled entirely with lentils and grain. It had been one of many such tents, but now that the army was on the move again, all the stores had been emptied and loaded onto wagons. The braying of donkeys, squealing wagon wheels, and the shouts of thousands of men marching and tearing down camp all around the tent threatened to invade on Badru's peace, if he let it. He would not. There was only one sound that could shake him from his trance.

Someone fiddled impatiently with the ties on the flaps at the entrance. One flap flew open and extra light flooded the interior. There was a pause before the man spoke.

"Where is Baydara?" Turuntay demanded.

Badru turned his head. The general's stocky form filled the entrance completely, but dust swirled in the light that managed to push past his bulky silhouette. Beyond him, a frantic world of man and beast rushed past.

"You," Turuntay said.

"Baydara is not here. He never was," Badru said.

There was a moment of silence while the two men stared at each other: Badru, half-naked, sitting on the ground cross-legged while Turuntay stood in the doorway with one hand holding back the tent flap. Most men would have let that flap go, turned around, and walked away. But Badru knew the old general could not have done that any more than Badru himself could have.

Turuntay stepped inside the tent and the flap slid back into place, choking out the light and once again separating the interior of the tent from the outside world.

Turuntay paced a full, slow circle around Badru. When satisfied with whatever he had seen, or not seen, he unknotted his sword belt and stood it up against one side of the tent. Still wearing his waist sash, with his khanjar tucked within, he walked to stand in front of the still kneeling Badru.

"I assumed you were gone. Has the boy recruited you to him, then? Or, do you act alone?" Turuntay asked.

The question puzzled Badru. "Why would I want you dead? I am here at the bidding of my sultan. Nothing more."

Badru remembered Turuntay from his youth. He, too, was a product of the Cairo Tabaqa, albeit twenty years before Badru undertook his own training. By the time Badru came along, Turuntay had already risen high in the sultan's Royal Bodyguard and had very little to do with the military school itself. Still, he had been around enough for Badru to recognize him the moment he saw him again in Qalawun's tent two days ago.

Turuntay shook his head. "You may be here at the boy's command, but this," he cast his eyes around the tent, "is your doing. I have been waiting for Khalil's assassins to find me in my sleep. He would never give me a chance to fight for my life."

"I only give you a chance to die in the manner of one who has lived by the code of the Furusiyya. Make no mistake. You will not walk from this tent alive."

Badru could tell by the way the older man's eyes caught fire that Turuntay had not been spoken to like this for a very long time. In fact, it brought some youth back into his face, and his body. In a blur of motion, he pulled his khanjar with his right hand and held it at his left hip, with his left hand above it.

"Stop making threats, *Northman*. Stand up so I can finish something I should have a long time ago."

Badru let out a breath. If he succeeded in carrying out

the sultan's command, Badru would once again be a true Mamluk.

One who is owned.

His life would no longer be his to live. All masters of Mamluks are favored in the eyes of Allah, but this master would be special. The Sultan of Egypt was subject to no other power on earth, save for the will of Allah, Himself. And by giving himself to the sultan, Badru would become, by default, a servant of Allah. For to serve one is to do the bidding of the other. No Mamluk could ever wish for more.

He reached to the ground in front of his knees and slowly drew his own khanjar.

And so it begins.

While still on his knees, Badru slashed at Turuntay's legs, simply to create some room between them. He was no longer certain the old warrior deserved the respect he had given him. He still wore his armor and there were riddles in his words.

Turuntay jumped back from the slash and settled into a hidden leg stance. Badru faced him with an open stance with both his right hand, the one holding his khanjar, and his left raised in a high guard. Of course, Badru's high guard was a modified one because of his great height. The top of Turuntay's head only came up to Badru's neck, but this was not a disadvantage in the small confines of the tent.

Turuntay came on fast and hard. He knew he did not have the endurance to last more than a few minutes with someone as skilled as Badru. Badru also knew this. He also knew the older man expected him to draw out the fight, use his youth and strength to advantage. Instead he stepped forward and met the seasoned warrior with a charge of his own.

Turuntay's eyes went wide. The two men's hands slashed and struck out in a flurry of cuts and blows that made their limbs blur together, like the blades of a windmill in a thunderstorm. When they separated, the stocky general's chest heaved with effort. He was cut on both sides of his face and blood leaked from under his right armpit. Badru had a thin red line running across his bare chest, but other than that, he was neither winded, nor hurt.

They circled each other, making two complete revolutions around the dim tent. The only noise was Turuntay's ragged breathing. Badru initiated the next assault. The curved blades flashed in the low light, again and again. The sound of metal on metal increased as the men tired and their technique became sloppy.

Badru struck Turuntay with his off hand, then elbowed him across his jaw with his blade arm. The older man took the blows in order to rake the point of his blade across Badru's stomach. Badru hopped back, but the blade snagged his skin and ripped another red line to match the one on his chest.

Badru's eyes narrowed as he looked at his blood on the point of Turuntay's khanjar. It could have been his intestines on the tip of that blade. Somewhere in the last exchange, the older man's face had taken on a detached look. He no longer flinched at Badru's feints and his body had stopped trying to suck in great gasps of air. Turuntay knew he was going to die, but his body did not. It was pooling its resources, saving itself for one last desperate attempt to preserve itself. He had never been so dangerous.

Badru dropped down on one knee and backhanded his blade underneath Turuntay's lamellar armor, opening up the major blood vessels on the inside of the general's leg. Turuntay tried to lean back, lift his leg out of the way of Badru's slash, but his effort only resulted in him falling over backward, with his life blood painting one wall of the tent.

Turuntay lay there, his chest heaving once again as his heart tried to regulate the flow of blood. All Badru had to do was wait. He would be dead in less than two minutes. A celebrated warrior, a *fāris* who had served the same sultan for over twenty years. Turuntay had fought to turn back the Mongol horde not once, but twice, and was on the verge of driving the Christians from his sultan's lands. But he had failed. His life taken by a man whose greatest deed was to strangle a Frankish woman. Badru had succeeded in killing a great man, a man who did not deserve to die at his hands. But Badru's fortune was about to change. His time had come, and he made a silent vow that eventually, he would be remembered as a man worthy of taking the life of the mighty Turuntay.

Badru bent over and retrieved Turuntay's khanjar. The old man watched Badru with clear eyes as Badru took his hand and placed the blade in his grasp. He helped him wrap his fingers around the ivory handle and then pressed his hand to his chest.

"Do you know… who you are?"

Badru nodded. "I am no one."

"Your mother's name was Astred."

Badru blinked. Turuntay continued, speaking quickly, for he knew he had little time.

"Qalawun was forced to overwinter in Dane's Land. He met your mother then. He wanted to bring her back with him, but she refused. Three years later she brought you to us…" His face was pale and his words began to slur. "When she died, I tried to have you killed… but Qalawun…"

The name of his sultan was the last word to pass Turuntay's lips. He died there on the ground, his blood clumping with dirt and sand, with only a confused and shaking Mamluk warrior to bear witness.

I have seen the white rain.

CHAPTER THIRTEEN

The Hospitallers owned a minor estate near Limassol, on the southern edge of Cyprus. Located near the sea, it had a small natural harbor and a dock large enough to tie up the two merchantmen. The galley had to be anchored a short distance away in deeper water. The wooden dock was weathered, and badly in need of repairs, but it was still floating.

The estate was listed in the kingdom's registry as a castle, and King Henry taxed it as such, but the property was little more than a large manor house surrounded by a six-foot-high wall. The wall offered very little security, both because of its insufficient height and the fact that it was assembled using a dry-stack method, which meant there was no mortar holding the irregular stones in place. In the event of an attack, the best Foulques could hope for from this first line of defense, was that it would crumble as the attackers climbed it and cause them injury.

Foulques claimed one of the rooms in the manor house for himself, another for Brother Alain. Three more he reserved for visiting knights or other high-ranking individuals. That left eight more rooms besides the large common area, which he left unassigned for the time being. He decided to focus his energy, and the few resources he had been granted by the grand master and King Henry, on building a barracks for the Schwyzers.

He hired two carpenters from Limassol and gave them the labor of his men from early morning until noon. The afternoons he put the Schwyzers under the direction of Vignolo.

For the first two weeks, no one set foot on a ship. Instead, Vignolo spent each afternoon teaching the men how to swim. He said the condition of their fleet demanded it. Foulques had thought it a waste of time at first, for he knew very few sailors had ever learned to swim. However, by the end of the second week Vignolo staged a demonstration where a group of Schwyzers wearing mail hauberks jumped into the deep water at the end of the dock. They sank like stones, but soon surfaced with their hauberks removed and tucked under one arm. They then proceeded to swim the cumbersome chain armor to the dock. Breathing heavily, each man successfully hoisted his hauberk out of the water and deposited it on the wooden dock. Foulques was impressed.

After the demonstration, Foulques left Vignolo and the men to their exercises. He walked the short distance from the seaside to his new home.

The room he had selected for himself was large enough for a bed in one corner and a desk in the opposite one. He kept his clothing in two trunks at the end of the bed. He entered the room and removed his Hospitaller cloak, hanging it on a hook on the wall, then sat down at his desk. A small, cloudy window let in enough light that he could write during the daytime with no need of a lantern. The desk had no drawers, only a large cubbyhole beneath the writing surface. He reached to its back and felt around until he found what he was looking for. He pulled out the rolled up parchment and untied the ribbon keeping it closed. Spreading it out on the desk's surface, he began to read through Thomas's list, visualizing each young man's face as he did so.

He had been so busy of late. First, with preparations for the move, then the voyage itself, that he had put little thought to the task he had been charged with. As he read through the list, he became acutely aware of how ridiculous his position was. He shook his head. Counting today, Foulques had only been on a half-dozen sea voyages in his entire life. Who was he to teach anyone anything about sailing? Who was he to transform one hundred boys born in the land-locked valleys of the Alps into able-bodied seamen? He looked down at the list and noted how Thomas had crossed out two names with a thick, meticulously drawn out line.

Pirmin Schwyzer. Gissler Schwyzer.

Curious, he thought.

He knew why Pirmin's name had been crossed out. At the last moment, Marshal Clermont had not allowed Foulques to take him. He said his natural talents were needed to help defend the city. He would have to make do with ninety-nine. Foulques had shrugged, and did not even bother with a counter argument. How could he when, deep down, he envied the lad for being permitted to stay in Acre. Pirmin had narrowly escaped banishment. But Gissler? Why had he been removed?

A knock sounded on the door.

"Enter," Foulques said, without looking up from the parchment.

Seconds passed. Foulques eventually looked up to see why whoever had knocked had not come in. He started, for a man stood before him, two feet from the front of his desk.

He was no Hospitaller, nor Frank for that matter, for he was wrapped in loose linens of white and cream. Foulques knew who he was even before his eyes settled on the curved dagger hanging from his side. He looked up, expecting to see Monsieur Malouf's placid smile. It was indeed Najya's father, but his face was the gray of a stormy sea rather than its usual still pond.

"Foulques. Forgive me for disturbing you."

Foulques stood. "Not at all. Peace be upon you, Monsieur Malouf. I did not expect—"

"I know. I apologize for my unannounced entry. But I must speak with you."

"Of course. How did you get here?"

"None of that is important now." He paused. Foulques said nothing, but encouraged Malouf to continue with a nod.

"I have made a grave mistake," Malouf said. "We all have. You know of Sultan Qalawun's death, of course?"

"Yes. Through King Henry. We were both very much

relieved to hear of it. It should take some time for them to choose Qalawun's successor."

Malouf shook his head and turned his back on Foulques. "Then I was right to come. You have not heard that his son, Khalil, has proclaimed himself sultan?"

Foulques lowered himself into his seat. "No, I did not know. When did this happen?"

Malouf turned back to the desk. "One week ago. I was not surprised that Khalil would make a play for the sultanate. Nor even when he was awarded the title. But, Allah as my witness, I never imagined he would be able to keep that title. The emir never should have allowed it."

"What does this mean?" Foulques asked. "Surely they must return to Cairo and observe the mourning rites?"

Malouf shook his head. "However he did it, Khalil has seized control of the great army and marches toward Acre as we speak."

Both men were silent. Foulques felt that same doubt about where he was, and what he was doing, renewed. A hundredfold.

"When will they arrive?"

Malouf looked at him. "Sooner than any messenger you send. Sooner than you yourself can."

Something about what Malouf said did not make sense to Foulques. "Why did you say you made a mistake?"

Malouf turned his back on Foulques, once again. "Because I am responsible for Qalawun's death."

Those words left Foulques speechless. Then he realized it was not so much that Malouf had a hand in assassinating the sultan, but that he would admit to it.

"Why?" Foulques said, finally.

When Malouf answered, his words were barely a whisper. "There is nothing a father will not do for his daughter."

Malouf moved to the small room's single window and stared out. "I knew the only way the great army would disband, was if the man who had brought it together was eliminated. So I mixed the poison and set a plan into motion."

"You poisoned him? How could you have gotten to him? I have heard it told that he has tasters for every drink, every piece of food he puts in his mouth."

Malouf let out a sigh. "He does. But every evening he has a cup of tea before bed, which of course, is tasted. What few know, however, is that the sultan used to have a sweet tooth. He drank his tea with honey for years, until his hakim told him it was ruining his health. He gave it up, but he always kept a few long pieces of dried honeycomb next to his bed. There was no honey in them, mind you, for he was diligent in heeding the advice of his hakim. So they were little more than wax, but he considered it an acceptable treat to stir his tea with one. In his mind, it became sweeter."

"You poisoned the wax," Foulques said.

"Not me. I promised to provide a lifetime of care for the family of one of his slaves if she exchanged the pieces of wax for ones I provided."

"You provided?" Foulques did not like where this was going. "Where did you get the honeycombs?"

Malouf locked Foulques in place with an unapologetic

stare. "There is a certain art to what I do, Brother Foulques, whether you see it or not. It was only fitting that I use my daughter's property to save her life."

"Only you did not save her life. You may have made things worse. Qalawun was known to be a fair man. Sometimes, even merciful. If the things I hear about Khalil are true, he will not rest until Acre is burned to the ground, along with everyone in it."

Malouf looked away. "Now you understand why I have come."

CHAPTER FOURTEEN

F OULQUES HAD BILLED it as a training run. He had Vignolo man the faster of the two merchantmen with a skeleton crew and then he joined them on board. Some of the lads had looked at him strangely when he boarded in full armor, wearing his red Hospitaller war tunic, but most, including Vignolo, thought he was merely playing his part as admiral. Once they were out on the water, Foulques had Vignolo set course for Acre. Understandably, Vignolo had almost thrown him overboard.

When they finally sailed into Acre's harbor, Foulques could not believe how crowded it was. Never in his life had he seen so much activity. There was not a single open slip, and ships of all sizes jockeyed for positions as berths opened up. Vignolo decided it was safer to anchor away from the docks since he had an inexperienced crew. They lowered a skiff and he set two wide-shouldered sergeants to row him and Foulques to the dock.

Foulques kept his eyes on the people streaming near the water's edge. It seemed that ships carrying supplies were coming in, and leaving riding even lower in the water, loaded down with people.

Vignolo had his looking glass to his eye. "This may have not been such a bad idea, Foulques. I sense there is good coin to be made by offering passage out of the city to those who want it."

"You will not, under any circumstances accept payment from these people," Foulques said. "In fact, I specifically want you to take as many women and children back with you as you can. Select only those who cannot afford payment. The rich can find their own way from the city, if they must leave."

Vignolo closed his eyes and rubbed at his temples with the thumb and forefinger of one hand. "Oh, Foulques. Do you ever do anything that makes any sense whatsoever? What if it is a father with his two daughters?"

"Take the girls, but not the man. Tell him to report to the City Watch to help man the walls against the Mamluks. That will be how he pays for his daughters' safety."

"What if it is a priest who, for all that is holy, begs me to take him away?" Vignolo had raised his voice.

"He can stay in the city and pray for its deliverance. We will need men of God as well as soldiers. And once you are away, return directly to Cyprus. Do not, under any circumstance, come back to Acre. Am I clear on that?"

Vignolo nodded enthusiastically. "Finally you have said something that makes sense. I would not have it any other way."

They found an opening on the lower dock area and Vignolo hopped out of the boat with the bowline in hand.

He did not tie the line to a mooring, but he held the boat steady while Foulques climbed out.

"Thank you, Vignoli," Foulques said. "I would appreciate it if you would look after things until I get back."

"I cannot make any promises," Vignolo said.

"Then consider that an order. Remember who controls the purse strings that feed you and your creditors."

Vignolo rolled his eyes. "I suppose I am off to find my passengers, then."

Foulques nodded. He turned to go but Vignolo said, "One more question, Admiral."

"What?"

"If I have the choice between a beautiful woman and a homely woman, do I have your permission to choose as I see fit?"

"Choose the homely one, of course."

"Of course," Vignolo said. He gave Foulques a bow with an exaggerated flourish and turned away to finish tying up the boat.

Foulques's legs swayed as soon as he planted his feet, a motion he attempted to conceal by taking a moment to unknot and re-tighten his sword belt. The sail from Cyprus was but a few hours, however Foulques had not taken well to his new life as a seaman. He felt his normally solid foundation to be unsteady, compromised, like someone had stolen the bones from his legs. He was the first Admiral of the Knights of Saint John, and it was all he could do to keep the contents of his stomach to himself after even the shortest ride in a stable skiff. He took in a deep lungful of the warm spring air, spit out a small piece of ginger that he was certain had saved his dignity, if not his life, and looked around with horror at the city he had once called home.

Acre, the trading jewel of the Mid-Earth Sea, with its deep-water port and colorful bazaars filled with citizens of every nation imaginable, had always been a loud, vibrant city. With well over a hundred thousand people, it teemed with an intoxicating energy that Foulques had known since childhood, and one which he found lacking in all other places he had experienced in his life. But as Foulques made his way along the docks, stepping into the chaos swirling all about him, he realized that that energy had been replaced with something else entirely: sheer madness.

The harbor was crammed with boats of all shapes and sizes. Many had seen better days, but with thousands of people trying to evacuate the city, anything that could float had been put to sea. Some of the captains were good-hearted fishermen, or the occasional merchant, who were trying to do their duty and rescue fellow Christians from the hordes of Islam. Most, however, were privateers offering passage only to the highest bidders. Acre was a rich city so there was no shortage of desperate patrons.

A tremendous boom sounded behind him, shaking the ground at the Hospitaller's feet. A nervous cheer rippled through the crowd and Foulques turned to see a massive catapult erected on a platform at the edge of the Pisan Quarter. Men scurried around its base while it rocked back and forth, its arm still quivering with spent energy. It had not been there the last time Foulques had been in the city.

The Pisan engineers had been busy.

Foulques was wondering at the effectiveness of the catapult blindly launching its missiles over the walls toward the enemy camp when a group of armed men pushed through the crowd toward him. In their midst was a slight figure dressed in a simple brown robe, with the hood pulled up obscuring his face.

"Out of the way," one of the armored men shouted. His hand rested on the pommel of his sword and he swatted frightened people aside like flies with the other. Foulques was about to step in front of the guard when the figure he escorted looked up and Foulques caught a clear glimpse of the face under the hood. It was His Eminence, the Archbishop of Acre himself, God's chosen representative for the people of the Kingdom of Jerusalem. And he was fleeing.

The Archbishop saw Foulques staring and quickly ducked his head. Before Foulques could say or do anything, the Archbishop's bodyguards whisked him away through the crowd toward one of the many waiting ships. Foulques had to fight against the impulse to spit in the direction the old man had fled. Did he have so little faith in God and the good men and women who fought for Him? What kind of holy man could believe that God would allow Acre to fall to the Mohammedans? Foulques would demand answers to these questions, and more, the next time he saw him.

Foulques began to make his way north, upstream against the crowd, but there were so many people and animals swarming toward the docks that he was forced to take a wide detour west through the Genoese Quarter. His destination was the castle. That is where the war room may be set up and where he was most likely to find King Henry's marshal or the grand masters of the Hospitallers, Templars, Teutonic Knights, and other leaders of the defensive forces.

His path brought him in front of Acre's great church, the largest one in the city, and the one in which the Patriarch would oversee the most important ceremonies of the Lord. That is, if he had not fled like a kicked dog. Now, the high arching doors were barred from the inside, but that did not stop a crowd from gathering on the steps beneath them. Foulques felt a bitter taste rise at the back of his throat. As he neared, he saw several large vats lined up at the foot of the church's stone stairs. They were filled with cold water and bald, half-naked children stood shivering in the tubs, while monks chanted verses from their bibles.

In addition, all manner of self-proclaimed holy men hovered about, shouting to be heard over the crowd. The sour body odors of one such man forced Foulques to hold his hand over his mouth and nose as he came near. The fanatic's once-white robe, shredded at its hems and seams, had fresh, rusty splotches hardening on its back where the man had recently whipped himself bloody. Foulques walked alongside a long line of crying mothers holding wide-eyed children of all ages. At the front of the line, nuns with knives, scissors, and razors went to work on the innocents' hair until the scalps of their small skulls glistened in the sun. All the while, the fanatic preached to any who would listen.

"God has brought the heathens upon us! They have been sent by the heavens to punish not only those who have lived in sin, but those who tread upon its cusp, as well. We can turn a blind eye no longer. To bear witness to sin, and do nothing, is to partake of it. Repent! Repent I say, or they will come for us all!"

As if on cue, a shadow grew over the man and something heavy whooshed through the air high overhead. All eyes turned skyward to see a boulder launched by a Saracen catapult smash through the thatched roof of a nearby house. The thunderous crash of splintered wood and broken thatch was followed by an eruption of flame as the collapsed roofing material came into contact with a broken oil lamp or some other source of open flame. The spectacle punctuated the fanatic's rambling so perfectly that the crowd let out a collective gasp. The fanatic himself was shocked into silence for a few seconds, but he soon recovered to continue his tirade with renewed enthusiasm.

"They come! Who will they take? Repent, repent, I say!"

A small girl standing in one of the water-filled vats screamed until a monk pushed her under. Her mother knelt nearby, hands clasped in prayer. When the monk brought the sputtering girl back up for air, both mother and daughter wailed in unison.

What is happening here? Foulques asked himself. He pushed on, past the burning house, determined to put the madness behind him and talk to someone in power.

Since his altered route had brought him so near the gates of the Hospitaller compound, he decided to make a brief stop. It was not yet midday, but its heavy timber gate was closed. Sentries standing on the walkway above recognized

Foulques and immediately shouted down to the gate men. The side door opened and Foulques stepped through, where he was greeted by Brother Jimmy Goodyear. The big man slapped him warmly on the shoulder and wrapped Foulques in one of his bear hugs. After Jimmy released him, Foulques noticed there was a large gathering of men-at-arms in the main square.

"What is happening?" Foulques asked.

"Longshanks's lapdog is addressing the Schwyzers. I assumed that was why you were here," Jimmy said.

"Lord Grandison?"

Jimmy nodded. "Who else?"

"That explains you volunteering for gate duty. But I do not think you need worry. Grandison no doubt has more on his mind than a fugitive from the Poll."

"I am not a fugitive. I relocated to take the cross."

"Then I shall tell Grandison there is a wistful guard at the gate that would love to talk with him about all that has happened in England in recent years."

Jimmy shook his head, a movement that resembled a boulder about to detach itself from a mountain. "Why did I ever open this gate?"

Brother Jimmy had fled England years ago, when King Edward began taxing the common man. Grandison being in Acre did not surprise Foulques, for word had reached him in Cyprus that the King of England had dispatched a contingent of knights and men-at-arms to Acre's aid. Longshanks himself had not made the journey, but he had sent his most trusted general and friend in his stead, Sir Otto de Grandison. Putting the English forces under the command of a Savoyard knight from Lausanne had no doubt upset Edward's advisers, but Longshanks was a stubborn man, and was well known for acting independent of those in his court. What Foulques did find surprising though, was that Grandison wanted to address the Schwyzers. Foulques's curiosity was piqued. What could a man like Grandison hope to gain by addressing them?

Foulques set off for the square. He squeezed between two monks and found himself standing beside Sir Jean de Grailly, the commander of the French knights. He was a tall, fit man, perhaps sixty in years, and he too was a long time friend of Grandison and a member of Edward's court. Unlike Grandison, however, Foulques had met Sir Grailly on several occasions. He was a regular player in the politics of the Kingdom of Jerusalem and had fought at the recent siege of Tripoli.

Sir Grailly raised his eyebrows in recognition. "I was told you were in Cyprus."

"I was," Foulques said.

"You should have stayed there. I suspect we will all be there before long."

Foulques was about to respond, but Sir Grailly nodded toward Grand Master Villiers as he approached a raised platform at the head of the square. Another knight followed a few steps behind. The thought Foulques had when he set eyes on Sir Otto de Grandison for the very first time was how young he looked. He expected him to be a much older man, closer in years to Sir Grailly. Grandison was in his early fifties, but no one would blink if told he was ten years younger. He was average in height, build, and looks, so much so that Foulques found himself a little disappointed. The stories about Grandison were many and some bordered on the ridiculous. Now that he had seen the man in person, Foulques wondered if the bards had more to do with his fame than his actual exploits. It would not be the first time the legend of a man grew from only a seed of truth.

"Does not look like much, does he?" Sir Jean de Grailly said, as though reading Foulques's mind. "Not everything you have heard about him is true. How could it be? But I can tell you a lot of it is, for I was there myself. And that bit is more than enough to earn the man his reputation. What I often wonder, is how much truth there is to the many things I was not present for? Let me give you some advice. If you are ever in a tight spot and Grandison is nearby, follow him. He has the uncanniest aptitude for survival."

The grand master introduced him as a special guest, a distinguished knight from the Schwyzers' own part of the world. Grandison stepped up to the platform under a polite, but hesitant, applause. The Schwyzers were just as confused as Foulques. Some of them undoubtedly could not remember a thing about their alpine beginnings. Their home was Acre now, and Foulques found himself doubting the wisdom of bringing up the past by allowing Grandison to address them. Foulques had found himself unimpressed with the man thus far, but that all changed when he heard him speak.

"Enough of that," Grandison said, raising his hands for silence. "My name is Otto, and I have been waiting a long time to meet you all."

As soon as he uttered his first word, he looked a little taller to Foulques. There was a power in his voice. Many skilled orators project their speech with the deep rumbling of a thunderstorm. Grandison's words came out soft and steady, but with a force all the same, like the wind that bends the trees before a storm.

"You, friend. What is your name?" Grandison asked, suddenly pointing at a boy standing in the front row.

"Peter, my lord."

"I am not your lord, Peter. You are a Hospitaller. You have only one lord, and I am most definitely not Him." He smiled in a way that let the tension out of the room like someone had popped it with a needle. "My name is Otto, and that is what I would have you call me. If you cannot bring yourself to address such a magnificent man as myself by my Christian name, then 'sir' will suffice." He laughed at this, and the honesty and richness of it infected many of his audience to follow in his stead.

"Do not be misled. There is only one man, outside of my family, who I permit to call me Otto," he said, his voice losing all traces of laughter. "His name is Edward, the King of England." The earnestness of his tone drew in his audience like water to a dry sponge. "Peter. Where are you from?"

The young lad flinched like he had been hit in the back of the head with a thrown rock. Grandison waited patiently for the boy to respond.

"Aarau, my—sir."

"Truly? I doubt the Habsburgs would let a strong lad like you out of their capital city."

"Well, not exactly. But you would not know my village's name…"

"Tell me, and we shall see."

"It is called Baden, sir."

Grandison laughed. "Baden? On the Limmat river? Of course I know it. The Romans called your home the 'Waters of the Helvetii.' I have soaked my aching body in its hot springs on several occasions, and the inn there has quite possibly the best mutton stew I have ever eaten in my life. I talk about it all the time. Ask the King of England how tired he is of hearing about Baden's mutton."

Peter smiled at this and his spine straightened just a little.

"And you, friend. Where might you have come from?"

"Appenzell, sir," Marti, a youth small for his age, said.

"Ah, Appenzell. You must be a giant of your people! They may be short there, but God had to do that because he blessed them with too much speed and honesty. I imagine you are imbued with a surplus of one of these, if not both?"

He continued picking faces from the crowd, asking where they were from, and then made it clear he not only knew of each place, but had also traveled to it. Foulques did notice that Grandison picked the older ones. He did not know if Grandison did this on purpose, but it was a wise move if he did. It would have disturbed his momentum if a youth could not recall anything of his roots.

"You are a strapping lad. What might your name be?"

"Well, Otto, I am fairly sure I am Pirmin Schnidrig of Tasch!"

The grand master and the monk next to him started at Pirmin's familiarity, but Grandison laughed. "You have an honest feel about you, son, mixed with a lion's share of trouble, I suspect. I have never been to Tasch, but I have seen the Matterhorn from afar, and I have heard many stories about the men and women that dwell in the valleys below." He addressed the crowd with a voice turned serious and he thumped his chest with a clenched fist. "Stories of great honor and courage." He looked at Pirmin. "With a fair bit of mischief, I might add. It pleases me greatly to finally meet one." Pirmin grinned.

Having tamed the big youth, Grandison moved on. He once again addressed the entire host of young men.

"I know you all," he said. "Perhaps not yet in name, but I will before the end of today. I know you, because I am you. My home too is in the Alps, near the shores of Lake Constance. And I too, was sent away by my family. Not because they did not love me, but because they loved me more than anyone or anything in this world. My father wanted more for me than he himself could give. To that end, he sent me away to a damp, cold, miserable place called England." This earned some chuckles in the crowd. "Forty years later, I have the honor of standing before you all. I will not lie. My life has not always been easy. I have worked hard to be what I am today. But if I can make a life after being sent to dreary England, surely you can build one here in the sun and splendor of the East!"

The Schwyzers were dismissed after Grandison's talk. They filed out of the square slowly. Grandison took the time to clasp arms with each and every one of them and hear their names. It took a while, for there were over two hundred Schwyzers in attendance, but Foulques remained nearby, long after Sir Grailly had left. Whether out of respect, or envy, he found he could not take his eyes off Grandison. He was a true leader of men. After only a short time with the Schwyzers, Foulques was certain they would gladly fall over one another to do his bidding. Foulques now understood why King Edward entrusted the soldiers of England to the care of Otto de Grandison, a foreign knight.

Grand Master Villiers appeared in front of Foulques. "Admiral. What are you doing here?" His words came out harsh and strained. Foulques blinked once before deciding it was indeed the grand master who was speaking.

"I heed the call. You sent word to the world that all Knights of the Grand Cross are needed in Acre."

"You will return to Cyprus immediately. Be thankful the marshal is not here to see you defy his orders."

"Where is the marshal?"

"On the wall."

"That is where I should be," Foulques said. "Not hiding on an island in the Mid-Earth Sea."

Grand Master Villiers stepped in close. Foulques could smell wine on his breath.

"You will return to the harbor and board your ship before the hour is up. That is my command. Do you understand?"

"Of course, sir. But my ship has already sailed for Cyprus with a full passenger load of evacuees. And I do not know if you have been to the harbor of late, but securing passage on a ship of any kind is not a simple task."

The grand master said something but Foulques did not hear it, for the last of the Schwyzers had departed and Grandison was marching directly toward Foulques and the leader of the Hospitallers. Foulques was surprised when the veteran knight addressed him directly, virtually ignoring the grand master.

"And you are Brother Foulques. Well met, sir. You have done well with these lads. They are a fine bunch and I shall be honored to stand on the wall with them."

"I… thank you, Sir Grandison," Foulques said. "But I am only one of many responsible for their training."

"Ah, but without you they would not be here," Grandison said.

"I understand you were the one who suggested recruiting the Schwyzers in the first place," Foulques said.

"I was. The Alps breed hearty men and women. They have to be strong to survive in that terrain, but more importantly, they must learn to rely on one another. That is what makes them ideal soldiers." He paused, then said, "Your Uncle Guillaume sends word. He was gathering more men when I saw him last, and intends to set sail as soon as he can. He looks forward to seeing his nephew when he arrives."

"He is coming to Acre?" Foulques had not seen his uncle for over seven years. Brother Guillaume de Villaret's duties kept him traveling, forever negotiating with kings and lords, trying to get them to take up the cross or support the Hospitaller cause financially. The last time they had seen each other was when Foulques was still recovering from his wounds after his disastrous encounter with Badru Hashim, the Northman. Of course, Foulques was the only one who truly considered the incident a disaster. Most others considered him a hero for rescuing the children. But they had not been there to see Foulques humiliated in the eyes of God. Foulques knew the truth, but he had learned to live with his shame.

"Then I shall be here to meet him," Foulques said. The grand master gave him a scathing look.

"You do not have to return to Cyprus?" Grandison asked.

A horn sounded in the distance, so small and insignificant at first, Foulques found himself automatically blocking it out. But then the City Watch Tower's bells started echoing its blasts, followed by more bells as the city's churches joined in. The three men looked at one another as the ringing escalated, culminating in a violent frenzy.

"What is this?" Foulques asked, having to almost shout over the din. When the grand master spoke, his words were a whisper.

"The Mamluks are coming for the wall," he said.

CHAPTER FIFTEEN

"SAY SOMETHING," BADRU said.

He had wanted to tell Yusuf what Turuntay had revealed to him sooner, but he had been forced to wait until this moment, for he knew he needed total privacy. Looking at the disbelief on Yusuf's frozen face as he stared into his teacup full of cold tea, Badru was glad he had waited. They had marched with the army to Acre and now sat across from one another in their newly erected tent. It was in disarray, for their belongings were not yet unpacked, but Yusuf had spread a thick, silk carpet on the ground for them to sit on. In an army of a hundred thousand men, this was as alone as they would ever be.

"Yusuf?"

His eyes fluttered upward to meet Badru's. "And you believed him?"

"He had no reason to lie," Badru said. "And it would take a lot to drive a man like Turuntay to lie."

Yusuf shook his head and let out a long, slow breath. "Then this would make you and Sultan Khalil brothers."

"Half-brothers," Badru said.

"You being the elder."

Yusuf stared at Badru. His large hazel eyes seemed to grow larger still. Badru knew where Yusuf's mind was going, and he did not like it.

"No one need know," Badru said. "I suspect only Turuntay had any knowledge of this."

"And if you are wrong? How long do you think you will live if the sultan finds out? No, Badru, the risk is too great. We must leave this place. Go far away, somewhere beyond his reach. We have a ship. We could go anywhere. We could—"

"Start over? Is that what you want to say? I am tired of starting over. And there is no glory in hiding."

Yusuf was quiet for a moment. His voice quavered when he next spoke. "You know I will support you no matter what your decision. But what exactly is it that you want, Badru? Do you wish to be sultan?"

"Sultan?" The question caught him completely unawares. He lowered his voice again. "Never would I wish that. I was put in this world to serve. I see that now, but I will not accept just anyone as my master. You taught me that."

Yusuf shook his head. He opened his mouth to say something, but decided against it and settled for shaking his head once again.

Voices sounded outside the entrance of the tent. Moments later, the guard Badru had posted ducked inside.

"Forgive me, Emir. The sultan has summoned you."

Yusuf closed his eyes as Badru rose to his feet.

"Do you trust him?" Ibn al-Salus asked.

"Of course not. I am sultan, now. I cannot afford to trust anyone," Khalil said. The two of them were alone, if a sultan could ever truly be alone, in the newly relocated Dihliz. The red tent sat atop a small rise near the southern shore of the sea, not far from the walls of Acre. It was well out of the Franks' crossbow range, but many of the Royal Emir did not approve of Khalil's choice of locations. They questioned the wisdom of putting the sultan's pavilion so near the enemy, but Khalil had argued it was a show of confidence. He said he wanted to torment the Franks by dangling himself before them, so near, but yet untouchable by any means within their power.

Four guards stood outside the tent's entrance, while another twenty patrolled the surrounding grounds. They were all Mamluks of the Royal Guard, trained since childhood in the Cairo Tabaqa. Their lives had been so dominated by the codes of the Furusiyya that it was said they were above politics, beyond all forms of bribery. They had one purpose, and one purpose only: to protect the sultan of Egypt from any and all threats to his person, be it in times of peace, or war. These men had sworn allegiance to Qalawun, and earlier that day, they had renewed their vows to his son.

Khalil had watched his father rule for his entire life, and he thought he knew what being sultan would be like. He had assumed it meant freedom. Freedom from his father, perhaps, but it was definitely not the freedom he had envisioned. Still, with this lack of freedom came a certain power. Power over the lives of others, if not his own. It would take some getting used to, but he felt he was adjusting quite well.

The first official act he had performed, of course, was to dismiss Turuntay as vice-sultan. He was not worried about upsetting the other emir, as this was not an unusual act for a new sultan. A sultan needed to appoint a respected and capable man as vice-sultan, for if anything happened to the sultan himself, the vice-sultan must be able to rule until the emirs elected their new permanent leader. Khalil had promoted Baydara, his father's vizier, to the role. It was not a popular move, for although Baydara was a Mamluk, he was a scholarly, thin man who spoke in nasal tones. He had been recruited by Khalil's father fifteen years ago, and was a new breed of Mamluk at the time. One who had been brought up with a quill in his hand rather than a sword. Qalawun had realized the need for men such as Baydara early in his reign. Many of the emir looked down on Baydara and joked openly to his face. But Baydara did have his supporters, for he had made many connections during his time in Qalawun's court.

Promoting Baydara to vice-sultan provided a certain continuity to the sultanate and therefore, Khalil's detractors could not risk protesting openly. Baydara, himself, was overjoyed at his good fortune. Khalil could still feel the unpleasant dryness of his lips pressing against the back of his hand over and over again, his annoying voice swearing to serve him faithfully as he had done Khalil's father for so many years.

With the vice-sultan position filled, that left an opening for the vizier. As personal secretary and head adviser to the sultan, the vizier's duties were as varied as they were vague. When Khalil appointed his boyhood friend, Ibn al-Salus, to the position, there was a general grumbling in the assembly of emirs, but no one really cared enough to make it a public point of dissension. Yes, Ibn al-Salus was only the son of a merchant, but a very rich merchant. Truth be told, Khalil felt many of the emir were happy they had not been chosen for the task. Who wanted to be the personal scribe for the new boy-sultan? He was, after all, not even a true Mamluk.

"Have you learned anything new about Badru Hashim?" Khalil asked.

"Only that he was indeed at the Royal Tabaqa. I have sent messages to some of my father's contacts in Cairo. Perhaps they will know something, but I am doubtful. It has been almost twenty years since Badru Hashim was sold. What about Baydara? As vizier he may have known why he was sold. He could have even done it without the sultan's knowledge."

Khalil shook his head and leaned back in his cushioned chair. "He did not become vizier until a couple of years later. Of my father's court, only Turuntay was around at the time."

"And now he is dead," Ibn al-Salus said.

"And now he is dead," Khalil echoed, unable to resist a slow smile from spreading across his face. He stood up. He needed to move. These past few days had lifted a thousand pounds of weight from around his neck, weight he had endured for as long as he could remember. Now, it was time for Khalil to open his wings and fly.

He stretched his arms wide, took a deep breath, and paced a circle around Ibn al-Salus, who watched him with curious eyes. How quickly one's life could change. He had been scared when his father died, for the sultan had told him time and time again how difficult it was going to be for Khalil to win over the emirs and become sultan. But it had proved to be simple. Maybe it was only Qalawun who did not want his son to become sultan, and when he died, Allah was able to see Khalil and shower him with favor for a change. Why else would a Mamluk such as Badru Hashim, an educated emir with no political affiliations, suddenly appear out of nowhere at exactly the moment Khalil needed him? He even commanded thirty seasoned Mamluk warriors who worshiped him, along with a handful of foot soldiers. How could Badru Hashim not be a gift from Allah?

"Call him in," Khalil said.

A moment later, Badru Hashim knelt before the sultan and his vizier.

"Imagine for a moment, that you were sultan, Badru Hashim. Imagine this were your army. How would you direct it at the Christian forces?"

The man's unnerving gray eyes snapped up and looked directly into Khalil's own. The breath caught in Khalil's chest and he focused all his power of self-restraint to not look away. Just as suddenly, Badru dropped his stare to the floor.

"I would not know, My Sultan. I have no experience in commanding such an immense body of soldiers."

"No one has," Khalil said. "But you have met the Christians in battle, yes?"

Badru nodded.

"And the knights of their holy orders. You have come up against them as well?"

"Many times, My Sultan."

"Then tell me of your experience. That is all. Tell me what you have seen, what you have learned from these encounters."

Badru took a breath and a moment to think before he spoke.

"Their knights are formidable warriors, especially those of the cross. The Templars, Hospitallers, and the Germans. They are all dangerous and very difficult to unhorse once set in their saddle. I would imagine they are even more difficult to remove from a wall."

"Go on," Khalil said, when Badru's words slowed down.

"Some men give up hope when they are cornered. There will be many of those in the city. But the men of the cross fight like cornered lions when others would lie down. It will cost our army dearly to take the walls of Acre."

Khalil considered the Mamluk's words for a moment. He leaned forward in his chair.

"Picture in your mind, Emir, that you stood before, not a thousand, but only one of these knights. He stands upon a wall looking down at you. How will you defeat him?"

Badru replied without hesitation. "I would get him to come down off his wall, make him face me on open ground, where my speed and strength could not be diminished, and his could not be enhanced."

Khalil sat back in his chair, rolling his eyes. "Unfortunately, he would have to be a fool to do that. The Christians are many things, but I do not consider them fools."

Badru shrugged. "I may not know how to command great armies, My Sultan. But I know more than one way to make a man go where I want."

Khalil's eyebrows arched. He told Badru Hashim to continue with his train of thought. He listened, and as he did so, he settled back into his chair. A voice in the back of his mind kept repeating the same thought.

How could this man not have been sent by Allah?

CHAPTER SIXTEEN

THE CHURCH IN the Hospitaller compound took up the alarm. Its bells rang with a frenzy that sent shock waves through Foulques, shaking him to the marrow in his bones. The grand master shouted at a nearby sergeant standing guard at the door to the main keep. The brown-robed brother ran to where Grand Master Villiers, Grandison, and Foulques stood. "Tell the stable master to ready three horses as fast as possible." As the sergeant turned and began to run toward the stables, the grand master shouted at his back. "And tell him they need not be destriers—any pacer will do, and if he has none available then saddle up mules!"

Grand Master Villiers turned to Grandison and Foulques. "Do you need anything, gentlemen, before we join our brothers at the wall?" They shook their heads and the three men set out at a fast walk toward the stables.

Three Icelandic ponies were saddled and waiting. Short, strong animals, normally used for traveling long distances because they had an extra gait somewhere between a canter and a trot, which was exceptionally smooth, and was a pace the sturdy horses could keep up all day. Foulques was debating which of the other men to help into his saddle first, but Grandison grabbed a handful of mane and swung effortlessly into his saddle with no help from the stirrup. The grand master also mounted with the ease of a man twenty years younger. "Follow me," he shouted. The two men were already galloping out of the Hospitaller compound before Foulques was in the saddle. He swung up onto his own horse and put her into a full canter. There would be no need of a traveling gait this day.

Foulques caught up to the two men as they turned east and rode parallel to the wall that divided the city in two. North of that wall was the district of Montmusart, and near its center was a tiny home and workshop with a few bee hives standing outside. Foulques wavered when he passed the gate leading into Montmusart. His urge to check on Najya was strong, but he was needed at the wall. He decided that he would serve her best by seeing to the defenses of the city. After he helped turn back the first wave of the Mamluk attack, there would be time for him to search her out and make sure she was all right. He urged his pony on east, past the castle, and then toward the Gates of Saint Anthony.

Acre was situated on a large tract of land that jutted out into the Mid-Earth Sea. Its deep harbor and rocky coastline protected it from the west, north, and south, and a long line of two parallel walls ran from the north all the way down south to the water, cutting the city off from the east. Over the years, various powers that be had constructed towers along the walls to further add to the city's already impressive fortifications.

The three men galloped through the first gate, leaving the guards scrambling to get out of their way. They veered left and pulled up at the base of the Hospitaller Tower.

As they all dismounted, the grand master looked at Grandison. "Will you not go to the English Tower?"

Grandison shook his head. "Sir Grailly is there with some of his French knights. The lads will fight for him as well as anyone."

They dropped the reins of their horses and ran toward an open, man-sized doorway. The brilliant spring sun was high in the sky, illuminating everything around them except that rectangular patch of black at the base of the massive tower. One after another, with Foulques at the rear, the three men plunged into the darkness.

There were lanterns on hooks spaced evenly along the circular stairway's wall, but it still took Foulques's eyes a moment to adjust to the low light. Keeping his hand on one wall, he followed the two older men up the stairs. They took them two at a time, and after what seemed an eternity, Foulques emerged once more into blinding sunlight. As overloaded as his eyes were by the brightness, it was his ears that caused him the most pain, followed shortly by his chest. For the sight of the Mamluk army stole the air from his lungs and the blood from his heart.

The Sultan of Egypt had assembled a siege force two hundred years in the making. A hundred trebuchets and mangonels blotted out the far horizon, coming ever closer under the power of man and beast. In front of them marched what looked like four or five distinctly separate armies, enough men to spread along the entire length of Acre's walls. Thousands of drummers beat their instruments as the sea of men and animals flowed inexorably forward.

Foulques stared open-mouthed. The sultan's forces had to number more than a hundred thousand men. The last Foulques had heard, Acre's defenses consisted of no more than twelve thousand, most of which were men-at-arms, or city militia. There were only eight hundred knights in all of Acre. He felt his faith waver. How could they possibly hold against such a formidable threat?

It was an unseen force that finally made Foulques tear his gaze from the fields below and look along the length of the wall. Fifty paces away, Marshal Clermont locked Foulques in place with a venomous stare. The marshal looked like he wanted nothing more than to cross that fifty paces and skewer Foulques with the sword he held at his side, but fortunately, they were separated by ranks of Hospitaller knights and sergeants. Most were in red tunics, some in black. Many of the brown-clad brother-sergeants were armed with crossbows. The wall was wide enough to comfortably ride a horse along, if one could ever get an animal up the narrow staircases, but the crossbowmen worked in teams of three so it was crowded at the moment. One man would shoot from between the crenellations, while the other two stood behind him holding goat's foot levers and bolts to reload the weapon. Sometimes they had a second crossbow to put into the mix.

The drums stopped all at once.

"Put me where you want me, Master Villiers," Grandison said.

The grand master drew his sword. The lines on his face smoothed out and the weariness in his eyes brought on by the last few restless nights faded away. The waiting was over.

"Here is as good a place as any," the grand master said. "May God hold you both in His graces on this day."

Foulques, too, drew his sword and his arm hummed with energy he felt travel all the way to the base of his skull. Despite the odds, this was where he was meant to be. On the wall, defending his city from the enemy. He had never been so sure of anything in his entire life.

The great arm of a single trebuchet slung its load high into the blue sky with a grating whoosh of its counterweight. Its head-sized boulder gracefully sailed past the Hospitaller tower and disappeared somewhere in the city. Where it struck, Foulques could not hear, for the moment the missile passed overhead, the Mamluks charged. Their screams were so loud Foulques thought he might topple off the wall backward before the battle had even begun.

The first ranks of the approaching armies picked up their pace and began to separate from the main host. Each man carried a large shield at his side, and as they closed to within two hundred and fifty yards of the city walls, they swung the large, rectangular shields to the front. Then they slowed their approach and tightened their formations, banding together in groups of fifty or more to form shield walls. Completely protected from the tops of their heads to their ankles, they ceased their forward momentum and stood firm.

"Crossbowmen, hold your bolts!" Foulques heard the marshal's voice rise up over the deafening shouts and jeers of the army below. Very little noise came from the defenders themselves.

"Hold firm. Do not waste your bolts on the shield bearers," the marshal said.

With a new series of shouts and cheers, another wave of infantry broke away from the main group and sprinted toward the shield lines. Many of them clutched wickedly curved Saracen bows in one hand, while bags of arrows hung from their opposite shoulders. When the archers arrived, the shield men began their shuffling approach toward the walls. As they closed the distance the archers began loosing arrows at the defenders, but the marshal still would not allow his crossbowmen to launch their own volleys.

Like the others around him, Foulques pushed himself up against the wall for protection as arrows shot from powerful horn bows thudded against stone and brick, or whistled over the wall to harmlessly hit the second set of walls behind him.

From his position, Foulques could see Marshal Clermont hunched behind a crenellation, constantly leaning out to take stock of the enemies' actions. Foulques risked a glance around the wall. Thousands more men were sprinting toward them in groups of twenty or thirty. Some were archers, but most of them carried long, lightweight ladders and grappling ropes.

"Now!" the marshal commanded. "Train your bolts on the ladder men. Loose at will!"

The wall erupted in a series of clicks and grunts as men

shot and reloaded crossbows. Aside from the occasional curse as someone missed his mark, the wall was surprisingly quiet. But Foulques had been atop enough walls to know this relative peace would not last. He had seen thousands of ladders, far too many for the number of crossbowmen. Even if they had every Genoese crossbowman alive in the world today, it would not be enough.

The intensity of enemy arrows flying over the wall increased, as did the curses spewing forth from the defenders. Then, Foulques began hearing grunts of pain as men began to take wounds from enemy arrows.

"Ladders on the south!" came a shout. Foulques heard the marshal bark out a series of commands to the men around him and a small group of Schwyzers, crouching low, made their way to where the grand master, Foulques, and Grandison crouched near the tower. The giant lad, Pirmin, was there, and in his hands he held a long, wooden pole with a forked end.

"The marshal said we are to report to you," said another Schwyzer to the grand master. The young man had small eyes and straight, black hair. It was Gissler, and though he was exceedingly thin, Foulques knew him to be more than a fair hand with a sword. In fact, he was one of the marshal's favorites because of that skill.

"Good lads," the grand master said. He pointed to Pirmin and two of the other Schwyzers. You three will be on the pole. The rest stay close to me or Brother Foulques. If you lose track of us for any reason, do whatever Sir Grandison requests."

Foulques was grateful the grand master did not refer to him as "Admiral." Perhaps it was a slip, or maybe it was on purpose. At the moment, that title held no meaning for Foulques, here on the wall. It belonged in a different world, to a different man, even. He flexed the fingers around his sword hilt and felt them relax into position. Everything was as it should be. Despite the escalating sounds of a charging army and the nervous energy all around him, Foulques felt more at peace than he had for a very long time. He looked one crenellation over at Grandison, who had his arms crossed over his chest as he leaned his back against the wall. He had not yet drawn his sword. The older warrior looked at Foulques and winked. Foulques was immediately reminded of a certain mariner who swore he would not be caught within a hundred leagues of Acre anytime soon.

Grandison drew his sword and Foulques saw the tips of the first ladder arc through the air and bounce against the wall not five feet from where he stood. He stayed in cover and waited for the head of the first enemy to appear. However, with a loud cry, Pirmin charged forward and caught one of the ladder's upper rungs with his forked pole. He continued to run forward and with a mighty heave sent it toppling straight back. Another appeared, and he attempted to repeat the process, but there were already too many men hanging off it. Two other Schwyzers latched onto Pirmin and together they tried to tip it back, but it was no use. Then Grandison appeared beside them.

"Do not push them straight back!" he said. "Slide them to the side and it will take others with it." Together they pushed the ladder sideways and it toppled over, spilling the men on it to the ground. "And watch out for ropes on the upper parts of the ladders. They will try to steady them from below."

Foulques was still waiting for a head to appear over the wall when, to his surprise, a fully armored Saracen arose on the walkway six strides away. When another appeared behind him, Foulques recognized the source of their ascent: a grapple, with a thick rope attached, was wedged against the far side of the walkway. They drew their curved blades and Foulques charged. He was too late to stop the first man from slicing open the back of a brother-sergeant bent over loading a crossbow. But before the sergeant had fallen, Foulques plunged his sword through the Saracen's face. The second Saracen was struck down from behind by another brother. Foulques kicked the grapple to dislodge it, but it was stuck firm. The rope was taut and moving gently, hinting at a weight on its other end. Foulques drew his knife, not his dagger, and sawed at the rope until its last strand broke away. The thick hemp slithered across the walkway and disappeared.

Several ladders had made it to the wall and more of the enemy were leaping onto the walkway or stepping between the crenellations. Many crossbowmen were forced to drop their weapons and do battle with swords and daggers. The fighting was close and fierce, and Foulques, Grandison, and even the grand master himself were in the thick of it. There was no room for honorable knightly duels or one-on-one challenges. The Saracens who had gained the wall were the undesirables of the enemy army, the first wave of sacrificial conscripts and mercenaries. Most of them had never expected to get this far, but now that they stood on the wall, they held onto a glimmer of hope that they could take it, and live to see another day. They fought like madmen.

Foulques turned aside an attacker's blade with his own and swept his leg out from under him with his right foot. Then, holding his sword in both hands, he plunged his weapon straight down through the man's chest. He withdrew his bloodied blade only when he felt it come up against stone. He turned and his sword found the back of another assailant who was hacking at a young brother-sergeant trying to fight from his knees. The youth had a nasty wound on the side of his neck, and he collapsed at almost the same time as his dead attacker.

Foulques felt someone bump up against his back and he whirled with his blade in a high guard. Otto de Grandison stared back at him from a similar position. With no words spoken, they both turned away again, keeping their backs near enough to touch, and fought on.

Men were pouring onto the walkway from a new ladder while one of their number stood in front, slashing left and right with his scimitar to give his comrades time to make the wall. Foulques was about to engage the man when, seemingly out of nowhere, Pirmin came charging across the rampart with his pole leveled in front of him. The giant youth's forked stick caught the Saracen standing guard just above his hips. Pirmin lifted him into the air and continued running forward, eventually slamming the man into another as he climbed the ladder. Pirmin let loose a terrifying battle cry as he hooked the ladder and sent it toppling sideways with a dozen men screaming as they fell to their deaths.

Foulques began to hear horns sounding in the distance. At first he thought they were a signal from his own forces. Perhaps someone requesting assistance. Had part of the wall been overrun? He risked a glance north along the wall toward the Templars' Tower and then south. The horns belonged to the Mamluks. They were calling a retreat!

Saracens were scrambling away from the base of the wall, leaving ladders standing against the ramparts and the dead where they lay. Cheers went up all along the wall. Several men shot crossbows at the fleeing enemy, until the hoarse voice of Marshal Clermont ordered them to stop. It was quiet one moment, and then, when the reality of the situation had sunk in, everyone talked at once. Men slapped each other on the back and laughed. Others stood staring at the dead on the wall and shook their heads. Others worked in pairs to throw the bodies of the enemy off the battlements.

Foulques searched the faces around him until he saw the grand master. He was talking to a small group of knights and looked unharmed. Foulques sheathed his sword and found himself suddenly weary. Weary, but overjoyed. He offered a quick thank you to God and admonished himself for doubting the ability of the Christian forces to hold the city. This was Acre, the last of God's fortresses in the Kingdom of Jerusalem. Of course He would not let it fall.

As he stood there at the wall, looking out over the stragglers of the attacking force as they returned to the main army, Foulques felt his enthusiasm wane. They had attacked with only a pittance of their full strength. The bulk of the army still stood by. Watching, waiting. Then Foulques began to notice changes in the enemy positions that had occurred during the attack. The siege engines had moved closer and there was now a long line of ten-foot-tall screens directly in front of their position. Someone came to stand next to him.

"The battle has begun," Grandison said. "They are done feeling us out. How long do you think it will take before those are operational?"

He pointed toward the middle of the line of siege engines and Foulques suddenly realized what he was looking at. In the midst of all those mangonels and catapults, was a collection of timbers, ropes, and pulleys the size of which Foulques had never seen before. When he looked closer, even at this range, he could see the timbers were already carved and squared. They were gigantic. There were no wheels, because whatever they were building would be far too large to move. When assembled, the machines, for there were enough parts for more than one, would be five times the size of any engine currently on the battlefield.

Foulques had to still his heart before he could speak. "Have you ever seen an engine that large, Sir Grandison?"

Grandison shook his head. "No, but as worrisome as that might be, our real problem is over there." He pointed at the screens two hundred yards away.

"Sappers?" Foulques asked.

Grandison nodded. He looked up at the clear sky. "I imagine they will start digging tonight. I would."

CHAPTER SEVENTEEN

ON THE INNER wall, there was a large armory located in the base of the tower looming a short distance south of the Gate of Saint Anthony. Normally overflowing with spears, swords, and axes, the room now contained nothing save row upon row of empty weapon racks pushed against the walls to make space for the group of men gathered in its center.

Foulques followed the grand master and marshal inside the tower. No sooner had he set foot in the hastily created strategy room, then a gravelly voice called out.

"What is he doing here, Mathieu?" William de Beaujeu, the Grand Master of the Templars said, leveling a thick finger at Foulques. "The prince said this was to be a meeting of commanders only."

Unlike Marshal Clermont and Grand Master Villiers, Grand Master Beaujeu's beard was short and neat, like his hair, and less streaked with gray than either of the two Hospitallers, though all three men were probably similar in age.

"Foulques has recently been promoted to admiral. As

such, he has every right to be here," Marshal Clermont said, walking straight up to Beaujeu and staring him down.

"Admiral?" Beaujeu looked right past Clermont at Foulques. "And how many ships in this new fleet of yours, Admiral?"

"Say nothing, Admiral Foulques!" Clermont said. "For that information could be too easily traded for gold."

Beaujeu laughed, but the sound was dry and humorless. He took a step toward Clermont. "Be careful who you accuse of being a spy, Mathieu."

"Spies sell information to the enemy," Clermont said. "You, however, will sell anything to anyone. Is there a word for that?"

"I believe it is called a Hospitaller," Beaujeu said, crossing his arms and taking a step forward.

Grand Master Villiers put a hand on Marshal Clermont's shoulder and the Templar marshal also took a step forward. Whether he was going to attempt to rein in his grand master, or join in the fray himself, Foulques would never know, for in just that moment, a shout went up near the doorway.

"Make way for the prince! Clear a path!"

There were fifteen or twenty men in the room. Grudgingly, Clermont and Beaujeu backed away from each other to make space at the doorway.

Two fully armed Cypriot knights moved slowly into the room followed by Prince Amalric, a young man barely out of his teens. Behind him trailed two of his advisers. Foulques immediately saw the resemblance between the prince and

King Henry, his slightly older brother. Amalric was a fleshed out, more fully realized version of his older brother. Where Henry's eyes were sunken and his skin pale, Amalric bore all the signs of a man who spent a good deal of time in the outdoors. He was still a thin man, but his skin was browned by the sun and his eyes bright and quick as they took in the men surrounding his little entourage. So similar was he in looks to his older brother, it was as though God had made Henry first, who had proved disappointing, so He then went ahead and created Amalric.

The prince was unarmored, opting instead for blue hose and a matching velvet tunic, but he did have a sword belted at his hip. A sword, Foulques noted, that was too long and heavy for someone of his stature. Not that it mattered, for he was sure the prince had not once released it from its scabbard.

The Cypriot knights led their lord to the front of the room, toward the only chair. As the commanders in the room parted to make a path, Foulques saw Grandison and Sir Grailly standing beside each other at the front of the room. Also present were representatives of the Venetians, the Pisans, and the Genoans, although they were all at different sides of the room. The Master of the leper knights, the Order of the Knights of Saint Lazarus, was present, and though he himself did not have leprosy, he may as well have for how much space the others in the room gave him. Foulques saw a man he did not recognize wearing the black cross of the Teutonic Knights. He assumed it to be their newly appointed grand master. Apparently, the previous head of the Order had resigned and taken ship only days before the Mamluk army had appeared.

As the prince's advisers made a show out of dusting off the chair with scowling faces to ready it for their lord to sit, Marshal Clermont grunted and shook his head.

"Look at the boy. Thinks he is king already."

"He has been put in a difficult position for one so young," Grand Master Villiers said. "We should give him a chance."

"You forget," the marshal said, "that I was at Tripoli with him. Look at his face. He does not want to be here. I watched a lot of good men die in Tripoli and mark my words, he will let the same thing happen here."

"Then we had best advise him well," the grand master said. He narrowed his eyes and gave the marshal one of his stern looks that said, 'I have heard enough on this topic, so do not say any more.' Though generally known to be a calm, level-headed leader, Grand Master Villiers had an unnerving ability to sense what men needed to hear to keep them in place, and to make the best use of their abilities. There was a reason he had been their leader for so many years, Foulques thought. Even so, he could tell by the emotion in his voice, that the siege was beginning to have an effect on even the grand master's steel nerves.

One of the prince's advisers, a tall, elegant man wearing a yellow robe with voluminous sleeves, called for order in the room. He waited, staring out over the room with the stern look of a tutor waiting for his pupils to quieten down. When it was silent, he bowed to the prince and backed away.

"Marshal Levesque. Your report on the city's defenses," the prince said.

Marshal Levesque was the commander of the city's guard and militia. Foulques knew him well, for he was an elderly man and had been a presence on the city walls for as long as Foulques could remember.

"The Templars hold the wall in the north, the Hospitallers a long section in the middle, near the main gate. South of them are the Knights of Saint Lazarus and the Teutonics, and then the English and the French. Mercenaries and the city guard are stationed at the gates."

"Very well," the prince said. "How long can you hold the walls?"

The silence grew uncomfortable as the captain pondered how best to answer the question. "That is for God to decide," Levesque said, finally.

"We have enough men to man the walls completely?"

"Yes, Your Grace. I estimate our forces to be slightly over eleven thousand men."

"Good. Keep a reserve of the city militia back and on alert in the event they need to be sent to assist somewhere."

He nodded and stood up, apparently satisfied with his decision.

"Your Grace," came a voice from the front of the room. "Might I say a few words?" The speaker was none other than Otto de Grandison.

Amalric turned ever so slowly toward the voice, looking every bit a thief who had just been told his person was about to be searched.

"Of course, Sir Grandison."

Like the two men were joined by the same puppeteer's stick, Grandison stepped forward and the prince sat back down. Grandison angled himself so he addressed the prince but also the assembly of commanders. "My Lords, I have spoken with the Pisan engineers, and they reassure me that our walls are thick enough to resist the missile attacks from our enemy's siege engines for months. However, work is underway on two trebuchets the size of which neither the engineers, nor myself, have ever seen. If they are completed, and prove functional, the Pisans say our walls will crumble like dry cheese."

"Then we must destroy these machines before they are built," the prince said.

"Exactly my thought, Your Grace," Grandison said. "With your permission, I would like to put this before all here, to see if we can come up with a feasible plan of action."

A few murmurs shot through the room. "We should train our own catapults on the engines," a voice said. The idea was quickly dismissed by the Grand Master of the Templars. "Impossible. They are too far out of range." He strode forward to take center stage, ignoring the dark look from Prince Amalric's adviser, who had to abandon all vestiges of grace and practically leap out of the knight's path. "The only feasible way of destroying those engines is with a well-timed cavalry raid."

Several gasps cut through the air and open protests followed.

"That would mean charging directly into enemy lines. It

would be a death sentence," Marshal Levesque said.

"Not if it was done at night," Grand Master Beaujeu said. "A small force of men could steal out of one of the northernmost gates under cover of darkness and be on the first engine in moments. The machine would be in flames before the enemy even knew they were under attack."

"A bold plan," said the Grand Master of the Teutonics. "But who do you propose leads this attack?"

"Me, of course," Grand Master Beaujeu said. "I would trust no one else but Templar Knights with a mission of this magnitude."

Foulques heard the marshal next to him murmur under his breath. "William, you arse, there are two trebuchets."

As if echoing his thoughts, Grandison spoke up. "And what of the second engine, Master Beaujeu? With the first in flames, you will have attracted the wrath of the entire Mamluk army. You will have no hope of ever reaching the second one."

Marshal Clermont was on the verge of stepping forward when Grand Master Villiers's thick hand shot out and grasped him by the forearm. "I forbid it," he said. "You will be needed on the wall, Mathieu," he added in a less harsh tone.

Grandison was right, Foulques thought. It was a good plan.

"The Hospitallers shall target the second engine," Foulques announced, stepping toward the front of the room. "And I shall lead our men, if there are no objections."

Grand Master Beaujeu's eyes widened. "You will hear no

objections from me. I have seen you tip a lance, Brother Villaret, and you do a fine enough job of it. For an admiral." This brought some chuckles from the crowd, and more than a few confused glances.

Grandison stepped forward and looked at Foulques. "And I will have to join you both with a few of King Edward's men, for I fear if he were to hear how I missed the opportunity to go on a midnight ride with both the Templars and the Hospitallers, Longshanks would have my head." He bowed to the prince. "That is, of course, if we have Your Grace's permission."

The prince paused long enough to give the impression that he was actually weighing the pros and cons of the plan. Foulques knew, however, that it did not matter what he said, for neither the Hospitallers nor the Templars were his to command. And from what he knew of Grandison, the Savoyard knight would do whatever he thought best, as well. But in the end, Amalric simply nodded. He rose and magnanimously made the sign of the cross in front of the three men. "God be with you," he said.

As the prince exited the room, Foulques could not help but see the two very dark, and very furious faces of Grand Master Villiers and Marshal Clermont burning him with fire from their eyes hotter than any in all of damnation.

CHAPTER EIGHTEEN

THE RAID WAS planned for that evening, a moonless night lit only by the stars. Beaujeu, Foulques, and Grandison each led a contingent of fifty men. The Templars stole out of the northern-most gate in the wall, their target the northern siege engine. Grandison rode out of a gate in the south, his task being to destroy the southern engine. Foulques led his group of fifty men from the same gate as Grandison. He was to ride behind the screens the Mamluks had erected and destroy their sappers' tunnels.

Foulques and Grandison stood beside each other, their horses' reins in hand outside the walls of Acre waiting for the rest of their men to pass through a narrow doorway behind them. The sky in the distance was lit up by the light cast from thousands of small fires scattered over the plain. In front of the two men, however, lay only blackness, a thick curtain that seemed all the darker because of the light beyond.

"This seemed like a much better idea when we were on the other side of the wall," Grandison said.

"I am sure Beaujeu is thinking the exact same thing,"

Foulques said.

Grandison checked over his shoulder. Satisfied that his entire group was out of the city, he turned to Foulques and the two men clasped arms.

"Remember," Grandison said. "No one is to mount up until you either see your target or you hear one of us charging our target."

"Godspeed," Foulques said. "It has been an honor fighting alongside you."

Grandison cocked his head. "Are you always this morose, Brother Foulques? You talk like this is the last time we are ever going to do something unwise together." He gave Foulques a grin and led his horse away, a long line of English men-at-arms trailing close behind.

Since Grandison's siege engine was further away than Foulques's target, the Hospitaller counted slowly to one hundred before leading his own men into the darkness.

Foulques had asked for volunteers from amongst the Hospitaller men-at-arms for this mission. Since the marshal had forbidden him from taking any knights, which was eerily reminiscent of when he was tasked to choose men for his navy. Brother Roderic had been the first man to step forward and surprisingly, Jimmy Goodyear the second. Foulques was ashamed to admit to himself that his first thought when Jimmy had volunteered was that the big man was simply looking for a way to get outside the walls, and once he did, that would be the last anyone saw of the opportunistic tax dodger from Huntingdonshire. But then it occurred to Foulques that if he really wanted to desert the

Hospitaller ranks, it would be much easier to stow away on one of the ships coming and going from the harbor than it would be to flee over mile upon mile of open land. Especially when an enemy army blocked most of that route. One that had made it publicly known that no Hospitaller or Templar they took prisoner would keep his head. No, Jimmy the Rogue was many things, but mad he was not. He had a keen sense of self-preservation, but could it be he wanted to do his part in this war and make a difference? Stranger things had happened and Foulques knew from experience that in times of war, the most unlikely of people were capable of the most surprising feats.

Foulques held up his hand and signaled a stop. He turned behind him and motioned for Jimmy to join him at the front. Jimmy took his time getting there, for he only operated at one speed. Two, if you counted motionlessness.

To be fair, one of the reasons he was so slow was because he carried a hooded lantern in each hand and a dozen long wicks hung off his neck. Foulques relieved him of one lantern and half of his wicks. Every other man possessed two small ceramic pots of Greek fire.

"You and I will be the only ones with fire," Foulques said in a half whisper. "Remember to keep your distance from the others until they have emerged from the shaft and you are certain no one else is inside, then go ahead and lay your fuse."

Foulques had no idea how many shafts they would discover once behind the wicker screens. The plan was to burn the timber supports lining the shafts to hold back the earth.

Hopefully a cave-in would result, but even if it did not, the noxious fumes given off by the Greek fire would persist in the tunnels. Work crews would have to wait a few days before entering the shafts to make repairs and digging toward the walls could resume. All of this would take time. And with thousands of mouths to feed, time was the true nemesis of every besieging army.

They proceeded on foot, leading their horses, until Foulques could just make out the ten-foot-tall screens ahead by the way they blocked out the small fires of the enemy's camp. Once again he wordlessly commanded his men to halt. They waited.

From the north came the unmistakable shouts of men and the pounding of hooves. Foulques mounted his horse and put her into a trot toward the southernmost screen. They would start there and work their way north destroying as many shafts as they could. From there, it would be a straight shot back to the Gate of Saint Anthony. A hard gallop would get them there in a couple of minutes.

As Foulques came around the first screen, he reined his horse in to a walk. He was surprised to see no sign of guards. Surely they would have left someone to watch the shaft entrances? Just then, a bright glow lit up the sky in the north and he could hear the sound of heavy fighting. The Templars must have been successful in lighting up their engine.

There was no shaft behind the first screen. He commanded his men to stay where they were while he urged his horse forward, carefully picking his route through the shadows to the second screen. Now was not the time to fall into an open shaft and maim his destrier. But there was no shaft behind the second screen. Looking ahead, he did not see any mounds of earth, or other signs of digging, behind the third screen, either.

They will probably start digging tonight, Grandison had said when they saw the screens first moved into place. That was four nights ago.

Foulques looked to the north. He saw not one fire, but a half dozen.

No.

He whirled his horse around and jammed his heels into her side. The moment he reached his men, fire after fire erupted into the night sky in the south.

"This is a trap," Foulques said the moment he reached Brother Jimmy. He raised himself up in his stirrups. He twisted and looked at the fires far to the north. They could go to the aid of either the Templars or Grandison, not both. The Templars were too far away. Their fate would already be decided before Foulques could reach them. He extinguished his lantern and tossed it on the ground. He told Jimmy to do the same.

He addressed the men over Jimmy's head. "Wedge formation! We go to the aid of Grandison and his men. Hit them once hard to make an opening and then retreat back to Saint Anthony. Understood?"

"For God," came the response from the men, as if from a single breath.

And then Foulques was charging through the night. He did not look back to see where his men were. He could hear the snorts of the horses just behind him, on his left and right flanks. For the briefest moment he wondered if charging into the midst of a well-planned ambush was a wise course of action. It was, of course, not.

He could see the marshal's scowling face. Risking the lives of fifty men to save fifty was an irresponsible act. But it was worse than that. There was very little chance that all of Grandison's men still lived. Foulques was very well aware that he was taking fifty staunch defenders off the wall of his city. He had made a poor decision, he knew, but that was the difference between him and a commander like the marshal. Foulques was a soldier of God, not God himself. Sometimes a soldier was forced to make decisions, and when those times came, it was most likely in the heat of battle. Foulques knew he should have been riding hard in the opposite direction. But he was afraid. Afraid of what he would see in his dreams if he did not try to help Grandison and his men. It would take a braver man than Foulques to leave the Englishmen to die.

The sounds of fighting grew louder, and the smell of smoke strong as they came upon the battlefield. The area was well-lit by a long line of at least a dozen fires, built high and thin for the sole purpose of casting light. In front of the fires, hundreds of enemy silhouettes streamed toward a small group of men formed up in a square and already locked in combat with dozens of men coming at them from all sides. The ground was strewn with the bodies of horses. Some of them dead, others writhing in agony from fractures in one or more legs that left the whites of bones sparkling like stars when hit by the firelight. Foulques could see thin cordage, almost invisible in the low light, wrapped around some of the horses' legs and dangling off short stakes sticking out of the ground. It had been a trap all right, but there was no time for Foulques to slow down and carefully pick his way through. He had to hope Grandison's force had taken out most of the trip hazards. He raised his arms at his sides, signaling his men to fan out. The wedge became a line, and then they were amongst the enemy.

Foulques allowed his destrier to halt her momentum by knocking a Saracen to the ground and crushing his spine with her iron-shod hooves. He drew his sword as she whirled in a tight circle. He directed her forward as he slashed and cut on either side of him. A Mamluk fighting one of the Englishmen sensed something amiss and he turned just in time to avoid Foulques's blow. He was not so lucky with Brother Jimmy's hammer. With a loud cry Jimmy brought his weapon arcing down over the Mamluk's head until it bounced off the top of his spine, shattering the prominent bones between his shoulders. The Mamluk crumpled to the ground like an empty tunic dropped from a drying line. Foulques slashed a nearby man's face and when he dropped, Foulques realized they had reached the English line.

Somewhere to his left, Foulques heard Grandison's voice call out. "Now! Off with your hobbles, lads. Back to the wall!"

The English slid between the Hospitallers' horses and began a mad run for the walls.

"Buy them some time," Foulques shouted.

The Hospitallers broke away from the main enemy group and began galloping back and forth behind the Englishmen, slashing or running down any Saracen that crossed their path. But they could not do this for long, for hundreds of spear men would soon be upon them.

No sooner had the thought entered Foulques's mind than a soft whistle cut through the air a hand width from his face. He looked up and saw a group of horsemen coming on fast from the ridge. With the fires at their backs, he could see each man held a bow, and in the same hand, a dozen arrows fanned out.

Foulques looked to where the English were running. There were about thirty men, some limping and beginning to fall behind. Others recognized their plight and were on their way back to help. Grandison had already spotted the horse archers, for he and two other men stood with longbows in hand.

"Horse archers!" Foulques called out to his men. "To the wall. Double up with the English!"

He held back for a moment to make sure everyone had heard him, and then he set off after his sergeants. Grandison and his two fellow archers loosed volley after volley over the Hospitallers' heads into the ranks of the horse archers somewhere behind in the distance. The fearsome English weapons had the advantage of range over the horse archers for the moment, but that would not last long. Foulques did not look back, but he bent low over his saddle and rode with a constant cringing sensation in his neck as he felt the

Mamluk arrows getting closer and closer.

Roderic and Jimmy had stopped where Grandison and his two men were making their stand. Jimmy was waving his arms at one of the bowmen, a short, thin man who seemed to be doing his best to ignore the brother-sergeant.

Foulques saw Grandison toss his bow aside and say something to the man on his left. The archer reached out a hand and Roderic pulled him onto his horse.

Arrows began to rain down amongst the men when Foulques was only a few strides away. He barely slowed as he reached out his arm and Grandison hooked on. The old knight swung up behind the Hospitaller so easily, and settled into the horse's rhythm so quickly, Foulques twisted his head behind him to make sure Grandison had not fallen off. As he did he heard Brother Jimmy cursing at the last archer.

"Now will you go, you stubborn Welshman? Before we are so full of holes we can no longer hold our wine! Do you even understand a thing I am trying to..."

Jimmy's words faded away until they were completely drowned out by the sound of horse hooves pummeling the hard ground. Finally, Foulques heard the satisfying clicks of crossbows from the wall of Acre.

When he pulled his horse up outside Saint Anthony's Gate, he saw the horse archers retreating back toward the Mamluk army and Brother Jimmy trotting toward him. He carried a squirming little Welshman in his arms, like he was holding an infant in the midst of a tantrum.

CHAPTER NINETEEN

AFTER THE FAILED raid, Foulques returned his horse to the Hospitaller compound's stables. He took the time to wash his face and hands in a trough, and then set out for Montmusart.

He should have been at the wall. Instead, he stood outside a small hut with two beehives flanking the entrance. It was late, and still dark, but he could see candlelight glowing round the outside of the door. Suddenly, it flew open, and a form came rushing out to greet him.

"Foulques!" She threw her arms around his neck. He held her for a moment longer than he should have. It was always that way with Najya.

"Have you heard the noise of the catapults? Have you been to the walls and looked outside? I have tried but the soldiers will not let anyone up top. I..." Her eyes caught at something on Foulques's chest and he thought, at first, she was merely surprised to see him in his battle reds. He followed her eyes to where she was looking and saw that the white cross on his chest was half covered with blood.

Fool, he thought. He could have covered it before coming, or removed his tunic entirely.

"I see you have been on top the walls." She looked at him differently, then. She seemed a little more reserved, more guarded. He made a feeble attempt to turn the bloodied portion of his tunic away from her.

"Is it as bad as people say?" she asked.

Foulques nodded. "Worse. That is why I have come. You must leave the city. I will not take no for an answer, Najya." His voice was quiet, but firm. He held his emotion in check, but he knew she could sense he struggled with it.

She looked around her. First at the beehives, then out into the darkness of the street. "I love my home. My workshop. But I know you are right. People are saying the Mamluks will destroy us all if we stay. I had passage arranged on a ship three weeks ago, but I gave up my spot when the captain refused to let me take my bees. I honestly thought I could find some other ship." She shook her head. "That was before the harbor became the madness it now is. It takes far more than I have to secure a spot on even a small fishing boat. Or, at least, more than I am willing to give." She looked away, feigning interest in her bees while her eyes finished smoldering.

Foulques felt his own eyes burn. He could imagine only too vividly of what she spoke. He, too, had seen the desperate masses on the docks. This was a time for unscrupulous men to make their fortunes, or in the case of a young woman desperate to leave the city, to satiate unholy desires. The burning in his eyes spread to his throat. Why had he left this so long? He should have seen her from the city long ago.

"I have spoken with a man I know who is going to sneak a small group out of the southern gate," Najya said. "If we can get past the Mamluk soldiers, perhaps we can join with their camp followers. We all speak Arabic, not Turkic, but I think it could work," Najya said.

The thought of Najya sneaking past thousands of hard mercenaries, thieves, and murderers knotted his insides. These men would not have joined the sultan's army out of a sense of duty, or some sort of loyalty to Allah. No, they were there for the spoils of war. When the walls of a rich city fell, men could make their fortunes in gold, silver, and slaves. Strictly speaking of course, by the laws of Allah, Najya need not fear being enslaved if she were caught, for a Muslim could not enslave another Muslim.

Foulques knew the laws of Muslims almost as well as his own. And like those of his own church, he saw them broken again and again. If a Muslim with loose morals truly wanted to enslave another Muslim, all he had to do was find a Christian buyer. Perhaps, if he was truly in need of a slave, simply trade for a Christian one. So Najya was not safe from the slave market if caught outside the city walls. But Foulques knew the more likely scenario was much, much worse.

If a mercenary discovered a woman such as Najya sneaking though his camp, he would not bother with trying to navigate the complexities of the slave market. These men were not planners. For a man who made his life through war, the future was a fickle thing. He lived for today. He would simply use her, then and there, and when he tired of her she would be passed around all night, until someone eventually slit her throat and left her on the muddied ground.

Foulques hated that he knew this. But evil existed in the world and ignoring it did not make it any less real. The Devil fed off the ignorance of men.

"It could work," Foulques said, slowly. "But give me some time. I may be able to get you on a ship. Do not do anything until I say, all right? Promise me?"

Najya smiled. "My knight. Always trying to save me. But where would I go?"

"Does it matter? Anywhere along the coast would do. From there you could make your way anywhere you want and have a fresh start."

She looked sadly at her hives. "I do not suppose I will be able to bring them?"

Foulques shook his head. "As you have seen, it will be difficult enough to find passage for a single person."

Najya was quiet for a moment. "Thank you, Foulques. I appreciate all you do for me. You do know that?"

Foulques dismissed her gratitude with a shake of his head. "Any word from your brother?"

"He is safe, in Aleppo."

"And... your father?"

Najya's head snapped toward Foulques. "Why?" Her eyes narrowed. "When was the last time *you* saw him?"

Foulques looked up the street. "It seems like a very long time ago," he said.

"Why do you want to know about him?" Najya asked.

She had turned hostile, putting Foulques at a loss for words. "With the city in peril, I just thought maybe he would have been in contact with you. That is all."

"You know I would refuse to speak with him."

"What if he could help you? Maybe he could get you out of the city."

"I would rather die here, burned alive, than accept help from that man!"

Foulques recoiled at her choice of words. He had pushed her too far. He saw that now. He reached out a hand to her shoulder, which she promptly shrugged away.

"He let us believe he was a lentil broker. 'I help farmers get the best price they can for their lentil crops,' he told us. He lied to my face for years. And he would probably still be lying to me this day, if not… if not for that night." She glared at him a second longer, until tears welled up in her eyes.

Foulques knew the night well, though he wished he did not. As with most things Najya-related there was no small amount of guilt involved as he recalled that time. For it was the worst night of her life, but perhaps the best night of his. It was the night she had become family.

He and his Uncle Guillaume were woken up late one night by a frantic, yet quiet, knocking on the door. It was Monsieur Malouf, with a skinny little eleven-year-old Najya in tow. Foulques had met her a few times before that night, but he did not know her well. Her eyes were red and puffed up so much, he wondered how she could see anything.

There had been an accident, a fire. Her mother was dead.

She stayed with Foulques and his Uncle Guillaume for

the better part of two months while her father 'reordered' his household. It was highly unusual for a knight of the Order to have one child in his apartment within the Hospitaller compound, never mind two. One of them, a Saracen girl, at that. Threats were made against his uncle, both public and some the more serious variety. The type carried out in the streets, at night. But he paid them no heed, for he was stubborn that way. Foulques, too, was constantly getting into fights with other boys during that period. The conflict of those days brought the three of them together. And then, just as quickly as it was formed, their little family was broken apart when Malouf suddenly appeared again in the dead of night.

Najya wiped the moisture from her eyes, before the tears had fully formed, and took a deep breath. "I will not leave the city until I hear from you, Foulques." She turned and walked between the beehive sentries and entered her small home.

Her father would have been proud, Foulques thought.

He waited there until the light seeping out around the door winked out and he was left standing in complete darkness. Then he headed to the wall.

CHAPTER TWENTY

THE BOMBARDMENTS BEGAN in earnest the morning after the failed night raid. Foulques stood on the wall amongst the Schwyzers and watched helplessly as the spoon arms of dozens of mangonels were loaded with projectiles doused in Greek fire. The drums beat nonstop as engine after engine released its deadly load. The flames lit up the early morning sky as they arched high overhead and dropped deep in the city beyond the walls. Fires erupted occasionally when one of the incendiary missiles found a thatched or wooden roof. Fortunately, Acre was an ancient city and most of its buildings were made of stone and roofed with clay tile. And its inhabitants were still fresh, unwearied from the siege. Any fire that sprang up was quickly doused by hundreds of people working together in bucket brigades. But that would change soon enough, Foulques knew. There would come a time when the fires and destruction would overtake the resolve of the city's inhabitants, and fewer people would turn up for each new fire, or to pick through the wreckage of a building for bodies. Eventually, they would give up entirely.

"Brother Foulques," Roderic said, appearing suddenly on the wall. "I was sent to relieve you. The grand master would see you in the strategy room."

Foulques let out a breath and watched one last flaming stone the size of a man's head veer off course and crash into the harbor. It left a plume of steam as it sizzled ineffectually and disappeared below the clear blue waters.

"Very well," Foulques said. "While I am gone, see if you can disperse that rabble out there, will you Brother Roderic?" He waved his hand vaguely in the direction of the Mamluk army stretching across the entire horizon.

Roderic grinned. "I will see what I can do, Commander. Best you stay away for the better part of the morning though, if you expect results."

Foulques laughed and shook his head. At a moment such as this, what else could a man do? Still, he knew he had made the right decision in returning to Acre. This is where he belonged, where he was meant to live out his life, however long that turned out to be. In the company of good men, like Roderic, as part of a brotherhood fighting for what he believed. Still smiling, he looked along the wall at the dozens of Schwyzer faces staring out over the ramparts. Some stoic, some fidgety, some talking and full of false bravado. All of them frightened beyond measure. Foulques had watched them grow into men. He was proud of each and every one of them, and knew they were another reason he had to come back. He had a sudden image of himself standing in their midst when the end came, not as their commander, but as simply another one of their number, a brother in arms. That was the path God had laid out for Foulques de Villaret. He had never been so sure of anything in his life.

He stepped out of the morning light into the relative darkness of the tower and circled his way down to the bottom of the outer wall. The moment he emerged once again into daylight he was greeted by a great creaking boom. He looked up in time to see a large stone fly over the walls toward the Mamluk forces. The Pisan engineers had just fired their own catapult. It was the only one in the city capable of reaching the enemy in their current location. There were some smaller ballistae and catapults on some of the larger towers, but their range was limited. Their operators would have to wait until the enemy attacked before they could be used.

Foulques crossed the killing field between the inner and outer walls, exchanged a few words with the guards as he went through the gate, and then slowly made his way to the strategy room located in the base of the tower.

When he arrived, the grand master was there. So too, was Marshal Clermont. Stuck to his side, as was common these days, was the young Hospitaller Knight, Connor Westhill. He was the marshal's latest project for the tournaments. Every few years he would take one on, someone young and impressionable, who of course displayed an aptitude for blade and lance. Foulques figured this was a way for Mathieu de Clermont, the famously undefeated 'Mongoose' of a bygone era, to relive some of those glory days.

The three men stood over a new addition to the room

since Foulques had been here last: a table upon which a crude model of Acre and its defenses had been shaped from clay. The grand master wasted no time in getting to the point.

"As soon as we are able to secure you passage back to Cyprus, you will return there without question. Is that clear?"

Foulques stopped where he was.

"And do not come back unless you are summoned," Marshal Clermont said.

Foulques looked from man to man. "I believe my place to be here. The Order has put out the call for all Knights of the Grand Cross to assemble in Acre. That is my duty, and that is what I have done."

"I am sorry, Foulques. We believe otherwise," the grand master said.

"There is no need to worry for the well being of our men in Cyprus, or our fleet, such as it is. I left Brother Alain in command. If something should happen to me, they are all in good hands. Better even, perhaps, than if I were there."

"And once again, you have no say in this matter," Marshal Clermont said.

Foulques ignored Clermont and spoke directly to Grand Master Villiers. "You need me and every man you can get. I can be of use here."

Marshal Clermont stepped between Foulques and the grand master. "Like you were last night? Tell that to the men who did not come back." He brushed past Foulques, moving toward the door. "Come, Master Villiers. We have an appointment with the prince. Someone has to explain why our attack failed."

The marshal left without another word, but as the grand master walked past Foulques he put his arm on his shoulder. "Do not take his words to heart. It was a well-conceived trap. No one could have made any better of that situation. We welcome your help on the wall for now, but as soon as a ship becomes available you will leave. I expect you to obey me on this, Foulques."

The grand master too, left, and Foulques found himself staring at the model of Acre's walls. Small flags were stuck along the length of the outer wall to denote the factions of the defenders in that section. Tiny black flags bearing the white cross of the Hospitallers covered a long section in the center, near the Gate of Saint Anthony, a short distance to the north of where Foulques stood now. They were fortunate that the Mamluks could only attack along that length of wall. Running from north to south, it was long, and would take many men to defend, but this would have been a completely different defense if the Mamluks had had a navy.

Movement caught his eye and Foulques realized Connor was still in the room.

"What do you think our chances are, Brother Foulques?" Connor asked, coming to stand beside Foulques. He was a tall man and had a languorous stride. Foulques was immediately reminded of the marshal.

"Do you think we can hold them until reinforcements arrive?"

Foulques shrugged. "Acre's walls are strong and we have

enough men to keep them at bay for a time. But I would not hold my breath waiting for reinforcements. Everyone who would come is already here."

"I heard some of the English talking. They said Longshanks has a fleet on the way."

"Is that so?"

Connor nodded. "I pray they do not bring too many men, for I will never tire of wetting my blade with infidel blood."

Foulques looked back at the clay model as Connor kept talking.

"I confess I hope this siege is over in time for the King's Tourney to take place. I have been looking forward to this one all year."

"And training hard, I hear," Foulques said. Connor was one of the favorites to claim the prize. Any winnings, of course, would be turned over to the Order's treasury.

Connor turned his back to the table and leaned against it. "I do not believe you and I have ever crossed blades in training, have we, Brother Foulques?"

"No, we have not," Foulques said.

"The marshal told me you were something in the early days. He said there was no one in the Levant who could come close when you were on your game."

Foulques narrowed his eyes. "He said that?"

"But he said you quit the tourneys before anyone really knew your name. Mind if I ask why?"

Foulques thought about it for a moment. After a few wins, his uncle had forbidden him from entering any further contests. But truth be told, by that time Foulques's heart was not in it any more.

"I suppose I grew tired of focusing my energies on trying to best my own allies, when we were surrounded by true enemies."

Connor nodded sagely and interlaced his fingers at his belly like a Franciscan friar begging for alms. "I would have really liked to know you at that time. When you were in your prime." He turned toward Foulques, suddenly, like an idea had just dawned on him. "Perhaps, when this is all over, we could train together once, for old time's sake. Maybe see if we can knock some of that dust from your sword arm?"

Foulques turned to the marshal's protégé and gave him a curt bow.

"I would like nothing more," he said. "When this is over."

CHAPTER TWENTY-ONE

FOULQUES STOOD ON the outer wall staring out at the massive Mamluk war engines as engineers swarmed around them, bringing them nearer to completion with every passing moment. He tried to swallow but his throat hardened like he had not had water for three days. One crenellation to his left stood Marshal Clermont. Both men were silent, a rare occurrence when they were within shouting range of one another. The assault of the night before had been a disaster. They had lost good men, men they needed for the defense of the city.

Foulques looked to his right at Sir Grandison, who had come to extend his thanks to Foulques and his men. The leader of King Edward's forces leaned heavily against the wall for support and he shifted his weight from one leg to the other like he was trying to rid himself of a cramp. His normally clean-shaven face was covered in gray stubble and he had the far away stare of a man who was present only in body. He showed his age this day.

Foulques's gaze wandered past the old warrior, down the entire length of the wall, taking in the slumped figures of its defenders. Morale had taken a hit they could not afford.

Some time later, mere minutes after Grandison had returned to the English Tower, a solitary drum began banging out a steady beat from somewhere in the middle of the enemy's camp. A group of men began making their way to the front lines. They led horses, large horses. Foulques instantly recognized them as Templar, Hospitaller, and English destriers captured in last night's failed raid. The sight tore at his innards, for the line of horses was long, and every one meant that a brave brother or ally was dead.

The drummer continued beating out his forlorn rhythm and when the horses reached open ground between the besiegers and the castle walls, their handlers tied them together, head to arse, and forced them to march in an endless circle. Gasps and swearing on the wall made Foulques look more closely. He had assumed that every horse meant one dead man. But he was wrong, for hanging from every saddle were at least two or three heads. Some were tied together with clumps of their own hair and then thrown over the horse like saddle-bags. But since most were Templars, their hair was cut short. In those cases, the Mamluks had punched holes through the skulls and threaded them together with rope.

"*Mon dieu*," Foulques heard Marshal Clermont say under his breath. "The heathens will pay for this."

The drummer abruptly picked up his beat and a chanting began in the midst of a mob of Mamluk soldiers. A cheer pierced the air and several of the high-pitched cries that the desert dwellers were fond of using to terrify their enemies followed. Then, a solitary form emerged from the main group and began walking boldly toward the walls of Acre. Foulques blinked and shielded his eyes from the midday sun. He looked again, sure that his cruel mind had taken to haunting him during the daylight hours, as well as the night.

Badru Hashim, the Northman, strolled to just within crossbow range and stopped. He likely knew that it would take a lucky shot from a volley of at least fifty bolts to hit him. He also knew no army under siege would waste fifty bolts to possibly bring down one man. Foulques caught himself calculating distances and wind direction before he took a deep breath and flexed the tremor in his hands away.

It had been eight years since he had seen Badru Hashim in person. Every now and then he would hear of something he and his Mamluks had done. Mostly attacks on vessels at sea, but in the last couple of years, they had begun to terrorize caravans on land and even conduct raids on small villages. And it did not matter whether the owners were Christian, Jewish, Muslim, or Pagan. Their coin was all good, and he was afraid of no one. But now, here he stood fighting in the front lines for the Sultan of Egypt.

Foulques closed his eyes and scrubbed at the great tangles of hair on his head with both hands. If Qalawun's son had managed to call even men like the Northman to his banner, perhaps he was a far better leader than they had all given him credit for. If that were true, than this was going to be a much longer siege than Foulques had thought.

The drumming stopped after one last thunderous boom and the host of Mamluk soldiers went suddenly and ecrily quiet. Badru Hashim raised his arms and called out to the walls of Acre in a low, clear voice that shook Foulques to the core far more than any catapult barrage ever had.

"I am Badru Hashim. I come here to fight for my sultan, to honor Allah and His messenger, Mohammed, the greatest of all prophets. Is there a man amongst this stable of sheep I stand before, who dares to defend your false god?"

The wall erupted into a chorus of shouts and insults. Men drew their swords and threw rocks that had no hope of reaching the Mamluk. Foulques heard a Hospitaller knight call out to the marshal, "Sir! I would have your permission to go down there and skewer this piece of desert shit."

"No one is going to take him up on this challenge," Marshal Clermont called back. "We will not play into their hands."

He spoke with confidence and the authority of someone who knew exactly what he was doing. But Foulques watched his face as he talked the man down, and he saw something there he did not like: a furrow of the brow, a grinding of the jaw, and an inability to remove his gaze from the giant Mamluk before them.

Another cheer went up, but this time, it came from the very wall Foulques stood upon. He leaned forward and looked down to where others were pointing. A man armed with sword and shield had emerged from one of the small sally ports in the wall below, and he was donned in the blood-red battle tunic of a Hospitaller knight.

Both Foulques and Marshal Clermont realized who it was at the same time. "Connor! Get your arse back inside!"

the marshal called out, but his words were drowned out by the roars of encouragement raining down on the young knight from above. Connor turned and raised his sword to his unhelmeted forehead in a salute to the crowd. They responded with a fervor that made Foulques want to clasp his hands over his ears.

Foulques stared at Connor, willing the young man to look into his eyes so he could somehow communicate to him the folly of what he was about to do. But Connor was too enamored by the cheers of the crowd to acknowledge one single face. With a final wave and bow, he spun on his heel and marched toward glory.

"Fool!" Marshal Clermont said. "What does he think he is doing?"

Foulques saw a couple of sergeants cast questioning glances toward the marshal. He understood their confusion. Personal challenges were nothing new when it came to sieges. It was not unusual to pass the time between assaults on the wall with challenges where men would meet in single combat while the two opposing armies looked on. Winning one of these contests was a surefire way to increase morale amongst one's comrades.

Badru Hashim walked out to meet his challenger. When they were twenty yards away from one another, they stopped walking. Connor announced himself at the top of his lungs.

"Sir Connor Westhill accepts the opportunity to spit in the face of your sultan and to assist you in recognizing the divinity of our Lord Jesus Christ. And by His guiding light, I swear, it shall be the last thing you do on this earth!"

Everyone on the wall erupted in cheers once again. Badru Hashim had a buckler on one arm and he said something as he slowly drew his scimitar but the two men were too far away for Foulques to hear what he said. He could imagine it was something calm, unnerving.

"Close on him, boy," Marshal Clermont mumbled, and as though he had heard his mentor, Connor leapt into action. He slid in with a straight thrust followed by a high attack and then another. Badru parried with his buckler and caught Connor's second swing in a bind with his own sword. The men pushed each other away and began circling to the left. They clashed again, and Connor attempted to snake his blade around the Mamluk's scimitar and ride it into his throat. But the Northman was able to redirect the Hospitaller's weapon at the last moment with his buckler and disentangle himself from the bind.

The men on the walls of Acre shouted their support, screaming so loud it set Foulques's hair on end. Foulques was surprised at Connor's skill. He was a smooth, languid fighter with a technical knowledge one can only acquire by training from a very young age. Too clearly he remembered his own battle with the Northman, and thus far the young knight was acquitting himself better than Foulques had. Connor was about the same age Foulques had been when he and Badru had fought on the docks of Gibelet. The "Weasel" had done well with this one, he grudgingly admitted to himself.

The two combatants came together again, shields clashing, swords crossing, separating, and cutting. Badru launched a flurry of blows that Connor turned to the side or managed to dance away from. Onlookers from both sides shouted their approval.

"Good job, boy," Foulques could not help but say aloud. He was strong, fast, young. Maybe, just maybe…

Foulques turned to Marshal Clermont to see if he was thinking the same thing. The old knight was already looking at him. Clermont closed his eyes and took a deep breath. When he opened them he squinted away the remnants of tears and surrendered his body weight to the castle wall. He stared out toward the contest taking place, but Foulques felt he was focused elsewhere.

There was a break in the action and Connor took the opportunity to raise his sword in the direction of Acre in a premature celebration of victory. The men lining the walls went crazy and let out a cacophony of war shouts to lend their support.

At the height of the cheers, Badru sheathed his scimitar. A cold chill ate its way down Foulques's spine. Connor looked on as Badru drew his khanjar, the wickedly curved knife that is the most sacred weapon of a Mamluk warrior. It is the first weapon he is trained to use, and if given the choice, the last one he would hold in this life. But the way he walked toward Connor, Foulques knew Badru was in no danger of losing his life this day. He knew that walk.

Thus began the humiliation of a Knight of the Hospital of Jerusalem. Connor looked confused at first, when the Mamluk gave up his sword for a much shorter weapon. Perhaps he took it for a suicide wish, one that he was fine with granting. He sent a powerful thrust at Badru's massive chest, one that would be impossible to turn aside with a knife. Instead, Badru twisted his torso and let the blade sail past, then brought his buckler around from the side smashing it across Connor's face. He fell to the ground and Badru let him get up. When he was set, Badru stepped forward and brought his buckler across the other side of Connor's face. He allowed him to get up again. For the next two minutes Badru fought Connor using only his buckler and superior body position. He occasionally employed his khanjar to bind Connor's sword near its hilt, but he never followed through with a cut of any kind, and this was obvious to all onlookers. It was a masterful demonstration. One that Foulques found nearly impossible to watch at times.

When Foulques caught himself looking away, he would steel his nerves and force his eyes back to the front. Many men stopped watching the fight after Badru broke Connor's shield arm with his buckler. But Foulques kept his gaze locked on the combatants, if you could still call them that, for the entirety of the fight. Connor deserved that much, and more.

Connor managed to rise a couple more times, but finally, his body could no longer support the weight of his armor, and down he stayed. The Northman waited a few moments to be sure, then he knelt over him and began pummeling his head again and again with his buckler.

Foulques saw one of the Schwyzers vomit over the side of the wall. He was one of the brave ones who was still watching.

This had to stop. He turned toward the tower's stairway.

"Where do you think you are going?" Marshal Clermont said, blocking his path.

"I have something to do," Foulques said. "Something I should have done a long time ago.

"I forbid it."

"You have no say in this." Foulques tried to move around the marshal, but Clermont reached out his hand and grabbed him firmly by the shoulder.

"He has taken something from all of us today. I will not let him take you, as well." He looked down at his hands and lowered his voice. "You are not ready, Foulques." He gestured to the wall. "Come. We owe a brother our presence. That will have to be enough. For now, it is all we can offer."

Foulques and Marshal Clermont turned back to the grisly scene in the distance. They stood shoulder to shoulder and watched as Badru Hashim loomed over the lifeless body of Sir Connor Westhill.

The Northman walked a few paces away and bent down to retrieve something from the ground. When he stood, he held a scabbarded sword in his hand, but it was no scimitar. Its blade was straight and the sunlight gleamed along its length when the Mamluk pulled it from its sheath. He tossed the sheath to the ground and walked back to Connor, flicking the blade this way and that, displaying its balance and beauty for all to admire.

He need not have. For even at this distance, Foulques could tell from its pivot point that the blade was his. The one he had lost to the Northman eight years ago. The one given to Foulques by his uncle on the day he was knighted.

When the Northman used the sword to sever the head from Connor's corpse, Foulques felt the blow in his soul. His legs buckled and he had to catch himself on the wall. He still might have fallen if the marshal's hand did not reach out to grip him by the shoulder.

Wordlessly, the two Hospitallers watched Badru Hashim carry Connor's head over to the horses walking in their endless circle. He tied it onto the saddle of a fine black stallion and then walked away without a backward glance. Within seconds, Badru Hashim disappeared into a roiling sea of Saracens that stretched across the horizon, touching the ends of the world.

CHAPTER TWENTY-TWO

THE STENCH OF death hung heavy in the air as Badru approached the ring of horses still walking their endless circle. Clouds of flies feasted on the severed heads draped over the animals' backs, with the larger flies taking frequent breaks to sample horse flesh instead. The once-proud destriers could do little to discourage them, for each one's tail was tied to the horse's head in the rear, leaving them defenseless from the assault of the flies. So bad was the smell, and volume of insects, that the Mamluk soldiers standing guard had retreated a hundred paces away. Only one man stood nearby. He had a leather bull whip, which he twirled overhead every few minutes and unleashed its fury on the back of some unfortunate horse to keep the circle in motion.

This had gone on for the better part of two days and Badru could no longer stand by and watch. The horses had been the sultan's contribution to Badru's plan of luring the Franks out from their defenses to conduct an assault on the siege engines. Badru had suggested piling the heads of the Christians in a mound on the ground somewhere they could be seen from every section of the wall. A sight that would greet them from the east with every sunrise. The horses had never played a part in Badru's scheme.

As he crossed the open ground toward the whip man, one of the horses let out a strangled whinny and stumbled. Her front legs gave out but her back ones did not, leaving her in a prostrated position. The circle faltered, the leather cracked through the air, but the horse simply accepted the beating. She was too tired to rise.

Badru caught the man's wrist before he could snap it again.

The soldier turned on him, furious that someone had the gall to interrupt his work.

"By Allah, I will—"

"You will what?" Badru said, stretching the man's arm straight up in the air as far as it would go, forcing him onto the tips of his toes. When he realized who it was who held him, he wisely held his tongue. It was now well-known that the sultan had a new head emir, the man who had killed Emir Turuntay in ritual combat.

Badru pulled the whip from the guard's hand, threw it to the ground, and shoved the man in the opposite direction.

"If you ever strike a horse with a bull whip again, I will educate you in its proper use until you beg me for death. Do you understand?" He glanced down at the leather on the rocky ground and the thought of using it right then and there on the man was very hard to resist. He took a breath.

"I am sorry, Emir. I did not know it was you. I was only following Emir Lajin's orders to keep the beasts moving."

"For how long?"

"Until they drop. Then we are to section them up and launch their parts into the city with the catapults."

Badru closed his eyes and took another breath. If the man had any sense he would be gone when he opened them. He was still there, rooted to the spot.

"These are your new orders," Badru said. "You will cut the rotting heads from the horses' backs. Then, go to those soldiers over there." Badru pointed at the guards in the distance. He kept his hand pointed in their direction until they began to shift their feet and became fully aware of his attention. "They will help you bring water to the horses where they stand. Do not give them too much! Then lead them to shade, untie them from one another, and let them drink again. This time as much as they want."

"But, Emir Lajin will have my head."

Badru stepped in close and looked down at the soldier. "You are no longer his man. Do you understand? You tell him Badru Hashim has claimed you as his own. He will know what that means, and if he does not like it, he knows where to find me. Now, go. Never mention Lajin's name again. He is dead to you. Do you understand?"

The soldier nodded and began to back away. "Yes, My Emir."

"Now go! You have thirty minutes to complete your task."

The man turned and began to run toward the soldiers as Badru looked on.

CHAPTER TWENTY-THREE

During the second week of the siege, Grand Master Villiers asked Foulques to tour the wall and speak with the various commanders to get a reasonable estimate of the defenders' strength for each section. The commanders had all agreed that the City Watch would be used to bolster forces where needed as the siege wore on. His last stop was the English line, under command of Sir Grandison. Grandison, of course, made him feel welcome, and he found himself staying longer than he should have.

"You hear that?" Grandison asked.

Foulques tilted his head. He heard nothing, but then realized that was the point. "The catapults have stopped," he said. "They are massing for another attack."

Grandison stepped into an opening and looked out over the field. "I see them setting up, but you still have enough time to get back to your men."

"If it is all the same to you," Foulques said, "I would just as well stay here."

"Need me to protect you, do you?" Grandison grinned.

"Something like that," Foulques said. He could not put

his finger on it, but something about the old warrior made it easy to remain in his company.

"I suspect it is not the Mohammedans you seek protection from. I have seen how your superiors look at you. You are not supposed to be here, in the city, are you?"

Foulques shook his head. "Even though it is where I belong."

"Well, I am more than happy to fight at your side. Welcome to my little piece of England. Might as well give the old legs a rest since it will be some time before those camel riders get their arses over here." He held his sword out of the way with one hand, pressed his back up against the wall, and unceremoniously slid down it to finish up in a sitting position with his legs stretched straight out in front. "Ah, much better."

Foulques cocked his head and thought, why not? Seconds later, he too sat atop the wall looking out over the city. It looked quiet, peaceful even. The calm before the storm.

Grandison let out a sigh. "I have heard it said, over and over, that the fighting is the easy part, and it is the waiting that kills men."

"I still feel very much alive," Foulques said.

Grandison nodded in agreement. "I have always liked the moments before a big battle. It illuminates one's life with a certain perspective."

"I heard talk that King Edward is sending reinforcements. Is that true?"

Grandison turned his head slowly. Foulques noticed a change in his eyes, like someone had extinguished a tiny candle in each one.

"He would like nothing more. I can tell you that much."

"I suspected so," Foulques said. "Raising an army is never as straight-forward as one might think."

"It is not his army that has failed him. It is his heart." His voice broke and he looked away. "I received word two days ago that Eleanor has died of a fever."

"The queen has died?" Foulques caught himself before he blurted out more. The love King Edward had for his Eleanor of Castile was the stuff of legends. Foulques had never believed most of what he heard, but he saw the way Sir Grandison's eyes misted over as he spoke her name. She was "Eleanor" to him, not "the queen", or even "Queen Eleanor". Whether the old knight was saddened at her death because of his king's loss or his own, Foulques could not tell. Perhaps a little of both.

"My condolences, Sir Grandison. I have heard much about Eleanor of Castile. But she is with God now, and I am sure she is finding it much to her liking after her service here."

"Thank you Foulques. Still, I wish I could have been there. I owed it to her and Edward, both. He must be devastated."

Both men stopped talking, each leaving the other alone with his thoughts.

"May I ask you something about the last time you were in Acre with King Edward?"

Grandison turned to Foulques and smiled. "He was Prince Edward at the time. And you want to know about the assassin."

"I have heard so many versions of the story. I cannot pass up the opportunity to know the truth."

"Ah, you are after the truth, is it? Perhaps the reason there are so many versions is men, and especially women, have a tendency to believe what they want, no matter what one tells them. I tell you what, Brother Foulques. You ask a question and I will give you a straight answer."

"Did an assassin try to kill King Edward?"

Grandison nodded. "Yes. He was an ambassador of the Saracens. A man we both had come to like and trust."

"But the king killed the assassin?"

Grandison nodded. "Edward can be stubborn that way."

"Who sucked the poison from the King's wound?"

Grandison let out a sigh. "I do not even know for sure that the assassin's blade *was* poisoned. But I had seen Edward wounded before, and never had I known him to be in such pain. I opened the wound slightly with my knife, and before I could investigate it, Eleanor pushed me aside and began sucking and spitting out the prince's blood on the floor. It was quite the grisly scene."

"Was there actually poison in the wound?"

Grandison shrugged. "Does it matter?"

Foulques was quiet for a moment. "Did you tell me this version because you thought it the one I wanted to hear?"

"Absolutely not. Though I do admit, on occasion, I have done just that with others. But this, I swear, to be the truth. My truth. The one I shall remember Eleanor by until the end of my days."

The two knights retreated once again to silence. Foulques savored the relative coolness of the stone against his back as he looked down the line of English defenders.

Grandison had brought only a few hundred men with him. Very few were knights, but the rest were archers, Welshmen mostly. They were a hardened bunch, standing there with their six-foot-long bows of yew wood. They looked like simple sticks to Foulques. But they had a certain elegance to them. Carved from a single stave of wood, the back of the bow was pale white, while the belly was a rich honeyed amber color. Foulques recalled seeing Grandison use one of the weapons the night of the catapult raid.

"What is it like to shoot one of those?"

Grandison saw what Foulques was looking at and pursed his lips. "It is, honestly, the most frustrating weapon I have ever encountered. Yet strangely addictive, for when the arrow flies true to the exact spot you are looking, there is no better feeling in this world."

"Really," Foulques said. There may have been a trace of doubt in his response.

"Do not let the simple looks of the longbow seduce you, Brother Foulques. For if she gets her hooks into you, you will never look at another woman again." He caught himself, suddenly remembering whom he was speaking with. Grandison laughed as he pressed his hands together and bowed his head in apology.

"I picked up my first longbow over thirty years ago. Still, I am but an amateur compared with these men." He pointed to a short, wiry man looking out over the ramparts. Foulques recognized him as the man Brother Jimmy had carried back to the Gate of Saint Anthony during the catapult raid. "You and I together could not pull Haydon's bow. And with it, I have seen him drop men at three hundred paces all day long."

Foulques looked at Haydon. He was compact, but not overly stocky. "Impressive," Foulques said, not quite sure he believed Grandison completely. "You would not think him so strong, by the looks of him."

"He is not, really. Until he picks up a bow. He started so young his back and shoulders are unlike that of other men. Like a horseman, good bowmen are made before they are ten."

A Saracen horn blew somewhere behind them. Seconds later it was answered by several more in rapid succession.

"It looks like I will get to see his arrows in action," Foulques said.

The two knights nodded at one another and then used the wall at their backs to help them get to a standing position.

The archers along the wall began readying their arrow bags by untying the waxed cover and leaning them at their feet so the shafts were within easy reach. In the distance, across the open killing field, thousands of enemy soldiers began shouting and shrieking their high-pitched battle cries. Drums began beating somewhere deep inside the endless mass of men. The shrill note of a single horn sounded and the charge began.

"Easy, lads! Wait for it," Grandison shouted to be heard

over the din.

Foulques had not yet unsheathed his sword, for the attackers were still hundreds of paces away.

"Archers to your line!" Grandison said. "We will hit them with one volley together, then I will give you your reins."

Foulques could not yet see the individual faces of the men charging. Distance was a tricky thing when standing on a high wall, but he estimated the forerunners of the Mamluk army to be more than three hundred paces away.

"Nock!" Each man set an ash shaft on the string of his bow but did not yet pull it back.

"Draw and loose!" Grandison commanded.

Two hundred bowmen drew back their powerful weapons and let their arrows fly, and all Foulques could hear was a series of creaks and taps as ash shafts touched the sides of the yew bows. Foulques was used to standing in the midst of crossbowmen, and the relative quiet of the longbow men surprised him. And never would he have let his men shoot their quarrels at this range, even from the most powerful Genoese crossbows. As he watched the three-foot-long arrows of the longbows arch toward the enemy, he noticed how they glided on the wind, whereas the much heavier and shorter shaft of a crossbow bolt would have sunk. Foulques's eyes widened in awe as a long line of Saracen soldiers began to collapse in the midst of their charge, tripping those who followed too close behind.

"Loose at will!"

With a calm detachment, the archers nocked arrow after

arrow, pulling each one back past his ear before angling it up into the sky and letting the string go. Most wore gloves to protect their fingers from the heavy string, others gripped crudely cut pieces of leather, and a few of the older men used nothing at all.

Foulques felt a strange peace envelop him as he stood there on the wall, his arms crossed, with nothing to do save watch men die so far away they did not seem like men at all. Again and again, he listened to the whispers of bowstrings and the controlled breathing of men as they released their deadly volleys onto the world below. Until gradually, the world below converged with the one above. Long before the first ladder hit the wall, Foulques had his sword in hand. The almost tranquil scene of mere heartbeats before, erupted into swirling chaos.

The pointed helmets of Saracen mercenaries began popping up everywhere along the wall. Archers exchanged their bows for swords and maces, while some picked up slightly shorter, more maneuverable bows and began to train them on the men ascending the ladders.

Foulques thrust his sword into a man's face as he stepped onto the wall. He tried to kick the ladder away, but there was already too much weight on it. He had to turn away to ward off an attack on his left, and by the time he turned back, two more men had crested the wall. He caught the scimitar of one of the men in a bind and snaked his blade down to cut his foolishly unprotected forearm. Though only a wound, the set-up allowed Foulques to run the man through with a thrust. He pulled his sword free of the man's chest and brought it sweeping around in a two-handed swing to the side of a helmeted head belonging to a Saracen locked in battle with a mace-bearing English knight. Stunned by Foulques's blow, the Saracen staggered to one knee, but the English knight's mace found him there with a great clanging shower of blood.

Foulques slid away from that scene and into the next. He found himself having to take great care fighting amongst the English. It was unlike being on the more organized Hospitaller section of wall, where each man was responsible for controlling his specific space. The English seemed to run amok without thought. Or fear. They appeared reckless, charging to and fro, wherever and whenever they were needed. It took a few minutes to get used to, but soon Foulques was caught up in the frenzy. He dodged the weapons of friend and foe alike, going to the aid of any man in need. And more often than he was probably even aware, others came to his aid as well.

He was not sure how long the battle raged, but by the time his arms had grown heavy and his feet slow, there was suddenly no one left to fight. Like others, he charged along the wall looking for enemies, but they were going down the ladders instead of up. He stood in place breathing heavily, envious of the archers who still had bows in their hands and were able to continue the fray. Gradually, the sounds of battle diminished. Foulques found himself standing once again beside Grandison, his bloodied sword in hand. And like before, all was quiet save for the gentle thrumming of bowstrings.

CHAPTER TWENTY-FOUR

When Foulques got back to the Hospitaller section of wall, he expected spirits to be high. But for some reason, the somber mood hung in the air like fog. He saw Roderic, Jimmy Goodyear, and Glynn, the Hospitaller Weapons Master from Scots' Land, looking toward the Mamluk line. Glynn saw him approach.

"Missed you at the last run o' the wall, laddie."

"I found myself trapped near the English Tower. Ended up fighting with Grandison and his archers."

"Did you now? Hope you let your blade slip into a few English arses for me."

"That very well could have happened without me even knowing it. They fight like wild men over there."

"Bah, those were the Welshmen, then. The English are as soft as they are white and hairless. Easier to mistake one of 'em for a big loaf of unbaked bread than a soldier."

Jimmy and Roderic both shot him a look.

"You do realize we are both English," Jimmy said.

"So?" Glynn asked. "Look at the goosedown on Rod's face and tell me I am lying."

Foulques decided a change of topic was in order before Glynn got too far down his lane of hatred for the English.

"What are they up to over there?" He said, stepping to the wall.

"They just put the last braces on the big engines. Expect them to be slinging houses at us by morning," Jimmy said.

Jimmy the Neckless was rarely wrong when it came to building anything. Unfortunately, this was one of those times. Within minutes, not hours, a murmur began in the enemy lines, where the northernmost trebuchet was set up. The voices converged into a chant, and as more and more voices joined in, Foulques began to make out the words.

"Al-Mansuri! Al-Mansuri! Al-Mansuri!"

From the southern trebuchet, a new raucous chant began. It took some time, but within minutes it too drifted on the wind and Foulques recognized the words.

"Al-Ghadibah! Al-Ghadibah! Al-Ghadibah!"

"What are they on about?" Roderic asked.

"Looks like a competition of sorts between engineers," Jimmy said. "I think it is a race to see who can put their machine to task first. Can you twist your ears around what they are saying, Brother Foulques?"

"They have named the engines. The one in the north is 'al-Mansuri,' which means 'the Victorious.' The other is 'al-Ghadibah,' 'the Furious.'"

Jimmy crossed his arms over his broad chest. His war hammer rested against the wall in front of him. "I do not suppose that is Mohammed-speak for, 'we will be furious when we are not victorious.'"

No one laughed.

Thirty minutes later, the Furious won the race. Its operators, a long line of fifty men, heaved on heavy ropes rigged around pulleys and gears to crank its arm into place. Extra material was thrown into the counterweight box and a stone as big around as a man's chest was loaded into the sling dangling off the trebuchet's long arm. A torch was touched to the giant missile and it erupted into flames. The torchbearer jumped back and the missile was immediately released.

Its arc was low and fast. Whether by design and skill, or just plain luck, the flaming boulder smashed into the exact center of the Tower of the Countess of Blois. With a stunning display of fire and smoke, the tower took the hit, and survived, but Foulques doubted it could take another and remain standing. The entire Mamluk army roared with satisfaction, and then quieted down in eager anticipation of the next show, which was performed at dusk.

The Victorious overshot the wall by a tall margin, missing all of its towers as well. The flaming missile flew high into the sky, competing with the setting sun. Every defender on the wall turned his head and followed its path. It seemed to descend slowly, as though made of air, but it did eventually come down. And when it did, it crashed into one of the many churches in the city. One second the church was illuminated in its light, the next its bell tower was sheared off like it had been cut with a giant blade. Then the entire building exploded, sending flaming splinters of wood and stone into the sky.

Foulques shut his eyes, and then quickly brought a hand up to wipe at them before anyone saw. He need not have. All along the walls of Acre, from one end to the other, hardened Christian men who had spent a lifetime at war, dropped to their knees in terror and despair.

For the next week the Mamluk leadership contented itself with conducting the war at a distance. The siege engines roared to life at dawn and continued every day until dusk. Occasionally, deep in the night, the Victorious, or the Furious, would be called upon to deliver a flaming message from hell. These unpredictable attacks set the entire population of the city on edge. With the constant bombardments, the war had moved from only the walls to every square inch of the city. No place was safe.

This was a point Foulques had become painfully aware of. Every time he saw a missile fly over the walls toward the district of Montmusart, he thought of Najya. He wanted to go check on her. It was not as though he did not have the opportunity, for all the Hospitallers took shifts on and off the wall. When off shift, they would return to the Hospitaller compound to get a good meal and some much-needed sleep. During one of these times, Foulques could have easily taken the time to search Najya out. But in truth, he was afraid of seeing her when he had nothing to tell her, and no plan to get her out of the city. He thought back on how sure he had been that the Mamluks could never take Acre. He had allowed his ignorance to cause him to commit the sin of pride. How could he have been so foolish?

When the Saracens finally came at the walls after eight

days, Foulques, and many others, found it almost a welcome relief. Finally, they had a purpose, a target for their anger. They fought with a pent-up rage that lent them strength and sent the Saracens fleeing back to their lines. The enemy suffered great losses in that assault, and the two that followed the week after.

Foulques stood on the wall watching the Saracens scramble back to their lines after their most recent failed attack on the wall. Beside him, Marshal Clermont stared after the enemy with a troubled look on his face. Foulques slapped Roderic on the back as he walked past, congratulating him on a job well done.

"You should not be so pleased with yourselves," the marshal said to Foulques.

Foulques looked at his superior and decided not to voice the obvious. They had turned back wave after wave of the infidels in the last few weeks. They were doing far better in this siege than he had thought possible. Why should they not celebrate their victories?

"Have you not noticed," the marshal began, "that they are not sending any of their Mamluk warriors at us? This riffraff we keep turning back is mostly ill-equipped mercenaries and conscripted commoners. The Mamluks are being purposely held back."

"For what?" Foulques could not resist asking.

The marshal shook his head.

Once the remnants of the attacking force had retreated back behind the main lines, the siege engines wasted no time in starting back up. The defenders' good mood turned sour almost immediately. But then a shout went up somewhere along the wall and men started talking in excited voices while they pointed out over the city. Foulques and the marshal followed their outstretched arms with their eyes. There on the water, approaching the harbor was a long line of sails flying the colors of King Henry, the King of the Kingdom of Jerusalem.

As men began cheering and waving, Foulques shielded his eyes with one hand and counted sails. There were over thirty ships coming to their aid. He found himself joining in the celebrations erupting all along the wall.

The only one not cheering, Foulques noticed, was, of course, Marshal Mathieu de Clermont.

CHAPTER TWENTY-FIVE

THE STRATEGY ROOM was so crowded by the time Foulques arrived, he had no choice but to stand just inside the door, squeezed between a commander of the City Watch and a man wearing the green cross of the leper knights, the Order of Saint Lazarus. He bore no outward signs of the holy disease but the room was stiflingly hot, and the man still wore heavy gloves. Since Jesus himself was said to have appeared as a leper at times, caring for those so stricken was considered a great act of charity, one that would not go unnoticed at the gates of Saint Peter. Hospitallers, as well as Templars, who contracted the disease were expected to join the ranks of the Knights of Saint Lazarus. All the same, Foulques was in no hurry to exchange his white cross for one of green. He found himself leaning toward the City Watch commander.

King Henry was already seated at the front of the room on a raised platform, his pale face pinched and tired under the delicate gold crown on his head. He had on a suit of mail no more robust than his crown, but it was of a proper size for his physique and he wore it well. His brother, Prince

Amalric, was noticeably absent, for if he had been in the room, he would have no doubt been sitting at the front with the king.

The marshal of the city stepped forward and bent to one knee before his king. They exchanged a few words that Foulques could not hear, and then the marshal rose and turned to the crowd. He stomped the heel of his boot three times at the foot of the raised platform and all murmurs from the crowd ceased.

"King Henry has graced us with forty ships laden with supplies and soldiers from Cyprus, including lamb enough for every man on the wall. Tonight we feast on meat! Praise God for answering our prayers!"

A cheer went up through those gathered. "Praise God!"

The cheering went on for what seemed like a long time but not once did Henry smile or acknowledge it. He sat in his chair, staring straight ahead. Foulques wondered if, perhaps, he was having one of his seizures. But once the room quieted down, King Henry stirred, and pushed himself to his feet.

"I thank you, commanders, for your support and warm welcome. And God thanks you for your bravery and dedication to the faith of our lord, Jesus Christ. I have been to the walls. I have seen the unholy forces you have faced, and I commend each and every one of you. You have served the Kingdom of Jerusalem with honor and dignity. Now, go back to your men, repeat my words to them, and tell them their king said he finds himself blessed to have such subjects. Go with God. Marshal, clear the room."

Foulques turned, eager to step outside, but a hand on his shoulder stopped him. He turned to find a Cypriot knight he did not know.

"Admiral. The king requires your presence."

"Of course," Foulques said, unable to keep the surprise from his voice.

He and the knight pressed themselves up against one side wall to allow those leaving access to the door. Soon there were only a few men left in the room, standing before the king. Foulques and the knight joined them. Among a few others, those present included Grand Master Villiers, Marshal Clermont, and the Grand Master of the Temple.

King Henry turned to the marshal of the city. "Give me your report."

Marshal Levesque cleared his throat. "We are holding the outer wall, but for how long, I cannot say. Their cursed trebuchets are taking the towers apart stone by stone. Meanwhile, the Pisans' war machine has broken down again, though their engineers claim they will have it repaired soon. I suggest we use the two thousand soldiers you brought from Cypress—"

"Two thousand?" Marshal Clermont said. "With all due respect Your Grace, that seems a poor number for forty ships."

The other men cast stern glances at the marshal for interrupting, but the logic of his words soon had their eyes straying back to the king, who remained silent for a long moment before he spoke.

"I agree. It is a poor number. But it is all I had. Cyprus

has been left virtually undefended."

"Then why bring so many ships?" Foulques was surprised the voice asking the question was his own.

Henry looked at him. "In part, for morale, Admiral Foulques."

"And the other part?" Foulques asked.

"To evacuate as many of my people as possible before I capitulate the city."

The only sound in the room was the exhalation of every man present.

"The beginning of the end," Marshal Clermont said under his breath.

Then everyone spoke at once.

"What of Longshanks's forces?"

"Surely reinforcements are possible if we hold out long enough," Grand Master Beaujeu said.

"No one is coming," Henry said. "The Christian world has other problems, it seems. I have made up my mind. A party of my choosing will go to the sultan and negotiate terms for our surrender."

He met the open-mouthed stares of every man in the room. When he was convinced no one was going to interrupt, he continued. "My secretary, Robert, will be in charge of negotiations. Master Beaujeu, I would like Brother Guillaume de Cafran to accompany Robert as I hear his Arabic is excellent, and I am told the new sultan does not speak French. Admiral Foulques. You speak Turkic, do you not?"

It took Foulques a second to find his voice. "I do, Your

Grace. Though my understanding of it is better than my speech. I definitely do not have a diplomat's mastery of the language."

Henry waved his protest away. "Arabic is the language of diplomacy. I would merely like someone there that can understand what the infidels are saying behind our backs, if necessary. Will you go?"

It was framed as a question, for no king had the authority to command a Knight of Saint John or a Templar. They were the subjects of His Eminence the Pope, and God Himself, and by divine law accountable to no one else. But Foulques had learned long ago, when answering a request made by a member of a royal family, no matter who you were, there were very few choices in how one responded. No Christian in his right mind would willingly walk into a Saracen army's camp to beg for his life and the lives of others. But that was not the weight bearing down on Foulques's mind when he considered the question. He did not want to go because Foulques knew *he* would be there. It would be unlikely that Badru Hashim would be present for the negotiations themselves, but he would be somewhere in the enemy camp, and that was enough.

You are not ready.

Marshal Clermont's voice sounded so clearly in his head, Foulques glanced his way to see if he had spoken, but he was staring at his feet.

Foulques could not bring the king's frail face into focus as he looked in his direction and said, "Of course, Your Grace. When do we leave?"

BADRU WATCHED THE Royal Mamluks escort the Franks into the sultan's Dihliz. Their pale eyes flitted about nervously as they took in the decadence of color and fabric all about them. The awe with which they beheld the carpets and tapestries of the red tent only served to illustrate just how barbaric these people were.

The silk carpet they tread upon with dusty boots had images of a hundred different windows weaved into its design. As they trampled it underfoot, each window caught the light in a different manner, all but blinding the Franks with the splendor of the dancing hues of red and gold.

Badru shook his head. This was a tent on a battlefield. Whatever would they do if allowed into the sultan's palace in Cairo?

His heart picked up a beat when he saw the sharp blue eyes and long hair of the last man to enter. He was strongly built, with the rocking, easy stride of one who was equally at home on the ground, with sword in hand, or on the back of a horse. Confidence, not bravado, was built into his every movement, until his eyes settled on Badru kneeling on the floor at the sultan's side. He met Badru's look with a fierce gaze of his own, but not before Badru saw what was behind it.

This brought a keen sense of disappointment to Badru, for he and the Hospitaller had a shared past. One that had not yet resolved itself. The Hospitaller and his Genoan accomplice had humiliated Badru eight years ago, and lived.

Although he did not go out of his way to actively search for the Knight of Saint John, his face frequented Badru's mind, and he kept himself open to any news of his whereabouts. Their fates were intertwined in a way Badru did not yet understand, but he had faith that Allah would reward him by bringing the two of them together once again. And he had been right.

Though he had tried many times, Badru was never able to recreate the intensity of the experience he had felt when the two of them fought on the dock of Gibelet eight years ago. It was a hard thing to describe, even to himself. Simply put, he had never felt so… alive.

It had been a meeting worthy of the Furusiyya. Although he had been furious at the man's escape at the time, looking back on it years later, he was glad he had not taken the Hospitaller's life then. For it meant there was a chance they could meet again, and perhaps recreate that perfect moment.

But that dream died there in the sultan's tent, when he looked behind the eyes of the man called Foulques de Villaret and saw what he eventually saw in every other man: Fear. Badru had broken him in their fight and he had never regained his sense of worth. Or perhaps Badru's mind had simply painted his own memories with a fondness that had never existed in the first place. Whatever the case, he recognized that the Hospitaller was a broken man now, and it saddened Badru deeply.

Perhaps he should give the man back his sword. He once had fantasies of using it against him in a second battle, but that no longer held any interest for him.

No. No, he would not retrieve the weapon from his tent and return it to the Hospitaller. If he was as broken as Badru suspected, it would not be fair to the sword-smith who had put so much of his soul into the forging of that fine weapon.

Badru realized the vizier and one of the Franks, a Templar, had been speaking together for some time.

"My Sultan says seven days is too long. He will give you two and grant you safe passage. You may vacate the city by ship, or by foot from the front gate, but you must lay down your weapons and leave all your horses behind."

The Templar looked to the diplomat of the three, who shook his head. "That is impossible," the Templar began. "We cannot leave by foot, for where would we go? There are no cities in the Levant that would take us in. And we need more than two days to arrange for ships—"

A thunderous crash shook the earth and everything in the tent. A lantern tipped over and its glass shield shattered, spraying fire over the carpet at the sultan's feet. Men's screams could be heard just outside the tent.

The sultan let out a yelp and jumped up on his chair to avoid the flames.

Badru leapt to his feet, ripped a small carpet from beneath a table, and began beating the fire out before it could spread. Smoke billowed up, but he was successful.

A Royal Mamluk burst into the tent.

"What is happening?" the sultan asked in a high-pitched voice.

"The Franks have launched an attack with their catapult, My Sultan!"

Khalil's eyes went wide. He leveled a finger at the Franks and said in Turkic, "You dare attack during a peace negotiation?" His eyes grew wider still as a new thought occurred to him. "You waited until you knew I would be here and then you launched your attack. You are merely bait! Sacrifices!"

The Hospitaller was the only one who seemed to understand the sultan's Turkic.

"You are mistaken, Sultan. It was an accident. Our engineers were repairing our war engine and it must have unintentionally gone off—"

"Seize them!" The sultan said, growing more frantic with every second. His eyes darted madly about, like he expected a boulder to come crashing through the tent walls at any moment. "Execute them all! Send their heads back to their treacherous king tied to the balls of a donkey!"

Badru stood up to his full height. "Secure the prisoners," he shouted, then dared to put his hand protectively on Khalil's arm. "Come with me, Sultan. I will escort you to safety."

Khalil cast one surprised look at the huge hand on his arm, but then obediently climbed down off his chair. Vice-Sultan Baydara appeared on the other side of Khalil and took his other arm. "Perhaps I should accompany you as well," the older man said to Badru, looking every bit as disoriented as Khalil. "The sultan may have need of me."

"Of course," Badru said. He maneuvered the two of them through the flurry of activity erupting within the tent as the Royal Mamluks forced the emissaries turned prisoners to their knees.

As he passed by them, Badru called out. "Do not execute anyone until I return!"

His scimitar was in his hand and he used it to swat the flaps of the tent doorway aside.

CHAPTER TWENTY-SIX

THE ROYAL MAMLUKS dragged Foulques, Robert, and the Templar, Guillaume de Cafran, out of the tent and forced the knights to strip off their armor and boots. They left them squinting in the sun, bare-chested and on their knees with nothing on save their breeches.

Foulques and Guillaume resisted at first, but they had been relieved of their weapons before entering the sultan's tent so there was little they could do. And these were no ordinary Mamluks. They were the sultan's personal guard, highly trained and brutally efficient with the pommels of their swords. When they were finished, Foulques and Guillaume were both bleeding from their noses and mouths and Foulques could feel his right eye beginning to swell and color.

Robert, however, had not been wearing armor and had not resisted. Still fully clothed, he lowered himself to the ground between Foulques and the Templar, brushing pebbles from under his knees as he did so.

"Will they truly kill us?" Robert asked.

"Not you," Guillaume said. "You are headed to the sultan's harem, I suspect."

They remained there for the better part of an hour. By the time the large shadow of Badru Hashim fell over Foulques, his back was burnt, and he actually welcomed the reprieve. That feeling quickly dissipated when Badru walked around in front of the Christians and stared at each man in turn with his gray eyes.

Robert could not take the silence of the Mamluk's appraisal. "We are peaceful emissaries. Executing us is not the proper etiquette, no matter what your perceived offense. If you release us immediately, I guarantee King Henry will—"

Badru's hand snaked out and grabbed Robert by the throat, choking off whatever he was going to say next. He lifted the man to his feet with one arm, like he was nothing but a pile of fine clothes. Guillaume cursed and attempted to stand, but got the flat of a Mamluk blade across his back for the effort. Badru kept his grip on Robert and looked at Foulques, who was still on his knees and had not moved.

"I have convinced my sultan to spare your lives," Badru said.

"Why would you do that?" Foulques asked. The words came out with a slur to them. Apparently he had some swelling in his jaw he was not even aware of.

"Perhaps because you are already dead inside."

Badru gave Robert a shake and tossed him to the ground. He scrabbled around in the sand, coughing, and sucking in great mouthfuls of air.

"Do you still have my sword?"

Badru nodded. "Now I have two."

"And I have two hundred young men you once mistakenly thought were yours."

Badru smiled. The gesture looked out of place on his broad face. "There was a time when that statement would have driven me into a rage. Back when I was the simple pawn of a slaver. But that was a long time ago. Now I serve the most powerful man in the world and I have no need to live in the past." He put his hands on his knees and leaned over to look into Foulques's face. "Unlike some."

He stayed like that for a long moment, staring at the Hospitaller, looking for something only he could know. He must have found it, for he stood up abruptly and spoke to the Mamluks standing behind the three men. "Let them go. It is the sultan's command."

"Their armor and weapons, Emir?"

Badru shook his head. "I am sure their god will provide everything they need." He turned his back on Foulques and the others and began walking away.

"Hashim!" Foulques called out.

The large man's head turned back but his body did not.

"I will come for that sword some day," Foulques said.

Badru gave his head a sad shake. "No, Hospitaller. No, you will not."

Shouting in Turkic, the Mamluks pulled off Robert's boots and then kicked the men to their feet. They shoved and prodded them in their backs with the points of their swords. The message was clear, even to those who had no knowledge of the language.

Run back to your city.

The three of them marched barefoot and bleeding back to the Gate of Saint Anthony. Leaning outside the open gate was Goodyear Jimmy. He nodded and pursed his lips as he gave Foulques's near nakedness the once over. He handed him a full wineskin.

"So. Would you say your first peace negotiation went well?"

CHAPTER TWENTY-SEVEN

Much like any other day in the Levant, the sun rose into a sky bluer than the Mid-Earth Sea. However, there were two things that set this day apart from all others. First of all, it was Foulques's birthday. He was thirty-two years old. The second thing that made this day so different from all the previous ones, was the long line of siege towers on the horizon, blocking out the rays of the sun.

The enemy engineers must have had a sleepless night, for there were nearly a hundred of the structures. There was no uniform design to them. Some were tall and gangly, with large wooden wheels at their bases. Others were squat and broad enough to hold fifty men on their upper platforms. A third design was wheel-less, and really nothing more than a twelve-foot-wide ladder, but with rope netting instead of rungs. Its bearers would flip it up against the wall for men to scramble up like spiders.

The compact form of Glynn appeared next to Foulques. "Well, is that not a cheery sight to greet one with first thing in the mornin'?"

The knights and sergeants assumed their places at dawn,

but the towers did not begin their rumbling approach until three hours later. Instead, the Saracens unleashed "the Furious," "the Victorious," and countless "black bulls," the lesser catapults. The barrage was devastating.

The Tower of the Countess of Blois was the first to fall, crumbling in upon itself leaving nothing more than a great heap of rubble that no one could have hoped to survive. An hour later, "the Furious" made a direct hit at the base of the Tower of Saint Nicholas. It pitched forward, spilling thousands of pounds of stone across the killing field and creating an enticingly low obstacle for the enemy to target and gain access to the outer wall.

Then the barrage stopped. The morale of the brethren peaked and waned in those minutes like a rowboat fighting the surf. Foulques silently praised God when the Saracen horns and drums finally sounded and the siege towers began their short, ponderous journey to the wall.

A deep rumbling came from the south, followed by the shouts and screams of men. Foulques, Glynn, and several Schwyzers ran to where the wall curved south to get a better look. A cloud of dust hampered their view, but the cloud itself was enough to tell Foulques what had happened. The Tower of the English was gone, felled by the devilry of sappers. Foulques stepped from one side of the wall to the other, trying to catch a glimpse of Grandison and his men. But with the dust in the air he could see nothing.

"Back to your posts!" the marshal called out. "Fire bearers, spread out!"

Foulques gave up looking for Grandison. There was

nothing he could do for him now.

He ran back to his post amongst the Schwyzers. A few brown robes to his left was Glynn. Jimmy and Roderic were spaced between the young sergeants on his right. The beardless lad next to him, Lorenz, was fixated on the siege tower bearing down on their position at a pace much faster than its tall, unwieldy form should have been able to attain. Foulques gave him a firm grasp of the shoulder to shake him from his reverie, then reached into the wooden box at his feet and pulled out two earthenware jars stoppered with cork. A wax-dipped wick dangled off their necks.

"Here, Brother Lorenz, take one of these. Throw it exactly where and when I throw mine. And be very careful not to drop it on our side of the wall. I would rather not have my boots melted onto my feet. I suspect I will want to take them off after this day."

"Yes, Commander." Lorenz took the acorn-shaped jar carefully with both hands, like it was an egg containing a baby chick trying to peck its way to freedom. Foulques gave the boy another squeeze of the shoulder, hoping to instill a sense of confidence he was not sure he himself felt. The gesture did not have the desired effect. At his commander's touch, Lorenz tensed up and stared holes in the jar for fear he might drop it.

"Get ready," Foulques said. The tower paused twenty feet from the wall. It shook as men began to climb up its back side to get to the platform. It had a drawbridge style door covered in a patch-work of wet bull hides and heavy canvas soaked in some kind of fire retardant mixture.

"Remember," Foulques said. "We want the fire inside the tower, not on it."

The tower stopped trembling. Its invisible pushers chanted out a work rhythm beneath their cover and the weighted down tower began moving forward once again. Lorenz swallowed hard and looked at Foulques.

"How many men are in there?"

"The more the better," Foulques said, hefting the jar of Greek fire.

Shouting and screams came from different sections along the wall, but Foulques kept his eyes on the tower before him. It stopped two strides from the wall. Before they had been re-purposed, the bull hides had been soaking in tanning vats and the smell of urine made his eyes water.

"Hold steady," Foulques said, more to himself than anyone.

He lit his jar with a nearby lantern and Lorenz did the same. There was no more grunting from below and none of the defenders talked. The sound of far-off fighting was in the background, but in the immediate vicinity there was only complete silence. A warm breeze passed over the wall and the tower let out a slow, almost soothing, creak as it swayed hypnotically before them.

With no warning, the drawbridge began to fall. Slowly at first, until its weight caught up with it, and then it came on fast, crashing down upon the wall like the breaching of a whale. It bounced once and came to a solid rest straddling the crenellations.

There was a pause, and then the battle cries of the Saracens shook the tower, the wall, and every man on it. They streamed across the bridge with a mad determination, the whites of their eyes as large as the glaring sun overhead.

"Not yet!" Foulques shouted. He moved back, away from the bridge, pulling Lorenz with him. "Wait for the tower to fill."

He was not sure the boy could hear him, so he kept a tight grip on his wrist.

"Ready... now!"

He lobbed his earthenware jar deep inside the tower where it shattered against the side wall with a satisfying, musical crash. Instantly, blue flames erupted and began to spread. When Lorenz's jar hit the floor nearby, the two fires snaked toward each other and joined together as one. Men soon found parts of their armor or clothing aflame and the more they beat at it, the more it spread. Three other jars found their way inside, and within seconds the entire platform was engulfed in fire. Flaming figures began jumping off the backside of the tower trying to escape their plight, but once Greek fire had you in its grasp, it was nearly impossible to extinguish.

Foulques sent Lorenz to help fight those who had gained the wall, while he used up the remainder of his jars on another siege tower. This one failed to burn so spectacularly, and a steady trickle of Saracens were still able to cross from it. Foulques drew his sword and met them at the end of their bridge.

He sent man after man toppling off the unstable walkway before there were too many in front of him and he had to retreat further back onto the wall. Glynn joined him there and they fought shoulder to shoulder.

Foulques was aware of more towers appearing up and down the wall. Several were in flames and one collapsed, falling against the wall and sliding down it onto the Saracen soldiers below. The scent of urine was no longer in the air. The winds had turned much more noxious.

Glynn's sword whistled above Foulques's head and struck something behind him. "Look to your arse!"

Foulques half turned his head just in time to see a Saracen thrust at him with a straight sword. He twisted his body but the blade still rammed into his chest. The combination of his movement and the protection of the metal ringlets of his mail stopped the blade. His life was still intact but he could feel the bruises already spreading over his chest. He would feel it tomorrow. If he felt anything at all.

More and more enemies appeared on the wall and Foulques and Glynn were forced to fight back to back to protect themselves. Their goal was no longer to deny the Saracens the wall. They fought for their lives.

The trumpets of the Order began sounding on all sides. They blared away for many seconds before Foulques and Glynn risked a glance at one another over their shoulders.

"The marshal sounds the retreat," Foulques said.

But it was not only the Hospitaller trumpets that rang out. In the distance, other horns could be heard coming from the French, the Teutonics, the Cypriots, and even the Templars in the north. It was a general retreat. They were relinquishing the outer wall.

"Aye!" Glynn caught a man's blade with his and then ran him through. He lifted his bloody sword and pointed through the opening he had just created. Roderic and Lorenz were sprinting toward the nearest tower's door. "This way. We must gain the inner wall before they close the gates!"

And so, along with everyone else, they fled. Slowly, at first, for disbelief numbed the minds and muscles of many of the men. But as more and more Saracens appeared on the wall, the horns sounding the retreat grew frantic in their notes. The Christians sought out those towers still standing and fled down their staircases, or began the treacherous climb down the ruins of others. Once on the ground, it was a mad run for the nearest gate in the inner wall. For every man knew that at any moment the portcullis of that gate could be dropped, cutting them off from the city and leaving them to be cut up by the Saracens' curved blades.

Once on the ground, Foulques and Glynn joined a group of Hospitaller sergeants who had formed a protective guard around the grand master and marshal.

"Form up!" the marshal called out. "Crossbowmen to the front!"

They waited there for several minutes, and a few more Hospitallers and a couple of displaced Teutonic Knights joined their group. They became the targets of Saracen arrows and the marshal directed the unit to retreat orderly to a small gate a short distance south of their position. As they took cover from the Saracen bowmen in the open gate, the grand master called Roderic and Jimmy to his side and instructed them to take a half dozen men and hold the opening for as long as they dared. A dozen of the city's spear men were there as well, but Foulques could tell by the oblique looks of the grand master that he thought they would close the portcullis yesterday if they were given a choice. Looking at the trembling hands and wide eyes of the city guards, Foulques had to agree.

"When you are done here, and the gate is closed, leave it to them and join us on the wall," the grand master said.

"Where will you be, sir?" Roderic asked.

"We will ascend through the Accursed Tower. And God help us, pray it serves us better than it did Judas."

A short run later and the small group of Hospitallers stood at the entrance to the Accursed Tower. It was a pragmatic choice on the grand master's behalf, to choose this tower to gain the inner wall, for directly across from it on the outer wall were the ruins of the Tower of Saint Nicholas. The enemy would be coming hard through that breach.

Foulques paused and took one last look around the streets of Acre. He had been on the walls of Acre thousands of times in his life. But never had he gotten there by means of the Accursed Tower. He avoided it on purpose. For somewhere inside, coins were minted that had passed into the hands of Judas to buy the betrayal of his Lord Jesus.

Foulques hung back and waited. It did not take long for the grand master, marshal, knights, and sergeants to all pass through the narrow opening and begin appearing on the wall above. Foulques closed his eyes and said a quiet prayer, keeping his breathing shallow to lessen the pain in his chest.

Then he too entered the Accursed Tower, the birthplace of the ultimate treachery.

CHAPTER TWENTY-EIGHT

Two hours after the second wall was secured, the grand master called Foulques to attend him at the Hospitaller compound. As he had promised earlier, Grand Master Villiers had managed to gain passage for Foulques on a ship. Foulques had almost refused him outright, but when he heard who the ship's owner was, a plan began to form in his mind. To the grand master's surprise, Foulques accepted his orders without question.

As expected, the docks were swarming with people when Foulques arrived. He could hardly stand being there, for equal measures of desperation and greed assailed his senses on every level. A woman in fine clothing stepped up onto a barrel and began shouting.

"We have room for two! Arabic gold bezants only!"

Less than a minute later she had a group clamoring around her legs shouting at her. Negotiations were swift and to the point, ending with her pointing at a single noble-man. She descended from the barrel, took the man by his sleeve, and pulled him through the crowd as people cursed them both from behind.

Foulques wondered how he was going to find Grandison in this madhouse, but in the end, it was not difficult. There was a group of English soldiers restricting access to the walkway leading to the main wharf. When he questioned them, they told him at which berth Grandison could be found. Minutes later he saw Grandison helping load a group of women and children into a large rowboat. Grandison's face was a mask of welts and cuts, but he was still moving better than most knights half his age. His eyes lit up when he saw Foulques, and he grabbed him in a rough embrace.

"Glad to see you made it off the wall," Foulques said. "I feared the worst when I saw your tower go down."

"God smiled upon me yet again, I suppose. Seems hardly fair I should get let off the hook when so many young lads under my care did not."

"That was the Saracens' doing," Foulques said. "Not yours."

Grandison looked at Foulques. He nodded slowly. "I know it. But it does not make their loss any easier. Edward entrusted me with three hundred men and I will be taking less than a third of them home to their families."

A silence followed on both their parts, until Foulques broke it. "My weapons master tells me the English have no families. He says whenever room is made in their crowded cities for one, someone waits for the tide to go out and then turns over a rock. Whatever is there crawls up on land and swears fealty to the king."

"And a longbow is thrust into his slime-encrusted hand, I suppose." Grandison shook his head and laughed, but

Foulques felt it was forced for his benefit.

"Something like that," Foulques said. "In all earnestness, I heard the fighting was fiercer at your location than anywhere else when we lost the wall. Some say it was a miracle any of you made it."

Grandison gave him a doubtful look. "You think my archers are here because God called down a miracle?"

"I know better than to give God credit for the work of men."

Grandison nodded and put his hand on the younger man's shoulder. "If you will excuse me, Brother Foulques, I have preparations to make. We are leaving our horses behind and taking on as many passengers as we can."

Foulques looked at the rowboat now fully loaded with former citizens of Acre. "You are a good man, Sir Grandison."

"The sultan will definitely think so when he gets my horses." He raised his hands at his sides. "And unfortunately, even if I took my mounts, there would still be a lot of empty space."

"When is departure?"

"Two ships will sail for Cyprus this evening. The other, tomorrow morning. I will see you here for that one, then?"

"About that," Foulques began. "I know Grand Master Villiers said I would be joining you, but I am hoping you would be open to accepting someone in my place."

His eyes narrowed. "What are you planning, lad?"

"I need to remain here for a while longer."

Grandison shook his head. "It is time to leave, Foulques.

I can feel it. And when I get a feeling like that I act upon it. Even King Henry is making plans to leave."

"I appreciate your concern."

Grandison looked down at the wooden planks of the wharf and thought for a moment. "You are asking me to anger the Grand Master of the Hospitallers. That is not something I favor."

"Tell him I did not show up, if he asks. But I would wager that scenario will never come about. There will be more pressing matters occupying his mind very soon."

"So, you are a betting man, Brother Foulques. I am shocked! Tell me, who is this man to take your place?"

"*Her* name is Najya Malouf." He could have said more, but he did not know what that would be exactly.

"A woman?"

"Yes. A friend I have known for my entire life."

Grandison laughed. "My, my. You are full of surprises."

"It would mean a lot to me if you would see her safely to Cyprus."

Something in Foulques's tone, or expression, slowly robbed Grandison of the mirth in his face. Foulques endured an uncomfortable silence.

"She means that much to you?" Grandison asked quietly.

"More."

"I have room for you both. Why not escort her yourself?"

Foulques shook his head. "I cannot. But I can entrust that to you."

"I had to ask," Grandison said. "Very well. Tell her to

come here tomorrow and to look for the English colors. She should seek me out or any one of my captains."

He pulled off his glove and worked at a ring on his finger until it slid off. He handed it to Foulques. "This was given to me by King Edward. All of his commanders have one and the men will recognize it instantly. Tell her to show it to any one of my captains. I will warn them to watch for her."

A breeze blew across the water at the exact moment Grandison finished speaking. It provided an instant relief from the sweltering heat and took with it the constant dread and fear that had been eating away at Foulques since he had first learned Acre was under siege. His city would most likely fall, but Foulques swore he would not live to see that. And that was fine with him. For God had answered his prayers.

"Thank you," Foulques said. As much as he always protested whenever Vignolo called him a monk, Foulques found himself making the sign of the cross in front of Sir Otto de Grandison.

CHAPTER TWENTY-NINE

As Foulques climbed the steps of the Accursed Tower, the sun gave one last burst of red brilliance, before it was quenched in its entirety by the Mid-Earth Sea.

After seeing Grandison at the docks, Foulques had gone straight to Najya with the news he had found her a ship. She would go to Cyprus and seek out Brother Alain at the hospice. He would look after her until Foulques returned.

In an unspoken conspiracy, they accepted that last part as their truth. Foulques lingered there at Najya's small table, drinking tea and sharing memories, for the rest of the afternoon. Finally, it was time to go.

The grayness of dusk lasted mere seconds and Foulques found himself on the wall once again. The evening too seemed to be in a hurry, but the night itself was another story. When all that separates one from a hostile army is fifty yards of open darkness, it makes for a fitful rest.

As soon as the Saracens took the first wall they began to rain down arrows on the Christians as they scrambled to fortify the second wall. Because the outer wall was higher than the inner, they had a good angle of attack and could cover most of the walkway. The only place the defenders had protection was if they pressed themselves up tight to the wall and hid behind the crenellations. It was possible to move along the length of the wall without being too exposed, but it was awkward and nerve-wracking.

Foulques did not know how many men had fallen in the five weeks they had been fighting, but if the other factions had suffered losses like the Hospitallers, than he estimated there could be no more than five or six thousand men still able to use a sword. It was just as well they had lost the outer wall. They no longer had enough men to man it properly. At least now they did not have so much wall to cover. And the catapults would no longer be much of a threat, for they would have to go through the outer wall, which was now manned by Saracens, before it could do any damage to the defenders' last line of defense.

Foulques wondered if others were having similar thoughts to his. In the cold hours before dawn, did all tired, desperate men clutch at hope like it was the last rays of a warm sun on a winter day? Did their troubled minds create hope when surely none existed?

He looked to his left, at the marshal sleeping on his back with his fingers interlaced upon his chest. When darkness had fallen, the defenders had been given a reprieve from the deadly enemy arrows and the marshal was keen on taking advantage of that to get some rest.

"They will do one of two things, come dawn," he had said. "Either launch an all out attack on the wall, or pretend they have brains, and whittle our numbers down with their bows from above."

The marshal did the prudent thing and called up extra crossbows and bolts. There seemed to be a surplus of crossbows this far along in the siege; it was the bolts that were lacking. Two or three men were squeezed behind every crenellation along the wall. Foulques was not quite sure how he ended up being paired with the marshal.

After the crossbows were distributed, Marshal Clermont declared he would take first watch and Foulques should try to get some sleep. Lying there on the cold stones of the wall, Foulques did his best. He was exhausted and he kept his eyes closed, but when the marshal tapped him on the shoulder to take his turn at watch, Foulques doubted he had slept more than a few minutes, if at all.

"If you get killed while I am sleeping, try to do it loudly so I wake up," the marshal said as he lay down.

His words did not have the usual sharp edge to them. Foulques could have been mistaken, for there was only the light of the stars to go by, but he thought he saw a half-smile on the marshal's face. The darkness took twenty years off his face and Foulques was instantly reminded of the Mathieu de Clermont he had looked up to as a youth. Foulques had been the envy of all the other young knights when the marshal had invited him to come train with his select few.

"Foulques," the marshal said suddenly.

"Yes?"

"Quit staring at me. I am not the one that is going to kill you."

"No?"

"I do not need to, since you are so intent on doing it yourself. Do not forget you could be on Cyprus, in a warm bed, at this very moment."

The marshal's words had the tone of banter to them, but there was a deeper layer as well. The marshal had still not forgiven him for coming to Acre from Cyprus.

"Can I ask you something, Marshal?"

He grunted, which surely meant yes.

"Was it my uncle who suggested creating the admiral position within our ranks?"

"What are you talking about, Foulques?"

"Did he suggest to you and the grand master that I should be admiral?"

The marshal said nothing. Foulques nodded in the darkness. It was as he thought.

"And why would he have done that?" Marshal Clermont asked.

"To protect me. To make sure I was not in Acre when the Mamluks attacked."

The marshal laughed. "Well, if that was his intention, he does not know you very well."

Probably not, Foulques thought. How could he? They had not seen each other but once in eight years.

"I am going to sleep," the marshal said. "Remember. Gurgle and thrash around a lot if you get killed. Good night."

✶

DAWN CAME AND went but no Mamluk attack came. Even

though their wall was lower than the one the Saracens now controlled, Foulques could still see the army encampment because of the slope of the land. Thousands of tiny spirals of smoke lifted into the morning sky. Cooking fires. Foulques heard, and felt, his stomach growl as he pictured some Mamluk warrior holding a spit of meat, its juices dripping into one of those fires, getting ready for just another day of work.

"Foulques!" A voice turned gravelly by the night called out on his right. Jimmy the Neckless held up a leather wineskin. Jimmy sat with his broad back pushed up against the wall. He had his crenellation all to himself, for there was no room for another man.

Foulques nodded and held up his hands. Jimmy lobbed the skin toward him. Three arrows slipped through the air on all sides of it as it began its downward fall. Foulques clapped the wineskin together in his hands and inspected it. He gave Jimmy the all right sign, removed its stopper, and took a long drink. He noticed the marshal leaning around the edge of the wall for a quick view of the enemy.

"Looks like they have decided what option to pursue," he mumbled.

Foulques offered him the wineskin, which he gladly accepted. He took a long swig, nodded appreciatively, and then took one more for good measure. Then he called out to the two men next to him. He lobbed the skin to them and watched two arrows narrowly miss it.

"You remember how to operate one of those monstrosities?" He pointed down at the crossbow beside Foulques.

Foulques answered by using his goat's foot lever to draw back the string and lock it in place. He loaded in a bolt and looked at the marshal.

"Say the word, Marshal, and that wineskin is as good as dead."

One of Marshal Clermont's eyes almost twitched out of his head before he realized Foulques was not serious. "The shots came from a position directly in front of Brother James."

Foulques nodded. He rolled onto his stomach and pushed his crossbow along the stone walkway until he could see around his crenellation and had a good view of the outer wall. Being higher, the enemy bowmen had a superior position, but Foulques had the better weapon for this particular contest. The Saracens usually used a composite bow made of horn and wood. It was short, with curved limbs that made it very powerful. But to loose an arrow, the archer must see his target, draw the bow, and release it, all within a few seconds. The draw weights of these bows were too heavy for a man to draw his arrow back and hold it until a target appeared. But with his crossbow already fully drawn and loaded, Foulques could do precisely that.

He trained it on the wall and waited.

"They will be passing it along in three, two, one," Clermont said.

A Mamluk came into view to the left of where Foulques was aiming. He made the necessary adjustment. Foulques flipped up the tickler on his weapon just as the archer was coming to full draw. The morning sun glinted off the wooden vanes of the crossbow bolt as it glided across the distance from one wall to the other. It took the man in the face before he released his arrow. The violent shock dislodged the arrow from his string. The force of the fully drawn bow being released with no arrow in it to absorb that force, caused the bow's limbs to explode into several pieces. The Mamluk staggered and fell off the wall to the killing field below.

Jimmy the Mouth's voice cut through the morning's silence. "Yes! Never shoot at another man's wine you godless bastards!"

Other taunts followed. Even the marshal had been taken in by the simple moment, for he clapped Foulques on the shoulder. "Nice shot, Foulques. We needed that one."

That one, and a hundred thousand more just like it, thought Foulques.

The marshal had been right. There would be no attack on the wall that day, but many men on both sides would die all the same. Thousands of arrows filled the sky throughout the day. Not all at once, but in ones and twos, as each side tried to best the enemy from afar.

For the first half of the day, it was a welcome change for Foulques and the other Hospitallers, for they enjoyed a definite advantage shooting their crossbows from behind cover. But stocks of bolts were running low, and by midday, the marshal gave the order that only one man of every two should employ his weapon. By nightfall, the game of inches had become old, and the morale of the men began to wane.

Darkness came, and found Foulques and the marshal,

once again, taking turns trying to sleep. But the sounds along the outer wall this night were far different, and much more disconcerting than the night before. Some time after dark, the enemy had brought in thousands of laborers with picks, axes, shovels, and beasts of burden. On the far side of the outer wall, lanterns were set and the work began. Shielded from the Christians' ranged weapons by the outer wall, the Saracens were able to go about their task with relative impunity. Occasionally, a man would scream as he earned himself a bolt or an arrow because he stepped into a gap he should not have, but for the most part, the Christians could only stare helplessly at the long, demonic shadows of the infidels as they proceeded to tear great gaps in the outer wall. Wherever there were wooden gates, they set them aflame in place or tore them from their hinges and burned them in bonfires. There was no attempt to preserve anything.

The purpose of the Mamluk army was clear: they were preparing for an all out assault on the inner wall. They had no intention of claiming the city for their own. They would kill every Christian within, enslave who they wished, and burn Acre to the ground. And they would do it at dawn.

"Foulques. I know you are not asleep," Marshal Clermont said. He sat propped up against the wall in his usual spot. Foulques was lying on his back with his eyes closed, listening to oxen and men tearing the walls down around his home. Of course he was not asleep.

"I need to tell you something."

"I am awake," Foulques said.

The marshal grunted. It was long moments before he

spoke. "It was I who demanded we create an admiral position in the Order. And it was I who insisted you be chosen for the role."

"You?"

"We have sent a messenger, but as of yet, Guillaume does not even know the admiral position exists."

This made no sense, Foulques thought. He was so sure it had been his uncle…

"But why would we need an admiral? We do not even have a fleet."

"Not yet. But if the Order is to survive, we must. This war will not end when Acre has fallen. And when the infidels have taken all our land, there is only one place it can continue."

"I can understand that," Foulques said, "but with our past, why would you choose me for the position?"

He heard the marshal sigh. It was dark, but Foulques could tell Clermont was looking at him.

"Do you think I hate you? Is that it?"

Foulques did not answer.

"I hated your uncle, for a time. I hated him because he took you away from me, Foulques. And I hated myself, for thinking I could have done a better job of raising you than Guillaume did. But I could never hate you."

After a long pause, Marshal Clermont spoke in a voice just above a whisper. "In the end, he did all right, your uncle. He did all right."

The marshal said no more, but Foulques heard him exhale, and strangely, with that sound, a peace washed over

Foulques. Clermont was done talking, and Foulques did not know what to say. So the two of them sat there in silence, trying to enjoy the moment and ignore the sounds of the oxen, the picks and the shovels, and the occasional scream of a dying man who had stepped into the light.

CHAPTER THIRTY

"Admiral? Admiral?"

Foulques was aware of small hands tugging at his armor, attempting to rouse him from his sleep. Not that that was what he was actually doing, for these days his rest consisted of a trance-like state where he hovered somewhere between sleep and wakefulness. He was not sure he would ever sleep again.

Foulques opened his eyes to see a young boy, his dirty face lit by nothing but moonlight, was inches from his own.

"What is it?"

"I am to give you this. He said you would know what it meant. He also said do not lose it. You might have need of it again some day."

The boy pushed something small and hard into his hand.

"Who said that?"

But the boy was already moving away through the darkness. He disappeared so quickly Foulques thought it may have been a dream. But he squeezed his hand and felt the hard lump in his palm. He took it between two fingers and held it up to the stars. It was a ring. A ring of the English king.

Najya was safe. For the first time in many nights, Foulques slept.

✷

FOULQUES WAS WOKEN by drums in the cold, pre-light hours, when the desert dwellers say only the dead walk the earth. The first thing he did was to check the pouch on his belt for Grandison's ring. It was still there. He had not imagined the boy in the night. He could have lifted the world.

He rose to face a dawn that was two hours late in coming. Wave after wave of Saracen troops gathered against the eastern horizon and the dust billowing up from the feet of man, horse, and camel rose into the air and choked out the sun.

Foulques joined Marshal Clermont at the wall. Together, they cautiously peered out from either side of the crenellation that had been their salvation for the previous two nights. There were still Saracen archers on the outer wall, but they had not fired a single arrow since first light. Someone had ordered them not to, for that same someone wanted the Christians to witness the force that assembled against them.

A new, deep boom began to sound and echo across the plain. It grew in volume and Foulques found his shoulders involuntarily rolling forward as the sound hit him in the chest and penetrated deep within. The hairs on the back of his neck and hands stood upright. Out of the great wall of dust came a line of camels, at least three hundred of them, with massive drums strapped to either side. Their riders were dressed entirely in black. Their flowing robes fluttered around them and masks covered the lower halves of their faces, leaving only the slits of their eyes exposed. Each man carried a long stick with a fattened head. With a wide circular movement of his arm, he would pound first one drum and then circle his arm high into the air, letting it bounce off the drum on the other side of the camel. The long-legged beasts lurched ahead in their seemingly clumsy manner, their necks reaching forward and back with every stride.

And behind them marched the army of Islam. Banners and flags held high, trumpeters blaring their instruments, colorful silks floating on the wind. The line of men stretched the entire length of Acre's remaining wall and extended deeper than the eye could see.

Shouts rang up and down the defenders' wall as knights relayed the orders of their commanders. The Templars defended the north wall, the Hospitallers a long section south of them up to the Accursed Tower. To the south of the Hospitallers were the Knights of Syria, and the Leper Knights from the Order of Saint Lazarus, and beside them was the Teutonic Order. Interspersed throughout were the city militia and a mix of Christian men-at-arms from all nations.

But at this stage, day forty-three of the siege, most of the defenders were not knights or trained men-at-arms. They were merchants and shopkeepers, fathers and husbands who hoped to buy enough time for their families to escape.

"Look," Marshal Clermont said. Foulques could barely hear him, but he followed his finger to the center of the approaching army. The troops directly in front of the Hospitaller line. "Those are the Mamluk elite, their most hardened troops. All massed together in one spot." He shook his head and his eyes narrowed. "They will attack all along the wall, to spread out our forces, but the middle section of the wall, right here, is their true target."

He stepped back and shouted to get his men's attention. "Knights of Saint John!"

"The heathens think this is the weak point in the city's defenses!" He raised his voice even more. "You hear that, Hospitallers? The heathen think we, God's Warriors, are the weak point of the Kingdom of Jerusalem! What say you to that? I, for one, have words for their unholy sultan: We *are* the Kingdom! And God knows it!"

The nearby Hospitaller knights and sergeants raised their swords and screamed in defiance. Foulques was swept up in their exuberance and he began shouting his voice ragged. Further down the wall, though they could not have heard the marshal's words, more men joined their own voices to that of their brethren. In times of war, it was not the words that held the most meaning.

The trumpets and drums began to lose the battle against the voices of men. The camels stopped moving forward and the sea of men flowed around them and charged toward the city, screaming for all they were worth. Foulques let loose a battle cry of his own just to see if he could hear his own voice. It was a futile effort.

From his vantage point, Foulques could no longer see

open ground between the outer wall and the enemy. Seconds later, Saracens began streaming through all the gates, holes, nooks, and crannies of the outer wall. Thousands of ladders, which must have been brought in under cover of darkness, suddenly appeared. The wall shook under Foulques's feet. On the other side of the Accursed Tower, the Teutonic Knights were already locked in battle with hundreds of men on the wall. Looking north, the Templars too were engaged. Foulques hefted his crossbow and searched out a target. But no one was there.

A few strides away, Marshal Clermont had a strange look on his face. Foulques could not hear him, but he knew what he was thinking, for Foulques had the same question in his mind.

Where are the Mamluks?

Foulques stepped forward and leaned around the crenellation cautiously, expecting to see a ladder full of Mamluks. But not a single man was there. Yet he could feel the wall sway with the weight of the attackers north and south. He looked up and saw the Accursed Tower also tremble. It was the slightest movement, but it was there, and in that moment, he knew why no Mamluk had set foot on the wall.

Sappers.

It was the last thought to go through his mind before the world spun a thousand times in a second, and hurled him tumbling, over and over, through darkness. Gone were the sounds of battle and men's voices. All that remained was the darkness, punctuated again and again by pain, and the crashing roar of what sounded like the massive waterfall at the edge of the world.

CHAPTER THIRTY-ONE

THE LAST THING Foulques felt like doing was opening his eyes. His body felt like he had been run over by a team of horses pulling a cart completely loaded with casks of wine. But he could hear shouts and voices around him. Some he recognized, but they were oddly out of place. Like Kas the Baker. What was he doing on the wall?

Foulques forced his eyes open, one at a time, afraid of what he would find. The amount of blood on his tunic shocked him, until he remembered very little of it was his own. He began flexing the muscles of his legs and worked his way up until he finished with his fingertips. He identified no breaks, but plenty of bruising. He took a deep breath, which elicited some pain on the left side of his ribcage, but he was fairly certain none of his ribs were even cracked.

He looked around him. Not fifty feet away was the door to Kas the Jew's bakery. And it was at eye level.

How was that possible?

He heard the baker's voice again, and this time, it was accompanied by a tugging at his elbow. Then Marshal Clermont's voice cut through the fog of his mind and the noise and confusion surrounding him.

"Thank the Saints! Foulques, can you hear me? Is he hurt?"

"I do not think so. His helmet took the brunt of it. Look at it. I had a hard time removing it because of the dents," Kas said.

Roderic and Jimmy the Neckless were with the marshal and they helped Foulques to his feet.

"How do you feel?" Roderic asked.

"Nothing a week in a bath house will not remedy," Foulques heard himself say. "What happened? How did I get here, on the street?"

Jimmy pivoted Foulques around by his shoulders. "Look," the big sergeant said.

Foulques squinted his eyes to protect them from the dust in the air. On his right was the Accursed Tower. To its left was a hundred foot section of rubble that had once been the wall attached to the Accursed Tower. The tower, itself, seemed to have developed a slight lean to one side.

"They undermined the wall," the marshal said. "Under our very feet. Come. We must hurry. They will be through the rubble in minutes. We must hold them at the breach."

Foulques shook his head to clear it. Quarried rocks worn smooth by centuries of foot traffic were scattered haphazardly on the street around them. Rougher rocks of all sizes stretched toward the wall in a hill of debris that rose no higher than ten or twelve feet. Somehow, Foulques had ridden the collapsing wall to where he now stood. His armor had protected him to some degree, but truly, his survival had the hand of God in it.

"I need a sword," Foulques said.

"Come. You can pick one up along the way. There will be no shortage of weapons where we go."

They ran to the lowest part of the debris field. Foulques could hear the Mamluks on the other side, shouting and removing rocks one by one. The marshal had been right. Swords were everywhere. Foulques retrieved one from the ground. Nearby, buried up to his waist in rock, was a dead Schwyzer. His head and face were too disfigured to identify, but Foulques knew he was one of the Schwyzer youths because his brown tunic did not yet have the cross of Saint John on it. The monks of the Order sewed crosses on the Schwyzer tunics and robes when they had spare time. It was not seen as a priority. Had eight years not been enough time?

As they waited for the Mamluks to clear a path into the city, rock by rock, Foulques knelt over the dead youth and prayed for his soul. He removed his glove and brushed the youth's eyelids closed at the same moment the first Mamluk stepped through a gap in the debris.

He was the first Mamluk to set foot inside the city, and the first to die on the streets of Acre. As the breaches opened up in the remains of the wall, it became a frantic search and destroy scenario. The defenders would plug one gap and a few feet away another would open up. A brave Mamluk warrior would run through, hacking at Hospitallers left and right, trying to penetrate further into the city so the men behind him had some space to fill. But all the remaining

Hospitallers had come down off the wall itself, and with their numbers concentrated at the fallen section, they managed to hold their own when it came to pushing back the Mamluks as they tried to establish a footing within the city.

Foulques stood between Jimmy the Mouth and Roderic, fighting to keep the enemy from passing through a space wide enough for one man. They took turns standing in the opening. Foulques picked up a shield and he tapped Jimmy on the shoulder with it to signal it was time for him to take a rest. He retreated and Foulques pushed into the space, leading with his shield.

Two Mamluks stabbed at him with their scimitars, but Foulques's shield protected him. There was only room for him to thrust in the narrow opening, so that is what Foulques did. Again, and again. The Mamluks were being pushed from the back by members of their own army. The constant jostling from behind caused one of the men to be closer to Foulques than he should have been. Foulques caught him with a thrust in the groin, up under the plates of his lamellar armor. The second man fell forward against Foulques's shield, and pressed as he was so tightly against the Hospitaller, Foulques had no recourse but to drop his sword and draw his rondel dagger. The Mamluk was even more helpless, for both his arms were wedged against the shield. He looked on helplessly as Foulques pierced the white of one of his eyes with the dagger, killing him instantly.

The dead man could not fall to the ground because of the press of bodies behind him, and Foulques, though he continued to lean forward with all his strength, felt himself losing ground. Jimmy and Roderic both put their hands on Foulques's shield and the combatants struggled back and forth like that for several minutes. Finally, exhausted, their boots slipping on cobbles slick with blood, the three men were pushed clear of the breach. Mamluks began to emerge through the opening one by one.

Similar things were happening all along the remnants of the wall.

"Hospitallers! To me! To me!" The grand master called from somewhere behind Foulques. Out of the corner of his eye he saw his brethren begin to break off their entanglements and run toward the grand master. The marshal was already beside Grand Master Villiers, organizing the men into a box formation. Mamluks were everywhere now, so Foulques, Jimmy, and Roderic kept their backs toward one another and fought their way slowly toward the grand master's unit. It would have been an impossible task, but the Mamluks emerging from the wall were more intent on pressing further into the city than they were on engaging three grim-faced Hospitallers. So the most frequent attacks they had to deal with were mad slashes from Mamluks as they rushed past. Eventually, though, it became clear that they were not going to make it to the grand master. There were simply too many Mamluks around them and too many of the enemy's commanders were now on site. Discipline began to take hold, and the three Hospitallers found themselves surrounded by Mamluks intent on taking their lives.

Seeing the reality of the situation, Foulques directed his

trio up against the wall of a building and prepared to make a stand. He fought with dagger and shield, Jimmy had his hammer, and Roderic, only a sword.

The Mamluks came at them the way trained soldiers should: in groups of as many men as space would permit. Their purpose was to rid the battlefield of an obstacle, and the best way to do that was to use their advantage of numbers. This was no honorable contest of arms. It was war.

In some ways, fighting with only a dagger in these circumstances, simplified Foulques's life. With his options limited, both in offense and defense, he found it easier to concentrate on the weapons and men within his immediate vicinity. Those even a stride away were no longer a part of his world. Using shield and dagger, he turned blades and maces aside that entered his realm as best he could. He focused on protecting his vitals and put his trust in his mail for the rest. When a face or a wrist came within his reach, his dagger would snake out and take it, but defense always took precedence.

Foulques used his shield to cover himself and Jimmy's flank as best he could. But Jimmy the Neckless made for a big target, and he was tiring. He no longer had the strength to use his hammer effectively as a weapon, so he had resorted to employing it like a shield to entangle and thwart enemy blades. It was not working well, but Roderic had stepped in with thrusts from his sword to save him several times. Roderic's mail hung open on his chest and right side, where it had taken heavy cuts, and without doubt, saved his life. But it was now on the verge of being useless.

Foulques did not see the blow that killed Roderic, but he felt it. When one is fighting so close to his brethren, often touching him occasionally to maintain an awareness of where he is, it is almost as though they meld into a single being. So when Roderic's right side was opened by a Mamluk blade, both Foulques and Jimmy cried out as though they, themselves, were the ones who had been cut.

Roderic, for his part, did not make a sound. He stood for a moment longer, half swung his sword one last time, and then he slumped against the wall of the building they were cornered against.

Foulques turned in time to see him hit the ground. Jimmy had dropped his hammer and had his thick fingers around the Mamluk whose sword still dripped red with Roderic's blood. Jimmy screamed and squeezed the Mamluk's neck. It cracked like a sack filled with fine glass. His face still flushed, he pulled the dead man in front of him to shield himself from the other attackers. Foulques stepped in front of Jimmy and drove at his attackers with his own shield to give the big man some room. It was not much space, but it was enough for Jimmy to push the dead man against the nearest Mamluks, causing them to step back. As soon as he could, Jimmy drew his own dagger.

They stood shoulder to shoulder now, with their backs against the wall. Each armed with daggers and one shield between them. Jimmy was panting like a rabid dog and his thrusts were wild, fueled by rage. His brown tunic had been reduced to rags, his mail little better, with great patches of his once white padded gambeson showing through, now stained red with the Englishman's own blood.

Foulques was better off, due mostly to the shield he still carried. But bearing it for so long had taken its toll. His shield arm had gone numb a long time ago. He was not even sure if he still clutched the strap or if it only hung there by the tether on his forearm. He tried as best he could to keep the shield centered between the two of them, but his shoulder muscles began to give out and the shield kept dropping.

So focused was he on trying to keep the shield up high enough to afford them some protection, that Foulques did not realize the number of Mamluks in front of them had begun to decrease. The sounds of battle had been loud before, but now they were deafening. At first Foulques thought the entire Saracen army had broken through, but suddenly, the Mamluk in front of him had no head. Another one to his right lost his arm at the shoulder and fell screaming to the ground to reveal a knight with a cross on his chest. But it was not the white cross of the Hospitallers, it was the red one of a Templar Knight. The knight wore a white tunic covered in blood, but not his own judging from the way he swung his sword about. He wore a helmet with a full face shield so Foulques could not tell who it was. Before he could breathe a word, the Templar was off again, chasing down and skewering a Mamluk through the back. More white tunics of the Templars appeared and battle waged all around Foulques and Jimmy for a minute or more. And then, like a great storm had touched down around them and then moved on, Foulques and Jimmy were left with no one in front of them.

They fell back against the wall. Jimmy hunched over, put his hands on his knees, and breathed. Foulques's shield arm gave out and he let it drag him down to one knee. The shield hit the ground, still strapped to his arm. Neither man said a word until Jimmy turned and tried to pick up Roderic's body.

Foulques pushed himself to his feet. "Jimmy. Leave him. We have to make it back to the grand master while we still can."

Jimmy gave Foulques a dark look, but then his eyes cleared. He nodded and eased Roderic back to the ground, with his back propped up against the wall like he was waiting for something.

Foulques cleared the emotion from his throat, and then said, "The angels will be along shortly, Brother Roderic. Then you will know true peace." He made the sign of the cross over his fallen friend.

Foulques and Jimmy re-armed themselves. Jimmy retrieved his hammer and Foulques selected a fine scimitar from the many lying nearby. Everywhere Foulques looked, Mamluks fled from the wrath of the Templars, whose white tunics and red crosses were all around them. Some of the enemy escaped further into the city, but most retreated back through the breaches in the wall.

They made their way as quickly as they could to where Foulques had last seen the grand master and Marshal Clermont. There he found less than fifty Hospitallers Knights still standing. Perhaps another hundred sergeants.

There was no sign of the grand master, but Foulques arrived just in time to see Marshal Clermont and Grand Master Beaujeu of the Templars stride toward one another and clasp arms. It was a touching sight, one he thought he would never live to see. They exchanged a few words, seemed to agree on something, and then they began to shout orders to their respective men.

As Foulques and Jimmy got nearer, Foulques realized why he had not seen Grand Master Villiers. He was lying on the ground at the marshal's feet. Brother Reynald, a skilled surgeon, knelt over him.

When Marshal Clermont saw Foulques and Jimmy approaching, he closed his eyes and muttered something to himself. Then he called out.

"Foulques. Quickly!"

"How bad is he?" Foulques asked as they approached.

Brother Reynald shook his head. "Not good. I must operate as soon as I can if he is to stand a chance."

The grand master's face was ashen. His mail and gambeson had been removed. Foulques could see the broken off shaft of an arrow protruding from the right side of his chest and a bandage wrapped his middle. The thick cotton grew redder by the second.

Marshal Clermont looked at Foulques. "The Mamluks are gathering right now for another assault on the breach. The Templars took them by surprise, but that is done. Once they have their formations, they will be coming."

"Where do you want me?" Foulques asked.

In three strides of his long legs the marshal was directly

in front of Foulques. He leaned in, locked eyes with the younger Hospitaller, and said, "Get the grand master to the docks. Do whatever it takes to get him out of Acre. Do not fight me on this, Foulques, for if you both die here today, the Order is finished." He stepped back and announced in a loud, clear voice. "Admiral Villaret, I charge you with getting the grand master of the Order of Saint John to safety."

Horns sounded on the other side of the breach. Templars and Hospitallers charged to reinforce the men already there. Marshal Clermont looked once over his shoulder and nodded to himself.

"Brother Gissler. Lay down your shield. Brother Pirmin, help put the grand master on the shield, then you and Gissler will help Brother Reynald and Brother Goodyear bear him wherever Admiral Foulques commands. Is that clear?"

The young men stowed their weapons and did as the marshal commanded. Brother Jimmy hung his hammer over one shoulder and bent down to grab one corner of the shield. When all four men had a hold of the grand master's makeshift stretcher they lifted him up.

Foulques looked at the marshal, who bent to the ground and picked up a flanged mace. It was one of Saracen design. It was then that Foulques noticed the marshal's scabbard was empty. He too had lost his sword in the earlier conflict. He pointed the mace at Foulques and shouted over the rising crescendo of voices. "Go with God, Foulques. And by all that is holy, cut your hair!" He turned and as agile as his namesake the mongoose, ran straight up a nearby mound of rocks to survey the battle.

Foulques pointed down the street toward the docks. "Go!"

The shield bearers hurried off. Foulques had difficulty getting his feet to begin moving. He turned one last time to look at his brethren fighting for control of the rubble that had once been a wall. The battle had already become intense. It seemed a ridiculous endeavor, and in that moment he caught a glimpse of the madness of the world.

He saw the marshal standing on his mountain, daring any to try and take it from him. His feet were at the same level as the heads of the men around him. He hefted his Saracen mace high into the air and shouted something, urging his men on to glory. Foulques stared for a moment longer, before he turned and fled after his shield bearers, wondering how it was that he could not bring himself to look away from a man he had spent a third of his life detesting. But he knew why, and the lump swelling in his throat confirmed it.

CHAPTER THIRTY-TWO

FOULQUES LED THE way at a fast walk while Pirmin, Gissler, Reynald, and Jimmy each held one corner of the rectangular shield supporting the unconscious form of Grand Master Villiers. The shield was large enough to support his head and neck at one end, but his legs dangled off the other at the crooks of his knees. They proceeded down the main road for a few minutes, until Foulques saw the first Saracen raiding party. A group of Saracen mercenaries kicked in the doors of a glass blower's shop and proceeded to scour the building for valuables. Foulques turned down a side street before the Saracens emerged back out of the shop.

The looting had begun. He was afraid of this. Scores of Saracens had penetrated the breach earlier and gotten past the Hospitaller line. Who knew how many had made it over the wall in other locations. Now they were doing what they had been waiting forty-three days for. They had gotten inside the city and now everything and everyone they wanted was theirs for the taking. But there was an urgency to their actions, for they knew soon the entire Mamluk army would be inside the walls as well.

Because of this, Foulques decided it was going to be nothing but smaller side streets all the way to the harbor. He had been born in Acre, and knew the city as well as anyone. The men followed him without question as they weaved up and down side streets and alleys. Even so, the further into the city they traveled, the more roving gangs they came across. Apparently, everyone was headed to the docks.

They entered the Venetian Quarter and narrowly missed being spotted by a half dozen Saracens bashing at the door of a well-to-do family Foulques knew. He could hear frantic shouts coming from inside. He gritted his teeth and pressed on.

He had no idea what he was going to do once he got to the docks. He supposed he would have to commandeer a ship, or at least a skiff of some sort. He was not looking forward to doing so, for it would mean robbing some poor citizen of his or her means of escape. But that was the task with which he had been charged. He was to take a turn at playing God.

A commotion, men shouting, the sounds of fighting, came from around the next bend. He decided it was best avoided.

"This way," he said in a low voice over his shoulder. He pointed to a narrow space between two buildings. "This path will put us near the Pisan Quarter, and from there it will be a short run to the docks."

The path was just wide enough to accommodate the shield and its precious cargo. The grand master's shoulders brushed against the stone buildings as they hurried through. The men's faces were wet with exertion. None of them talked as they focused on their task. Even the big lad, Pirmin, looked to be in pain, but then that may have been because he had to hunch over to match the carrying height of the others. Jimmy matched him in girth but Pirmin was a head taller.

The narrow path opened onto a main street up ahead. Foulques signaled a halt and stuck his head out to check both directions. He saw people running at the far end away from them so he decided to proceed down the road for a few strides and then turn south down the small street just up ahead.

"Quickly now." He led them down the road as fast as he dared, turned left, and ran into a group of Saracens. Foulques drew his weapon, a scimitar that he had thrust into his belt earlier at the wall. He did not even have a chance to warn his men, but he did not need to, for they skidded to a halt right on his heels.

The Saracens shouted in surprise, but unlike Foulques, they already had their weapons drawn. They outnumbered Foulques and his men two to one, so once they realized no more Hospitallers were coming from around the corner, they relaxed.

"What is this?" a thick-set man said in heavily accented Arabic. Like many mercenaries, he was from one of the lands in the east. He spoke just enough Arabic to negotiate the terms of his contract and communicate with others like him.

"We get extra for Templar heads," he said, apparently mistaking Foulques's red war tunic.

"They are from the Hospital," another, more knowledgeable man said. He was a native Arabic speaker. "But we get extra for them too. Especially the wounded one. He looks to be someone of importance."

"Then you can have him," Foulques said in Arabic. "Let the rest of us go and you take the old man."

"Why would we do that?" the Arab said. "When we could have you all?" The first man had a dazed look on his face as he tried to understand exactly what was being said.

Foulques pointed his scimitar at the Arab. "Because we will kill at least five of you for your trouble." He turned his head and said to his men quickly in German, knowing fully well only Gissler and Pirmin would understand him, but he could not risk speaking French. "Put the master on the ground and be ready."

Pirmin and Gissler followed the order, and the other two caught on quickly enough.

"Do we have a bargain?" Foulques asked, gesturing to the grand master with his sword.

The Arab grinned. "You have some—"

As Foulques turned back towards the Saracens after gesturing at the grand master with his blade, he suddenly lunged forward in a long slide step, thrusting the point of his scimitar through the neck of the Arab.

His uncle had been a master with the scimitar and he made sure Foulques spent countless hours learning how to use it, as well. Guillaume knew that it was the favored weapon in the east, and would be the one his nephew was going to spend his life fighting against. He saw it as an indispensable aspect of Foulques's training, even though most of the other knights frowned upon training with the weapons of the infidels.

After stabbing the Arab in the throat, Foulques made good use of the scimitar's principal design function as a cutting weapon. He stretched it forward as far as his arm would reach, laying it across the face of a man in the middle of the group, and then he slide-stepped back out from the midst of the mercenary core, letting his scimitar drag across whatever, or whomever, it touched. When the blade bit into flesh, its curve made it dig in even deeper as Foulques retreated. One second he was right in the midst of the mercenaries, the next he was back out with Pirmin and Gissler at his sides. One man was dead, another dying, and one more severely cut across the face. In a narrow street where it was safe for no more than three men to fight side by side, Foulques liked the new odds.

Pirmin and Gissler were armed with hand-and-a-half swords. Foulques did not look back at Jimmy and Reynald, but he knew either one of them would be ready to step into the line if needed. But as he watched Gissler slice open both wrists and mark up the face of the man in front of him, he doubted it would come to that. Unlike Pirmin, Gissler was still growing into the man he would become. He was waif-thin and had a malnourished look about him. But by the Grace of God, could he whip a blade.

The mercenaries were falling over themselves now, trying to bring their weapons to bear on the three Hospitallers. Foulques stepped forward and the two lads followed a half step behind, as they had been taught. The stocky Saracen, the one with the poor Arabic, shouted something and lunged forward at Foulques. So intent was he on his target he underestimated the big man at Foulques's side. Foulques caught the Saracen's blade in a bind and Pirmin slammed him in the side of his temple with the pommel of his sword. The Saracen collapsed with a deep imprint on the side of his head. Foulques stepped over him, confident he would never rise again.

The Hospitallers pressed the attack. One more of the Saracens' number fell and the rest decided it was time to go and find easier prey. They turned and ran away up the street, leaving their dead and wounded where they lay.

The Hospitallers retrieved the grand master, and Foulques led them in the opposite direction. They turned left and proceeded cautiously toward the next corner. Foulques once again heard voices and signaled a stop. He could smell the water. The voices grew louder. He silently motioned for everyone to retreat back they way they came. They were in the middle of a long thoroughfare lined with shops. As they headed north, a large group of Mamluks entered the far end of the street. They spotted the Hospitallers instantly and began walking toward them, weapons drawn, and observing their surroundings cautiously. At almost the same instant, the voices Foulques had heard earlier rounded the corner from the south. It was another group of Saracens.

Foulques looked up and down the street for a side alley,

but he already knew none existed. He turned to his right and kicked in the door to the shop closest to him. It was the home of a butcher, and the smell of hanging lamb came flooding out as the door banged open. The silence of the street burst apart with the sound of Arabic and Turkic voices. Foulques could hear both groups running toward them as he led his men through the doorway. He did not look back.

"Jimmy! Bar the entry! The rest of you, find the back door and get out. Go right toward the water."

Pirmin took Jimmy's corner of the shield and practically dragged Gissler and Reynald through the shop, knocking dishes and tables aside as they made their way to the back.

Jimmy had his back up against the door, with his feet wedged against the heavy butcher's counter.

"I will find something to brace it," Foulques said, casting his eyes around the room.

"I already have," Jimmy said.

Foulques looked at him. The big man's face was red, sweat dripped into his eyes, and his chest rose and fell like the bellows in a blacksmith's forge.

"Help me push the counter over," Foulques said.

Jimmy shook his head. "You think it is easy dragging this much man around everywhere I go? No, Foulques, I think I will stay here for a spell."

There was a crash against the door as the first of the Saracens came up against it. Jimmy grunted and leaned harder against the heavy timber slabs.

"You are disobeying an order, sergeant!"

Jimmy shrugged. "It is what I do. Now get out of here, Foulques. And do not slam the door on your way out."

Another crash shook Jimmy. "Go!"

Foulques backpedaled away. "I will see you again, Jimmy."

"Are you still here?"

Foulques turned away and weaved his way quickly to the back of the shop. He slammed the door on his way out. He could have sworn he heard Jimmy the Mouth shout something after him.

He turned right and ran hard to catch up to the others.

"Where is Jimmy?" Pirmin asked.

Foulques shook his head and Pirmin looked away.

"Can you run?" he asked the three of them.

"The faster, the better, for the grand master's sake," Brother Reynald said.

"Stay close, then," Foulques said. He led the way with a slow jog. He ran just fast enough that he could still hear the men's heavy breathing and shuffling steps a few feet behind him. They hit their stride, and by the time they turned the next corner Foulques was moving at a good speed.

They were near the water. One more turn and they would be able to see the docks.

And then he slid across the cobblestones as he did everything within his power to stop. Twenty Mamluk warriors stood directly in their path. They were spread out, four or five men deep, stretched out to fill the whole width of the street.

Foulques turned and the shield bearers almost ran right

into him. "Back! Back!" Foulques shouted.

They spun and began running back the way they had come.

"More up ahead," said Gissler.

Sure enough, an even bigger group was headed toward them. From this distance, Foulques had no idea if they were Mamluk or mercenaries, but he did not want to wait and see.

"This way!"

He turned back toward the first, smaller group. The sudden change in direction made the shield bearers lose their grip and the shield slipped from their fingers. The grand master let out a loud exhalation of air as he hit the hard street. The three of them looked at each other with shocked expressions. Pirmin was the first to recover.

"I got him." He bent low and threw the grand master across his broad shoulders like he was a bag of flour. "Which way?"

"To the left, down that street. Move!"

They had to take a few more steps toward the now charging Mamluks. It was not a good feeling, but the street on the left opened up before the Mamluks could catch them. Foulques looked over his shoulder to make sure Pirmin was still on his heels. The big lad was there, all right. He had to swerve to avoid running Foulques over as he slowed. The other two also passed Foulques, and then, suddenly everyone was shouting and backpedaling once again. Foulques cursed and looked to the front. But his head was in the middle of Pirmin's back. He could see nothing.

Suddenly Pirmin fell, as did Gissler, and Reynald. Foulques was left standing alone in the road, staring at a line of crossbows. At first he thought his men had been hit, but then his brain registered the uniforms of Genoese mercenaries. All of them wore matching green and red tunics and breeches, except for one man in front waving frantically to Foulques and pointing at the ground. It was Vignolo dei Vignoli.

"Get your stubborn, self-flagellated arse down!" Apparently, he was done asking, for the next word out of his mouth was, "Loose!"

Deadly crossbow bolts zipped by Foulques on left and right before he had the presence of mind to throw himself to the ground.

"Loose!"

Another volley flew overhead. The eight or so crossbowmen who had just shot their weapons turned sideways and retreated back in the ranks. Another eight men stepped forward and raised their crossbows.

"Loose!" Vignoli had to shout to be heard over the screams and shouts of the Mamluks as they tried to organize themselves into a fighting unit.

"Infantry, advance!" Vignoli said, and a dozen brown-robed Hospitaller sergeants, armed with sword and shield, ran up the street. They stepped over Foulques and his men, putting themselves between them and the Mamluks.

Foulques jumped up to his feet, suddenly realizing these sergeants were his men. His Schwyzers.

"Pirmin, Gissler. With me."

The Schwyzers were two rows deep, six men wide. Foulques went to the center and put his hand on the back of the man there. It was Urs, a strong, stocky lad. Two men to the left was Thomas.

"Hold here, Hospitallers!" Foulques yelled, more for the men to hear his voice, and to know he was with them, than anything else.

The Mamluks charged. They still had the numbers, but the Hospitaller line held firm. They fought for a full minute in the cramped confines of the street, before Foulques called a line change. The new line came in and the old line fell back, dragging out two wounded men as they came.

The green and red had reloaded their weapons and were now directly behind the Hospitallers.

"Loose when you will!" Foulques called out. The Genoese spread out to either flank and began picking off Mamluks whenever they could find an opening. Once the crossbows were brought into play, the Mamluks quickly became aware of how much trouble they were in. The pyramidal iron tips of the bolts tore into them, penetrating armor like the prow of a ship pushing through lily pads. Already in disarray, the Mamluks panicked. Their commander called them off and they promptly retreated down the street and disappeared.

There was no time for celebrations. The grand master was back up on a shield, but he was looking paler than ever.

Foulques found Vignolo. "I sure hope you have a ship nearby."

The Genoan rolled his eyes. "Of course I do. The finest vessel in the entire Hospitaller Navy awaits your command, Admiral." He bowed, and then added, "May God help us all."

CHAPTER THIRTY-THREE

THE LAST TIME Foulques had been at the docks, the English were still there to maintain some semblance of order. Now, with the Mamluks in the city, the situation had deteriorated beyond saving. People ran left and right for no purpose, it seemed, other than to scream in a new spot. Fist fights broke out between men and women as they argued over seats in tiny vessels that were just as likely to cause their deaths as any Saracen sword.

"Go back to your homes! There will be no more ships!" A knight of the Order of Saint Lazarus shouted.

His entire face was wrapped in gauze and his affliction caused him to limp everywhere he went, but he wore the green cross of his order with pride and carried out his duty with dignity.

"Find somewhere to hide and wait out whatever is to come! Do not seek refuge in the churches!"

Foulques spotted his hulk of a galley anchored a long row off the main dock. She rode low in the water. Vignolo assured Foulques that he had already taken on as many evacuees as was safe. More even. They were crowded into the hold to keep the weight balanced.

They made their way to a waiting trio of large rowboats, where ten grim-faced Genoese crossbowmen stood guard, their weapons loaded and ready. The frenzied crowd gave them a wide berth, for everyone knew they were the most disciplined, yet ruthless, mercenaries gold could buy.

"Where did you pick them up?" Foulques asked as they headed swiftly toward the Genoese.

"Cyprus. They were already here two weeks ago, but got passage to Cyprus with some noble."

"How did you convince them to come back?" Foulques knew very well Vignolo did not have the coin to entice men such as these.

Vignolo untied one of the boats, avoiding looking directly at Foulques. "I gave them an hour to loot when we first arrived."

"Vignoli!"

"What? Better than the Mohammedans carrying everything away. Do not look at me like that. I specifically said, 'No churches and no women.' Are you getting in this boat or would you rather sit here, take off your boots, and dangle your feet in the water for a bit?"

A helpless silence descended over the rowboat Foulques rode in as they pushed away from the dock and drifted by scene after scene of hell. They passed the main berth where several overloaded merchant ships were making preparations to leave. A naked woman ran from ship to ship, crying and begging for someone to take her away. Another woman holding a baby waited until one of the ships had untied and pushed away. Then she threw the bundle in her arms across five feet of open water. From where he sat Foulques could not tell if the infant landed on the ship or not, but the vessel continued to ease gracefully away, while the woman collapsed to her knees and held up her hands in prayer.

The rowboat continued on. In the distance, a large group of men and women began jumping off the dock and swimming to nearby boats. The boats were already overcrowded and attempted to maneuver away from the splashing figures. One dangerously unbalanced fishing vessel rocked precariously as several people hung on its side, trying to hoist themselves up. The crew began to methodically beat them back into the water with the flats of their oars, the slapping sound of wood against skulls carrying over the water like the flapping of giant wings.

Foulques brought his own hands together in prayer and looked at the grand master. He was still on the shield, on the bottom of the boat. Brother Reynald held a blood-soaked cloth to his side and dabbed at his forehead with another. It seemed to take an eternity, but eventually, the steady work by the oarsmen ate up the distance to their ship.

Once on board, Brother Reynald whisked the grand master away to the captain's cabin to perform surgery. Vignolo began shouting orders and his small crew unfurled the sails. Foulques joined Vignolo at the helm, as did Thomas, who had become Vignolo's man for relaying orders to the different parts of the ship.

As they waited for the sails to be set, the three of them stared wordlessly back over the port. The late morning sky, though blue as always, was thick with clouds of smoke hanging low over the city, the red glow of fires dancing off their underbellies. Foulques could tell that the source of at least two of the black plumes were churches. He wondered how many had sought refuge in those buildings, despite the warnings of the leper knight. How many were even now being burned alive?

Foulques could feel the flames lapping at his soul. As well he should, for it was he and his kind who had failed the people of Acre. The tradespeople, artisans, merchants, servants, and even slaves were now fighting for their lives. That was not God's purpose for them. That task belonged to His soldiers of the holy orders, and their king, all of whom had failed miserably in this divine calling. Aside from the few of them on board, the entire fighting force of the Hospitallers was still in the doomed city. Along with at least thirty thousand people who had been unable to escape.

"The city will fall," Thomas said, as though he had just come to that realization. "What will happen to them?"

It was uncharacteristic of the lad to speak when not called upon. Foulques decided he deserved the truth. "Every man will be killed, whether he raised a sword or not. Any woman found will be raped, young or old, and then sold into slavery. The children will be separated from their mothers, and they too will be sold at market."

Vignolo winced, but he said nothing. He knew Foulques spoke the truth. His surprise, no doubt, was that Foulques had declared it so openly to the boy.

"And our brothers?" Thomas asked.

"We have failed our Lord and His people," Foulques said. "What do you think will happen to them?"

The words came out harsher than Foulques intended. He took a breath and looked at Thomas. He was a hard lad to read at times, but at that particular moment, the pain in his soul was as apparent as the jagged scar disfiguring his face.

God in heaven. The list.

One hundred names penned in the boy's own clumsy hand. Before compiling the final list, Thomas had worked off of the scroll with the three hundred names Foulques had given him. Thomas had taken his quill and carved clean, deliberate strokes through two hundred of them. Foulques derided himself for not seeing it sooner.

The boy thinks he is responsible for the Schwyzers still in the city. He chose his next words carefully.

"We have lost everything, this day. And I do not think God is finished with us, yet. But for some reason we have been spared. It is not our place to question this. All we can do is rise tomorrow, remember the smiling faces of our friends and brothers who are no longer with us, and follow the path God has put in our hearts. If we set out on that path, and are careful to stray but a little, the world will become a better place than it is today. You will see."

That is all any of us can strive to do, Foulques thought. The words he had just spoken sounded strange to his ears, polished, like the sermon of a priest. Or, perhaps, a father?

He looked at Thomas, who stared straight ahead, his dark eyes unseeing. If anyone needed a father at that moment, it was him.

Vignolo suddenly spoke up. "Sails are hoisted. You want to take her out of the bay, Thomas?" He stepped aside, relinquishing the wheel to the lad without giving him much of a choice. He pointed at it as it began to turn with a mind of its own.

The melancholy on Thomas's face was replaced by wide-eyed surprise, and not a little fear. "But I never… I do not…"

"Best grab onto her before she gets away from you, boy," Vignolo said.

Thomas stepped forward and grabbed the nubs of the wheel with both hands, like he was climbing a cliff of granite by using a dagger in each hand.

Vignolo laughed. "That is a fine grip you have there, Thomas. But, perhaps ease up a bit on it so we do not have a need to replace the wheel every voyage."

He went and stood at Thomas's side and put a hand on his shoulder. He pointed at the mouth of the bay with his other. "See the opening? See how our bow is angled toward the rocks on the left? Keep turning, little by little, until our bow angles away from them. Bring her into the middle."

He stepped back and watched, giving words of advice often as Thomas got the feel for the wheel, and how many revolutions it took to bring about the bow of the ship. Vignolo gave him some space and scanned the harbor with his looking glass. He was quiet for an uncharacteristically long time before he spoke again.

"Well, sard me all the way to hell if that is not who I think it is. And one of yours, as well," Vignolo said. He handed his glass to Foulques. "Know him?"

Foulques put the instrument to his eye and focused it where Vignolo pointed, along the eastern-most edge of the harbor wall. Halfway to the open sea, two men sat knee to knee in one of the tiniest row boats Foulques had ever seen. It rode low in the water, with the waves occasionally lapping over its edges. The smaller man rowed, while the other, a larger man wearing the white-crossed robe of a Hospitaller sergeant, bailed. Focusing in further, Foulques realized the conically shaped bucket he scraped along the bottom of the boat was actually a helmet of Saracen design.

Foulques could not keep the smile from his face. There could be no mistaking the profile of Jimmy the Neckless, even though they were about as far away from Foulques's ship as they could possibly be within the harbor.

"It is Goodyear Jimmy," Foulques said. He kept looking through the glass as the rowboat receded slowly into the distance. The second man looked familiar but Foulques could not place him. "Who is the man rowing?"

"Stephanos the Greek," Vignolo said, a note of regret in his words. "Looks like my debt to him will not go down with the city after all. How in all the hells do you think those two ever got together?"

"God's miscreants have a way of finding one another in this world," Foulques said, the glass still held up to his eye.

There was not nearly enough room in the boat for the two big men. As Stephanos bent forward at the waist to power his oars, Jimmy had to interrupt his bailing to lean away to avoid knocking heads. After every few strokes, their rhythm would break down and they would stop their respective tasks to exchange a few choice words.

Foulques lowered the looking glass and handed it back to Vignolo. "Can we go back for them?"

Vignolo shook his head as he collapsed the instrument. "Not without taking down a half dozen ships in the process. But a betting man would say they will do just fine. If the Mamluks could not get Stephanos at the Massacre of Antioch, they will not get him here."

Vignolo turned back to make sure Thomas was still on course. He looked out over the water, using one cupped hand to shield his eyes from the sun glinting off the gentle waves. His face dropped.

"Oh, no."

"What is it?" Foulques asked, as he watched Vignolo's hands fumble to extend his battered glass once again. He held it up to his eye and before Foulques had time to repeat his question, Vignolo swore at every angel in heaven.

"Thomas. I am afraid the lesson is over for today." He stepped forward and took over the wheel. "Foulques. You had best get your men ready. I can delay them for a few minutes, but they *will* board us eventually. I cannot change that."

"Who will board us?"

"I am afraid an old friend of yours has come calling, and it is too late to climb out the back window."

Foulques snatched the looking glass away from Vignolo. Even before he recognized the ship, he had a suspicion of who it was. He could tell by Vignolo's voice.

"The Northman," Foulques said, unnecessarily. He

counted the men on the ship that he could make out. "I would say forty or fifty men." He slowly returned the glass to Vignolo.

"That makes it fairly even," Vignolo said.

Foulques closed his eyes and shook his head. "Normally, I would agree with you. But if the Northman is there, then he has his Mamluk warriors with him. We will be no match for them if they board us."

Foulques knew the Schwyzers were too young, too inexperienced, and the Genoese were masters with their crossbows, but the Mamluks would annihilate them once they closed the distance. They could not fight them and they had no hope of outrunning the Northman's ship. That left very few options. Foulques heard the marshal's voice repeating the same thing over and over in the back of his head. *You are not ready, Foulques.*

"What do you want to do?" Vignolo asked.

Foulques looked at the ship in the distance as it steadily grew in size. Now he could make out its two banks of oars dipping into the water and propelling it toward them. Their sails were up, but angled in tightly as they were sailing into the wind.

"Point us directly at them," Foulques said. "Thomas. Tell the men to prepare to board."

CHAPTER THIRTY-FOUR

Badru and Yusuf stood on the helm deck of the Wyvern as they left the open sea and passed through the mouth of the port of Acre. Badru lowered the looking glass from his eye and nodded at Hanif, the Wyvern's helmsman.

"You are right. It is a Hospitaller ship," Badru said.

Hanif's eyes were keen when he was on the water. It was a phenomenon that confused Badru for the man was almost sightless when on land. He could not recognize the faces of his own men at twenty paces and he was forever tripping over imaginary obstacles when he walked. But put him on a ship, out at sea, and somehow he came alive. He no longer stumbled, his back straightened, and years fell from his leathery face. He could tell you the nationality and probable cargo of a ship in the distance long before any man with a looking glass ever could.

"But they have a company of Genoese on board, no?" Hanif asked.

"Yes. They must be transporting something valuable," Badru said. He lifted the looking glass up to take another look. "Adjust your course, Hanif. They will be our next target."

"Is that wise?" Yusuf asked. "The sultan was specific when he said not to bother attacking any of the Christian Orders' ships."

"This one may have something valuable on board. They have hired mercenaries."

Badru had no idea if that was true or not. What he did know was that he did not want to insult his men by attacking another ship full of women and children fleeing the doomed city. There were no Venetian or Genoese merchant ships in the vicinity, for they were most likely the first to gather their treasures and run. But this one had Genoans on it, which meant it carried valuables. Rarely did you find one without the other. In addition to the Genoans, he had seen only one Hospitaller Knight and a dozen or so men-at-arms on deck. Because of all this, he could justify attacking this ship even though it flew a Hospitaller flag. In his eyes, he would not be in open defiance of his sultan's orders.

"They have changed course," Hanif said.

"Head them off before they clear the bay."

Hanif squinted into the distance, his eyes all but disappearing in the sun-browned creases of his face. "No, Emir. There is no need. For they are attacking us."

"Attacking us?" Badru lifted his looking glass up again to have another look. Sure enough, the Hospitaller ship had altered its course and was now coming straight at them. They had a slight advantage in numbers, but their captain obviously did not know Badru's ship or his men. His

Mamluks were experienced warriors, and unlike most others of their kind, they were experienced at fighting at sea. He would put his men up against an enemy with even numbers any day.

He trailed his looking glass down the length of the Frankish vessel. He could just make out men attaching hinged boarding planks to the fore and port sides. The ship itself was unimpressive, medium in size, and very old. Her best days were long behind her. However, the bow was unnaturally thick, appearing to be reinforced with several layers of material, perhaps even some iron. That was the one strength of the ship.

Badru saw the coming battle through the eyes of the enemy. They would use their reinforced hull to ram the Wyvern and then board from their bow. The extra boarding planks on the port side were a precautionary measure in case they could not stick their bow and were forced to come up alongside the Wyvern. Badru saw no reason not to accommodate the enemy in their wishes.

"Bring us to a standstill, bow to bow with them," Badru said. He sent a runner to bring him Safir. Moments later his most trusted Mamluk was at his side.

"Yes, My Emir."

"We are going to board a ship protected by Genoese crossbowmen. Tell the men to leave their bows. Every second we spend exchanging missile fire we put ourselves at a disadvantage. Instead, line them up under good shield cover, with orders to board the enemy ship as quickly as we can. We will use their own planks against them, but establish two of our own as well. The Genoans will try to stay back and use their crossbows, so we go for them first."

"It will be done," Safir said. He bowed and walked swiftly away to make the arrangements.

Badru felt Yusuf's hand on his arm. "Are you sure you want to do this? The bay is littered with other ships. Ones that look like much easier adversaries. Many of which would surrender without a fight."

Badru let out a sigh. There were some things Yusuf would never understand, no matter how many times he tried to explain. He looked him in the eyes and shook his head, but as he did so, Badru covered Yusuf's hand with his own. It was not his fault. He was not Mamluk.

"Must you go with them?" Yusuf asked.

"Of course," Badru said. "An emir fights with his men. A slave owner does not." The way Yusuf looked at his feet, and gave a resigned nod of his head, reminded Badru painfully of Yusuf's house slave beginnings. Though he had been a free man for many years now, there were still some things from that life that would not let Yusuf go.

"I will stay here with you and Hanif until the ships are tied together and my men have made the crossing. But then I too, must go."

"Of course," Yusuf said. But Badru's words had the desired effect, for his face lit up and he moved a step closer to Badru to shield himself from the wind.

Badru turned toward the helm and the wizened figure of Hanif.

"They are coming on strong," Hanif said. "They have

mistaken our slowing down as us trying to tack away and run."

"Good," Badru said. "Play into their thoughts. Make it look like we are trying to turn around to gain the wind. They have it now so they may attempt to flee if they see us as too difficult a target." He leaned over the railing and shouted to the Mamluks below. "Safir! Conceal half the men behind the railings."

The Mamluk bowed his head and relayed the message. Hanif began yelling orders at his sailors. They were a small group of men hand-picked by Hanif himself. They were not Mamluks, nor even warriors by any stretch of the imagination, but they did not need to be. Their job was to sail the ship. Badru's men took care of all things military.

The only other non-Mamluk crew members, if you could call them that, were the slaves manning the oars two decks below. Badru had always preferred to use his own men as rowers, but the sultan had insisted on giving him fresh Christian slaves from his recent conquests. He had enough slaves below decks to man every oar twice. And that was not even taking into account the more recent prisoners they had taken on. He was glad he was no longer in the slaving business, for the market was about to be overrun with Christians. It would soon be cheaper to buy a new slave than to feed an old one.

As the minutes passed the ship grew larger and Badru could make out the shapes of men without the need of his looking glass. There was a lot of movement near the front of their ship and the sun began to reflect off the steel of weapons and mail.

He had been dismayed when the sultan told him he and his Mamluks would not be storming through the front gates of Acre with the rest of the army. For one brief moment, he thought perhaps Khalil had learned the truth about who Badru was. But fortunately, that was only Yusuf's worries instilling themselves in his thoughts. The sultan wanted Badru to use his ship and men to stop any rich Christians, Jews, or even Muslims from escaping the city by sea with their family treasures. He said to especially be on the lookout for ships with members of the clergy aboard, for they would never leave anything of great value behind in their churches. Badru had accepted Khalil's command without question, but now he wished he had not been so accommodating. Of course he would never refuse an order from his sultan, but perhaps he could have suggested an alternative. Khalil had heeded Badru's advice before. Surely he would have understood the desire of Badru and his Mamluks to be in the city when it finally fell. Of all people, the sultan would have recognized the waste in sending celebrated Mamluk warriors against defenseless priests and peasants, if Badru had only asked. But he did not. He was in too much of a hurry to leave the sultan's presence. Was that how a faithful Mamluk should serve?

Caught up in his thoughts, Badru soon realized the Hospitaller ship was almost upon them. A quick glance below told him his men were in position. He put his looking glass to his eye and observed the enemy. When he got to the helm, and saw who was standing there, his hand dropped involuntarily to his side.

"By Allah's prophet," he said.

"What is it?" Yusuf asked.

Badru willed feeling back into his hand and lifted the glass back up to his face. His eyes had not deceived him. It was Foulques de Villaret. And standing beside him, his hands clutching a wheel older than Badru himself, was an Italian. It had to be Vignoli. He was sure of it. He had never seen the man's face, but he had been living with his name inside his head for eight years.

"Emir, what do you see?" This time the question came from Hanif. Apparently they were still too far away for him to make out faces, because he was the one man on board who could identify the Genoan.

Badru pushed the looking glass into his hand. "Tell me who that man is beside Foulques de Villaret."

"Villaret? The Hospitaller?" Hanif kept one hand on the wheel and did as he was ordered. He let out a low whistle and handed the glass back to Badru.

"It is him," he said. "Vignolo dei Vignoli. Both of them. In one place at the same time."

Had he misjudged the Hospitaller during the failed peace negotiations? He had to know whom he was attacking, and yet on he came. He looked through the glass yet again and studied the Knight of Saint John. His jaw was set, determined, and his blue eyes stared back directly at Badru. He knew exactly what he was doing. A thick rope was wrapped around his waist to brace him from the upcoming impact of the two ships colliding.

Badru lowered the glass and handed it to Yusuf. "Find something to hold on to," he said.

He turned to Hanif. "Do not let him hit us on either side. I do not know what that ship has under its bow planking so let us keep the damage to a minimum."

He did not know how the Hospitaller ship had been built, but he knew the Wyvern. She had a reinforced hull at the bow and could take an enormous amount of punishment there. This was something Badru knew from many encounters similar to this one, albeit he was always on the charging end.

"Now!" Hanif said to his runner. "Starboard oars, double time!" The young sailor took the stairs to the main deck in a single leap and ran to the opening leading below decks. He shouted down to another man at the bottom of the ladder and he, in turn, relayed the order to the master of the drums.

Two decks below, Badru heard the drum beat out a quick rhythm, and as the oars dipped into the water, the ship's bow began to reverse its current direction in a slow, ponderous arc.

Hanif's timing was perfect. The prow of the Wyvern swung into position to meet the Hospitaller ship head on with less than a hundred paces between ships.

"Both decks ahead slow," Hanif ordered and his runner was off again. Badru realized Hanif needed the smallest forward momentum to keep the bow of the ship from drifting in the waves.

He enjoyed watching a master work. Any kind of master. Hanif was a credit to his trade, and that is why when he turned to Badru with wide eyes and shouted, "They are coming in too fast! Hold on Emir!" Badru did not question his helmsman. He wrapped the crook of his elbow around a thick guide line and grabbed hold of Yusuf's wrist with his other. He stared ahead and braced for impact.

The Hospitaller ship was indeed coming in too fast. What was Villaret thinking? Did he hope to try and sink them both? That would never happen. Only a fool—

Hanif let out a string of curses. "Retract all oars! Retract all oars!" His runner was fast, but not fast enough.

The Hospitaller ship was under full sail, so her oars were stowed. But then Badru saw a bank appear out of her starboard side. They dipped into the water and slammed backward against the side of the ship as Vignoli spun the wheel in his hands like a man possessed.

The prow of the Hospitaller ship drifted to Badru's left and straightened out. It continued to bear down on them at full speed and the next thing Badru heard was the sound of the Wyvern's forward oars on her port side snapping off as the two ships came together side by side.

Badru was aware of everything happening at once. The deck under his feet heaved and he slammed forward into the railing, but somehow he kept his feet and maintained his hold on Yusuf. Hanif bounced around the wheel like flotsam in a whirlpool, until his grip failed him and he went sprawling across the deck.

"Loose!"

Badru heard the command come from the enemy ship as it scraped along the Wyvern's side snapping off oars and splintering railings.

"Loose!"

Badru steadied himself enough to see how his men were handling the crossbows of the Genoese. They were crouched in their positions, holding onto ropes of their own for balance. Surprisingly, no bolts flew in their direction.

"Loose!"

The sound of the bolts whistling overhead is what turned him on to what the crossbowmen were shooting at. He looked up and watched a volley tear through the sails above his head.

The squealing of the hulls grinding against one another reached a crescendo and Badru found himself looking straight at Foulques de Villaret and the Genoan. They were so close, if he had had a bow he could have put an arrow in either one of the men's eyes. Foulques stared back, his blue eyes brilliant and unreadable. Vignoli fought the wheel of his ship with both hands, but when he saw Badru staring at him, he made the effort to wrest one hand free to give the Mamluk a mock salute. Then their backs were to Badru, and after another deck-shaking crash and the sickening sound of more splintering oars, the Hospitaller ship broke free of the destruction and sailed noiselessly away. But not before sending one last volley of bolts into the sails of the Wyvern as a parting gift.

The entire event took seconds, but Badru's heart was pounding like he had just woken from the darkest of nightmares. His chest heaved under his mail, threatening to snap its leather ties.

Hanif was on his hands and knees five feet away. All around the ship, men began to move at the sides of his vision.

A whisper sounded at his side.

"Badru."

He realized he still held Yusuf's wrist.

He turned to him and said, "They will pay dearly for—"

Yusuf's soft brown eyes were wide and wet. "Badru, I…"

He took a hesitant step and that was when Badru saw the blood. The pale blue silk of his tunic had a dark shadow on one side near the sash at his waist. But that was not the source of the shadow.

Badru followed the diagonal cross-seam on the smooth fabric all the way up to its open collar, and there, on the left side of Yusuf's neck, was a small pyramidal hole. From the hole flowed a steady stream of blood, hardly visible against his dark skin as it rolled over his delicate collarbone and disappeared within the folds of his favorite tunic.

"Yusuf!"

Badru stumbled forward and caught Yusuf in his arms. He pushed his hand against the wound in his neck as Yusuf's eyelids began to flutter. He thought he was making a difference, but then blood began forcing its way around the sides of his hand, between his fingers.

"Yusuf!" His eyes were open but he did not respond. Badru pulled him to his chest with one arm, kept the pressure on the wound with the other, and called out again and again for the most skilled surgeon of his Mamluks.

He came. They all came. And did nothing.

Safir placed his hand on Badru's shoulder and tried to remove his hand from Yusuf's wound. Badru fended him off and dragged Yusuf three steps away, before his legs too began to give way. He fought with all his strength to stay standing, to keep Yusuf standing, but, in the end, he could bear the weight no longer. He crumpled, and fell crashing to his knees. Badru clutched Yusuf to his chest with both arms, sobbing silently, while something began to build in the depths of his soul. When it was ready, he released it to the world.

For the forty prisoners chained together in the darkness, ankle to ankle, in the cargo deck immediately below, Badru's scream was the finale to a series of truly terrifying events. A child began crying, ignoring the pleas from her mother to remain quiet. A man, shirtless and bloody, clasped his hands together and recited every prayer he knew. Two sisters took turns using their fingers to comb out the matted hair of their catatonic mother, even though the younger of the two could not stop crying. While another young woman pressed a wadded up piece of her own tunic against a bleeding wound in the chest of an older man.

She hummed to herself as tears rolled down her cheeks. But she smiled when she felt a soft buzzing against her breast. For under her clothing, she had concealed a small papyrus tube, and in that tube, was her favorite queen.

EPILOGUE

ON THE FORTY-THIRD day of the siege, the Mamluk army breached the second wall. The Hospitallers and Templars joined forces and fought together in a brave attempt to push them back. The mass of bodies became so packed in the narrow streets there was no room to swing a sword. Straight, vicious thrusts to the face or in the joints around armor, such as armpits and groins, killed most who died that day. Many resorted to daggers, some were strangled with mailed hands. Occasionally, someone would throw a jar filled with Greek fire into the midst, and a knight would burst into flames, screaming as he twisted and melted inside his metal helmet. The dry, hard-packed streets became muddy with blood and gore. As defenders were wounded in the front ranks, they were lifted up and passed to the rear. But as the morning wore on, men's arms became heavy from battle, their breathing ragged, and the wounded lay where they fell. The Mamluks pushed forward like the tide, stepping over the fallen and advancing inch by inch until the dead and dying were completely engulfed underfoot.

The fanatical bravery and skill of the fighting men of the religious orders held the breach from the early hours of the morning until the afternoon, and perhaps would have pushed back any normal enemy. But the endless stream of Muslims was fueled by hatred and the dream of revenge. They had suffered at the hands of Christian invaders for two hundred years, and in this breach, they saw a chance to rid their lands of the Franks forever.

The Marshal of the Hospitallers was eventually overwhelmed and killed at the breach, along with almost every other member of the Order of the Knights of Saint John. Only the gravely wounded grand master and a handful of other knights and sergeants were able to escape the doomed city.

The grand master of the Knights Templar also fell in battle, but a group of Templars managed to hole up in their fortified compound. Behind their thick walls, they held out for another ten days. But in the end, the Saracen sappers finally undermined their fortress and Sultan Khalil sent two thousand men in to finish off the troublesome knights. During the ensuing battle, the Templar fortress collapsed, killing everyone inside, Christians and Muslims alike.

In the days that followed, the sultan allowed his army to raze the once proud city of Acre. It had been in the hands of the Christians for a hundred years; it needed to be purged. Soldiers went door to door, ferreting out any who hid. Men were dragged into the streets and killed, mothers and their children were torn from each other's arms and sold into slavery, if they were fortunate. In the years that followed, so many Christians flooded the slave markets that a healthy Frankish woman could be bought for a single silver coin.

To those who mark the beginnings and ends of such things, the defeat of Acre was surely the end of the Crusades. But to a select few warriors of God seeking refuge on the island of Cyprus, it was only the beginning.

✠

The story continues in

***Hospitaller* (Hospitaller Saga Book 3)**

Sign up for the **New Releases Mailing List** (http://eepurl.com/hTAFA). You will **only** receive notifications when J. K. Swift publishes something new.

ABOUT THE AUTHOR

J. K. Swift lives in a log house deep in the forests of central British Columbia, Canada. When he is not busy cutting wood to survive the winter, he spends his free time making mead, shooting his longbow, riding Icelandic horses, roasting coffee, and writing historical fiction and fantasy.

website:
jkswift.com

...a message from the author:

Thank you very much for reading my work. Reviews and personal recommendations from readers like you are the most important way for relatively unknown authors to attract more readers, so I truly am grateful to anyone who takes the time to rate my work. I do not yet write full time, but I would like to, and you leaving a review or telling a friend about my work is the best way you can help me write more books.

Thanks very much for your support!

All the best,
James

Sign up for the **New Releases Mailing List** (http://eepurl.com/hTAFA). Your information will never be shared and you will **only** receive notifications when J. K. Swift publishes something new.

Novels:

The Forest Knights Series: Join Thomas and Pirmin as they return to the mountains of Switzerland and lead a rebellion against tyrannical overlords.

ALTDORF (Book 1):
jkswift.com/books/altdorf

MORGARTEN (Book 2):
jkswift.com/books/morgarten

Short Stories/Novellas:

Keepers of Kwellevonne Series: Why would anyone want to kill a healer?

HEALER (Book 1):
jkswift.com/books/healer

FARRIER (Book 2):
jkswift.com/books/farrier

WARDER (Book 3):
jkswift.com/books/warder

Printed in Great Britain
by Amazon